The RENAISSANCE of GWEN HATHAWAY

The RENAISSANCE of GWEN HATHAWAY

A NOVEL

ASHLEY SCHUMACHER

WEDNESDAY BOOKS
NEW YORK

First published in the United States by Wednesday Books, an imprint of St. Martin's Publishing Group

THE RENAISSANCE OF GWEN HATHAWAY. Copyright © 2023 by Ashley Schumacher. All rights reserved. Printed in the United States of America. For information, address St. Martin's Publishing Group, 120 Broadway, New York, NY 10271.

www.wednesdaybooks.com

Designed by Devan Norman
Case stamp castle image © Shpringel Olga/Shutterstock

The Library of Congress Cataloging-in-Publication Data:

Names: Schumacher, Ashley, author.
Title: The Renaissance of Gwen Hathaway: A novel / Ashley Schumacher.
Description: First edition. | New York : Wednesday Books, 2023. | Audience: Ages 12–18.
Identifiers: LCCN 2022038176 | ISBN 9781250840240 (hardcover) | ISBN 9781250840257 (ebook)
Subjects: CYAC: Renaissance fairs—Fiction. | Interpersonal relations—Fiction. | Grief—Fiction. | Friendship—Fiction. | LCGFT: Novels.
Classification: LCC PZ7.1.S3365545 Re 2023 | DDC [Fic]—dc23
LC record available at https://lccn.loc.gov/2022038176

Our books may be purchased in bulk for promotional, educational, or business use. Please contact your local bookseller or the Macmillan Corporate and Premium Sales Department at 1-800-221-7945, extension 5442, or by email at MacmillanSpecialMarkets@macmillan.com.

First Edition: 2023

10 9 8 7 6 5 4 3 2 1

To anyone who hasn't felt at home in their skin:
I hope this story helps you lay out a rug,
place a frame, hang up your coat, and stay awhile.
Ad astra per aspera.

And to Mom and Dad. Thanks for teaching me
how to tame the world before I knew I could.

The
RENAISSANCE
of
GWEN
HATHAWAY

PROLOGUE

I WAS TEN WHEN I FIRST MET the Wizened Old Wizard. I didn't know then that the old man was a Ren faire legend, a traveler who only sometimes popped up at faires, never announced, never traceable. No director would kick him out or refuse to let him set up shop because it meant an influx of visitors once word got out that he had arrived . . . if those visitors could arrive before he took a notion to leave.

In retrospect, perhaps there should have been a place to sit, somewhere for weary souls to settle and absorb the wisdom he claimed to possess. Instead, the old wizard stood behind a counter just like every other vendor at the faire, a variety of potion bottles promising love, luck, or hexes scattered between sachets of bundled pine needles and jars of brightly colored sand. Strange brass beads that shone thick and golden in the dim light hung from thin chains along the front of the counter, twinkling near my hips.

"Come to buy my wares?" the Wizened Old Wizard asked.

He didn't sound particularly wise, nor old, really. He sounded jolly in a subdued way, but much too young to be calling himself the Wizened Old Wizard.

I peered through the wispy haze of smoke that permeated the air. I tried to decipher if his long gray beard and matching bushy eyebrows were fake, but every time I thought I had settled on the dark complexion of his face, I found my view obscured once more.

"Choose wisely, child," the wizard told me, gesturing to the table. "Magic is not free."

Ten years of being a human was long enough for me to become self-conscious, especially in my street clothes. When I wore the faire costumes Mom made for me—even if I *did* refuse to wear slippers and hid sneakers beneath—I felt like one face in the crowd, just another maiden in the village of Wiltonshire, or Hollygrove, or Pleasance, or at whichever faire our big blue RV, Britomart, was parked at the time. But in modern clothes, in pants and sweaters and Converse that were always bought a half size too large, I felt watched by the world in a way that made my skin prickle.

I felt stupid standing in front of the Wizened Old Wizard in my faded thrift store jeans, but this shop was different than any other vendor I had seen at *any* faire, and by then, I had been to almost every single one in the United States.

There was something about him, about his stall, that felt like a step back in time, a true harkening back to a land with no electricity or fans or upright showers. I couldn't even hear the hiss of the smoke machine, no matter how still I made myself and how carefully I listened. There was only the wizard's occasional cough, the happy, distant shouts of the faire patrons out in the sunshine, and the gentle sound of my own breath.

"You have not heard of my name before," the wizard said suddenly through the silence, causing me to nearly drop the potion bottle in my hand.

"No, my lord," I said, an incorrect faire habit that immediately made me blush. "My lord" was only meant for nobility, which the wizard was technically not, but he had such a commanding presence, my tongue slipped.

The wizard didn't seem offended. He smiled in a way that made me wonder if he did so often, quickly and with only one side of his mouth quirked beneath his impressively dense facial hair. He seemed serious on purpose, like he hadn't meant to let the half-smile slip.

"Most who come to me have sought me," he said. "Some come from miles and miles away. But it seems as if fate brought you here today."

"I don't believe in fate," I said quickly.

Because I didn't believe in fate. I *don't*. And yet my mind wandered to the coin—*the* coin—the one tucked safely in the deepest, plushest part of my mother's jewelry satchel. The one my great-great-grandparents flipped to see if they should abandon their jobs and run away with the Renaissance faire in the first place. The one that my parents flipped to decide if they would get married, if they would have me, if they would homeschool me and raise me in the Ren faire circuit.

The one that I stole and flipped just two weeks before meeting the Wizened Old Wizard to see if Mom was going to get better, if the doctors were right and the cancer wasn't aggressive and was, in fact, highly treatable.

The one that said *no*. The one that I refused to believe and shoved back into Mom's drawer and swore to never touch again.

The wizard must have heard it in my voice, my uncertainty regarding fate, because this time he smiled with both sides of his mouth.

"I do not only sell potions," he said. "I also give advice."

I had seen the prices on some of the potion bottles. If this was an extra feature, a mysterious one that brought people from miles away, there was *no* way I would be able to afford it with the birthday money still sitting in my pocket.

"Advice?"

"Of a sort. You ask a question; I answer."

"Like a fortune?"

"I cannot see the future more than any other man," the wizard replied. "But I have been on this earth so long, I do know a fair amount of its patterns, yes. If it's a query of what lies ahead of you, I can do my best to answer."

I wondered if a new fate could cancel out another. I wondered if the Wizened Old Wizard could rewrite my destiny, if he could undo the power the coin held over my family and over me.

"How much?" I asked. "For the fortune?"

"*Advice*," the wizard stressed. He leaned forward, still somehow encased by smoke, and I felt like I was being evaluated.

"For you," he said, "I will accept exactly three tokens."

"Tokens?"

"Items," he amended. "Things of importance to you."

"That . . . seems like a lot," I said.

For the first time, I got a clear enough view of the wizard's face to see a twinkle—a literal *twinkle* of mischief—in his eyes.

"I am *very* wise, and as I said, magic is not free. Come back tomorrow with your chosen tokens, and I will answer your question."

I turned to leave, dismissed, but paused before I raised the heavy sheet from the walkway.

"If you are so wise," I said without turning, "if you know so many patterns, can't you guess what my question will be?"

He was silent for so long, I was afraid I had offended him.

"You doubt my wisdom, child?" he finally said.

I gulped, not intending for it to be so audible. "I don't know you," I said, trying to make my voice braver than I felt. "I didn't know you existed before today. And I definitely didn't travel miles and miles to be here to see you. My parents are in the Renaissance faire circuit. You just happen to be where I am."

If the wizard rarely smiled, then he never laughed. After a beat in which I entertained all sorts of fantastical deaths by lightning from the wizard staff he surely carried or from a magical curse, his chuckle started low and raspy before growing into a jovial howl that made me want to both laugh along and hide.

"I can tell already that what you seek is certainty," he said, still laughing. "I can also tell you that no such thing exists. Save your tokens, girl. Nothing is inevitable, good or bad. When you have a more important question, I am sure we will cross paths again."

But he must have been able to tell I didn't want to leave empty-handed, was too lost to step outside the tent with nothing. He grumbled something under his breath, bent beneath the counter, and came back with a closed fist.

"Give me your hand, girl," he said. His fingers, brown and hardly wrinkled at all, dropped a necklace into my open palm.

Not a thick bead like the ones for sale below me, but a tiny globe balanced at the middle of a delicate gold chain. It wasn't like anything Mom made to sell in our shop. Her jewelry was beautiful, but full of rubies and emeralds and would-be diamonds. This was something different. It felt warm, heavier than I would have guessed, in the palm of my hand.

"The world," the wizard said, startling me from my examination, "can be vast and cruel. But it can, sometimes, be shrunken and tamed. Sometimes, if you're clever, you can find ways to make it kinder. Remember that."

This made about as much sense to me as my latest biology homework.

"What am I supposed to do with this?" I asked, holding up the necklace. "What does that even *mean*?"

The wizard smiled, just once more. "You say you don't believe in fate," he said, "but I believe you do, and I believe it's your fate to decide what taming the world means for you."

And then, because I was ten and not intimidated by adults—but mostly because my mouth ran away without my brain—I asked, "What does it mean for *you*? How do you tame the world?"

The Wizened Old Wizard blinked once in a way that made me realize it wasn't something you *asked* adults, especially Ren faire performers, no matter how wacky their shop premise.

"I'm sorry—" I began.

"No," he said. "Many have come to me, but no one has ever asked me that," he said. And then, as quickly as it had slipped, his self-assured mask came back up and he smiled his wise smile at me instead of his bemused one.

"I think your fate will surprise you, my young friend. Keep the necklace. It is my gift to you."

And then, like a burst bubble, someone slipped through the curtain and we were no longer alone, the wizard moving on from me to welcome his next guests.

"Weirdo," I made myself say under my breath as I left his stall, because it was much easier to pretend like he was just another performer, that he was trying to sell his cheap bottles of sand for a ridiculous price, instead of believing that maybe he was right and fate was real or whatever.

Still, that night after Mom and Dad tucked me into my RV bunk—a ritual I was much too old for but loved all the same—I clasped the globe to my neck and lined three treasures on the thin windowsill beside my bed: a tiny elephant of blown glass no bigger than my pinky nail, Mom's and my favorite book of poetry, and a key to my aunt Tabitha's garden shed, the one nonmoving place of permanence I could call mine.

I wanted to go back and ask him if the coin was right. I wanted him to tell me, once and for all, if the coin held all the power of fate and decisions and time that my family lore promised. I wouldn't get distracted by his talk of *fate* and *taming the world* and all that little-kid stuff; I would get straight to business and ask him about what actually mattered.

But when I came to the Wizened Old Wizard's stall the next morning right after the gates opened to the public—this time appropriately dressed in one of the faire costumes Mom had made me—the stall was empty.

"Where is the wizard?" I asked a passing knight.

He stuffed a biscuit in his pocket that looked suspiciously like a McMuffin and shrugged. "Not here, mistress," he said. "Perhaps he has gone to chase magic in a faraway land."

"But he was here," I insisted. "Yesterday. I saw him yesterday."

The knight dropped his faire speak, looking a bit bored. "Look, kid, he ain't here. As far as I know, this spot is empty for the whole faire, okay?"

For the next seven years, I would look for the Wizened Old Wizard at each faire. But just as easily as he had stumbled into my life, he stumbled out of it. Sometimes I'd hear that he was at another faire than the one we were working. Sometimes I wouldn't hear of him for months. But I kept my treasures ready, always ready, and the necklace around my neck so that he would remember me.

Just in case.

Because I still had questions to ask. Maybe more than when I'd started.

CHAPTER ONE

I WONDER WHAT THE WIZARD WOULD TELL me now, if he could see me standing with my elbows resting atop the stone wall looking down below into the lazy river moat with *literal alligator floaties*. I wonder what he would say if he could see my swirling thoughts. I wonder how he would advise me to make the world tamer given that the whole world around me has changed.

The moat encircles a castle—again, *literal*. I shut my eyes and give myself a moment to recalibrate like Dr. Jenkins—my teletherapist and my closest thing to an *actual* wise wizard— suggested I do when I feel overwhelmed. *Close your eyes,*

breathe, and just let yourself exist in the moment with no ex-
pectations, Madeline.

I try. It doesn't really work. The huge stone castle doesn't
change back into a worn-but-loved wooden facade. The moat
doesn't dry up and disappear from existence to match the
Stormsworth Faire of my memory, the Stormsworth Faire of
last year, where Mom is sick but still here. Where she is slow
and tired but still sits in a folding chair stringing beads for a
bracelet.

Everything, *literally everything*, is different this year. And
I'm trying my best to take it all in and *accept* and *breathe
through the changes*, but it's hard. So hard.

A memory flashes of elementary-school-aged me being
perennially unimpressed by Ren faire structures and castles
and life-size papier-mâché dragons, and Mom asking what it
would take to thrill me.

A moat, I told her. *An actual moat.*

But here it is, the one thing I said it would take to make a
Ren faire stand out from all the rest, the one thing that would
impress me, and she's not here to see it.

Mom died last year, near the end of the Stormsworth
Faire, actually. It all seemed so sudden, even though she had
been in and out of hospitals for a while.

I breathe in, exhale, then take in the air again to fill every
minuscule space in my lungs while my fingers play with the
globe that still hangs from my neck. I tug fretfully at it, like it's
a chain I can pull to hear the wizard's low rumble or Mom's

light, smiling voice, but the only sounds that reach my ears are of people laughing and splashing in the water below as bored lifeguards watch from their mini turret-shaped stands.

"Please, fair maiden," an exasperated voice says from behind me, "for the love of the kingdom and also my sanity, do *not* tell me thou art thinking about dropping that hunk of greasy meat in the moat."

I jerk upward from where I was leaning against the wall, quickly taking in the paper-wrapped turkey leg in my hand that I forgot I was holding before turning around.

The voice belongs to a bard, but unlike most bards I've come across at faire, this one is young, like maybe-my-age young, and he carries a lute. It's rarer than you'd think to hear a proper lute at Ren faire. Lots of bards and minstrels are perfectly happy with their acoustic guitars, ukuleles, and the occasional accordion, but this is the real deal with a stocky pear-shaped body that blocks nearly the entirety of its player's slim frame.

He is the most ordinary-looking boy I've ever seen. If he was cast in a movie, he would be Teenager #3 or not credited at all. He would be a guy waiting in line for coffee, a blurry figure hunched over a book in the background of a library scene, or maybe, if the casting director was feeling particularly kind, the boy with one line of discernable dialogue on a crowded street. His hair is brown, his skin is white, and his eyes are that kind of muddy dark color that might be brown, might be black, but you're never going to bother looking closely enough to find out, especially because it's hard to get past the thick, very non-time-period black-framed glasses that are a touch too big for his face.

"I wasn't going to *drop it*," I tell him.

The bard shrugs and strums a note. "You wouldn't be the first to drop something in the moat just to watch it splash."

"It's opening weekend," I say dubiously, "and this moat didn't exist last year."

None of this existed last year. My finger twitches toward my hip, where my travel journal usually rests, eager to catalog another tally mark beneath the *things that are different at Stormsworth* heading I know I'll make tonight. Of all days to forget my journal in Britomart.

"I *know*," the bard says, oblivious to my thoughts. "It's brand new, and already *somebody* had the bright idea to drop in at least a dozen foam swords and shout, 'Fight, you fools!'"

I level a look at him. "You dropped swords into the moat? You know there's always a code of conduct for faire staff and entertainers, right? I'm guessing 'don't throw things in the moat' is on there."

He grins. "It's not."

"Probably because it's *understood*," I say. "You're going to get fired."

He plucks at a string without breaking eye contact. He's the kind of sunshiny that pisses me off: willfully cheerful. Stupidly optimistic and carefree like it's his only personality trait, which it probably is.

"It's fine. I know the faire owners."

And just like that, I'm tired of this conversation. Not because the bard is particularly exhausting—even though he is—or because it's two in the afternoon and I haven't eaten lunch yet—even though I haven't—but because most conversations make me feel tired since my mom died. Because every single one is another string of words that separates me from her last. Every new person I meet is another person that won't get to meet my mom or see her flitting from stall to stall at faires to laugh with friends.

Everything, *literally everything*, feels like a reminder that she isn't here at our favorite faire.

Which I knew, of course. I knew that this faire in particular would be the hardest to weather without Mom, because this is *Stormsworth*. This is where so many of Mom and Dad's older friends who have left the circuit come each year as a kind of homecoming. It also used to be one of the more humbly decorated faires, and for that reason, it was one of Mom's favorites.

She loved the ramshackle stalls, the dirt pathways, the baseball-diamond-turned-arena. She said it felt like home. And because I grew up coming here, grew up looking forward to it year-round as a place where aunts who were not aunts and uncles who were not uncles would scoop me up in hugs and say things like, *My, how you've grown* and *Already taller than your mother*, it felt like home to me, too.

And it was the last faire she attended.

So I'm too tired to play with this bard, even though it's a rarity to see someone my age who is not a patron and even rarer for it to be someone I've never encountered in the circuit before. He's definitely a local, definitely someone who got an "in" because he knows the new owners. I haven't met the new owners, but I'm nursing a quiet grudge against them because they scrapped every little thing about the old Stormsworth Faire in favor of this overproduced, *expensive* monstrosity.

"This is lunch for my dad," I say to the bard, meekly gesturing behind me with the turkey leg. "I'd better take it to him before it gets cold."

"Wouldn't want that, Gwen," he says, falling in line with me as I turn to walk back toward our stall. I open my mouth to tell him my name isn't Gwen—and I have *no* idea why he would think it is—but he cuts me off with a waggle of his eyebrows and "This sounds like . . ." He pauses for dramatic effect. ". . . a Journey."

I unfortunately recognize the first few notes he plays.

"God, *please* don't," I beg. "Also, 'Don't Stop Believin'' isn't exactly a song from the Renaissance."

"Eh," the boy says, still strumming, still *annoyingly* walking beside me. "Nobody cares, so long as you throw in a hearty 'huzzah' once in a while."

He loudly sings the opening line of the song, and somehow manages to yell "Huzzah!" even *more* loudly after the girl takes the midnight train going anywhere. The answering "huzzah" from nearby faire-goers is—as is typical—on the tipsy side of enthusiastic.

I envy the girl on the train from the song. I'd pay a hefty price to be anywhere else right now. People are staring at us,

smiling at us. The attention makes my skin itch, and I'm ach-
ingly aware of where my elastic faux corset digs beneath my
arms.

"Would you *quit it*?" I whisper-yell under my breath, grabbing the bard's arm.

My actions regrettably have no effect on his strumming,
but he does stop singing and turns to smile at me.

"Gwen, you wound me. Is it the song? Because trust me: I
know *plenty* of others."

"Just stop," I say. "Please. And my name's not Gwen. It's—"

"No, no." He holds up his hands, cutting me off. "Your
name is Gwen. I won't hear of you being anything else."

His tone is easy, jovial. Too jovial. Like we're friends. And
maybe it's because I was just thinking of her and Stormsworth
and everything, but it reminds me . . . It reminds me a little
bit of Mom. She was exuberant, too.

I don't mean to snap at him so harshly, but I do.

"Go *away*, bard."

My words must not come out as menacing as I thought,
because his grin only widens.

"Don't be mad, Gwen. We've only just met. I can't possibly
have annoyed you yet. That's not scheduled for another"—he
pushes back a sleeve and checks his very not-Renaissance
Apple Watch—"ten minutes."

We're almost to the stall now, and I can't bear letting him
near Dad. Dad, who will look relieved and happy and a bit
sad all at the same time when he sees me with someone else
my age.

He's worried about me. I know because he's been doing that thing where he hovers a little more than usual after my Thursday appointments with Dr. Jenkins. And he's constantly asking "All right, Maddie?" or "Called Fatima lately?" when he thinks I've been too quiet for too long, which is often. Which isn't fair, because *he's* quiet, too.

I stop in the middle of the stone path—the one that just last year was reddish-brown dirt—and face the bard.

"You're ahead of schedule," I mumble to him. "You annoyed me the second I saw you."

For a moment, he looks hurt. His eyes—decidedly brown now that I'm looking—squint a little at the corners and his lips curve down. He recovers quickly, though, and the bright smile of a bard with no worries or cares slips back into place.

"But I need a muse, Gwen," he says, holding up his lute. "For my songs."

"Then I suggest you keep looking," I say, turning on my heel. "Go bother someone else."

I blessedly don't hear his footsteps or strums following me. *Good riddance.* And yet something in my heart jerks sideways when I glance behind me and see him walking away, his shoulders slightly lowered. The nudge of guilt makes me angry, and when I hear the distant opening chords of "Dancing with Myself" on a lute, I get angrier.

"Here," I say, irritably stepping into our stall and shoving Dad's turkey into his hand. "Dennis said to tell you hi and to come get your own leg next time."

Dad's bushy eyebrows scrunch over his nose, the only in-dication that he has detected my foul mood.

"All right, Maddie?"

I try not to sigh. "Fine, Dad."

A long pause as he wrestles with the paper of his lunch.

"Not hungry today?"

"Big breakfast," I say. Which is true, but not the whole truth. I'm too flustered by the changes to eat—and by the *bard*, if I'm honest with myself—but there's something else that's been bothering me. With the stall momentarily empty of cus-tomers and my guilt-fueled anger bubbling in my stomach, I drag my workbench stool over in front of Dad's cash register.

"How did you not know about this?" I ask him.

Dad finishes chewing. "About what?"

I point over my shoulder toward the faire. "*That.*"

"Oh," Dad says. "That."

As if there would be anything else to talk about.

He pauses to take a bite of turkey, chews like he's trying to break the world record for slowest mouthful of food ever consumed, and then coughs into his elbow. "I guess I did know about it."

I figured as much, which leads me to my next question. "Why didn't you tell me?"

Dad isn't like Mom. His emotions don't flash across his face for anyone to read. You have to know where to look, and then *really* look, to get an inkling of what he's thinking.

"It was a lot, Maddie," he says after taking forever to chew again. "I knew Stormsworth would be different—the structures, the events, the setup, everything. And I didn't think you could handle any more . . . news."

"But *how* did everything change?" I persist. "Marge and David didn't have this kind of money. Where did they get the cash to revamp *everything*? And why would they sell it afterward?"

"They don't. They didn't."

I pause as my brain fumbles for answers. "Oh my god. They *died*, didn't they? Is that what you're afraid to tell me?"

Dad's eyes widen. "No, no. They just retired, kid. They were old, you know? This place was a passion project and then the new buyers swooped in with an offer they'd be crazy to refuse and *then* changed everything. It happened . . . Well, it happened last August. I heard about it through the grapevine, of course, but I didn't want to bother you with it when you were . . . when *we* were still . . ."

Dad gets quiet in the way he does when he looks too directly at the hole where Mom should be. I've never mentioned it to Dr. Jenkins or to Dad, but when he gets the faraway look in his eyes, the one where he's flipping back through his own memories of Mom, it makes me scared. It makes me worried one day he'll go into the memories and not come back.

The story goes that when Dad met Mom, he was reading a book and looked up to see a princess standing before him.

"Bright as starlight on a dark winter's night," he used to whisper to me when I'd request the tale of their meeting as a bedtime story. "But prettier. Much prettier."

Dad didn't want to go to the Renaissance faire. His friends dragged him out of their college dorm, away from his precious studies for a day of drinking beer and betting on jousting matches. As always, Dad managed to sneak a book with him and eventually lost his boisterous friends and sat in the corner of the smallest tavern alone to read in peace.

He was halfway through his latest reread of *The Lord of the Rings*, he said, when he felt someone staring at him.

When he looked up, there was Mom, shirking her princess duties to get closer to the long-haired, bespectacled boy with the frown between his eyebrows and the finger poised to flip the page.

"I *never* dropped books," Dad would say. "I always set them down, and I usually wasn't happy about it. But when I saw your mom for the first time"—and he would always pause to laugh here—"I forgot all about my book. I forgot about everything except her. Just her."

Mom would usually come in at that part of the story, folding herself tight into Dad's other side, all three of us crammed on the bottom bunk that served as my room. She would kiss his cheek, reach across to smooth back my hair, smile, and say, "It was only the once, but it was such a loud *thump* in the quiet tavern, we both jumped and he spilled his ale."

Sometimes I would demand to see Dad's copy of *The Two Towers*, the pages forever rippled by the upset beer, but usually I would just tuck myself farther into our little family nest, reveling in my parents' love story.

I try to remember the nest and keep some of the bitterness

out of my voice when I say, "You should have told me. You know it's my favorite faire, that this was Mom's *last* faire."

Dad flinches, but I press on. "Why the hell wouldn't you mention it was going to be different this year?"

"It's not *all* different," Dad argues. "The new owners have employed most of the usual crowd. It's the people who make this place special, you know? That hasn't changed."

It's cheesy, what he says, but it makes me think of the bard again, of snubbing him *and* his enthusiasm that reminds me of Mom. It's not Dad's fault—or the bard's, for that matter—that everything is different. It's not the bard's fault that his enthusiasm brushed up against memories of Mom.

I pull on the globe around my neck again.

"I've changed my mind," I tell Dad. "I'm going to go grab some lunch."

"Probably for the best," he says.

I keep an eye (and ear) out for the bard as I walk to the food vendors, but I don't see him for the rest of the day.

Maybe I want to say sorry.

I *definitely* want to find the Wizened Old Wizard and ask him how I'm supposed to make the world tamer and kinder if I can't even be kind to a complete stranger who meant me no harm.

And, honestly? I want to know what comes next. I want to ask him where my life is going from here, because from where I stand, it looks like a sea of Mom-lessness and peering around corners hoping to see her coming toward me, only to be disappointed.

I know she's not coming back. It's been a year. We're long past the three-day miracle of biblical proportions. So I guess I want to know *when* I'll stop counting every day, every moment that she's not here . . . but also what I'll do when I stop. If I even can.

CHAPTER TWO

DR. JENKINS—WHO, AS ALWAYS, STARTS OUR virtual
session by insisting I can call her Julia—is wearing the
sweater I hate. The white, cozy one with chunky sleeves that
makes her look like she should live in Norway or Iceland or
somewhere else you can see the northern lights. I don't know
why I hate it, other than the fact that I could never own something that would take up so much unnecessary space. My
faire costumes are too bulky to have room for more than a
handful of street clothes.

If I was honest with Dr. Jenkins, I would tell her that the
Hathaway family coin is in my palm right now, still cool from

where I just fetched it from its velvet pouch beneath my pillow. I would tell her how I haven't flipped it since Mom's cancer diagnosis. I would tell her how Mom slipped it to me in the hospital room on her Last Good Day. How she said, "It's yours now," and how I was more than a little afraid of it, because hadn't the coin predicted exactly this outcome despite what the doctors said?

I know what she would say, which is why I don't bother telling Dr. Jenkins about the coin. *You are in control of your own fate, Madeline, not a coin.* Which isn't true, of course. If I were, Mom would still be here and Dad's smile wouldn't be sad. So either fate isn't real or it's a real bitch.

Only you can choose what's best for you, Madeline, Dr. Jenkins would say. And I wouldn't have a good answer. I would just nod.

Because truth be told, I can't articulate how I feel about fate. Most days, it's a heavy dose of skepticism—because what is even the point if we can't make our own choices?—but now, especially with Mom gone, I feel like the stupid coin is all I have, the only shot I have of maybe knowing how *she* would feel about what's going on in my life if she were still here.

Like Mom is personally haunting a family heirloom.

Like people in the afterlife can control coin flips.

So, like always, I don't tell Dr. Jenkins about the coin. Instead, I slip it back into its pouch out of sight of the camera. Sometimes it's just easiest to *not* think about something, especially in therapy.

"Hello, Madeline. Tell me about your week," Dr. Jenkins says, just like she does every Thursday.

And like every Thursday, I sigh through my nose, surreptitiously draw another tally mark in my journal beneath the *therapy* heading, and stretch a smile across my face. It takes a half second longer for the smile to appear on my webcam viewer.

"It's fine," I say, and it's almost true now that I've updated my journal and put on sweatpants.

Dr. Jenkins purses her lips. "Why don't we start with where you are today? Physically, I mean." I can see her peeking down at the notes in her lap. "Looks like you're in . . . Oklahoma, is that right?"

"Yes," I say, looking out the window of Britomart. "We just got here yesterday. Today was the soft opening." My eye catches on Dad, sitting just beneath my window at the picnic table on the patch of gravel beside Britomart. He's using his leather polish to neaten up his handmade journals in the dying light of the sunset, preparing for a full weekend of selling to the good patrons of the Stormsworth Renaissance faire. We sold a couple of the bigger journals today, so he's whistling and in a good mood.

"How'd that go?"

I turn back to my laptop. "It's fine," I say again.

In an attempt to get me to talk, Dr. Jenkins does that thing where she asks mundane questions that I guess are meant to show she's been paying attention to me for the last almost-year:

"Did you have a chance to set up your stall when you arrived yesterday?" No, we did it this morning because we got in late and didn't have the energy to go to the fairgrounds any earlier. "This one is your favorite, right?" Yes, I'm guessing migratory birds have favorite ponds, and this is mine. Eventually, she tries to sneak in the hard hitters, like I won't notice or maybe I'll "open up" and "really talk through my feelings." "Must be a relief to be at a place that is familiar and comforting to you as we come up on the anniversary of your mom's passing, huh?" Yeah, sure. I guess. "Do you want to talk about it?" Not really, Dr. Jenkins.

I give her questions only half my attention, nodding where I can as I quietly flip through my journal to find the heading marked *Dad working*. There are twenty-three tallies beneath it, mostly in black pen, some in purple, blue, or red, and it's the number twenty-three that gives me pause.

So few. Out of the last 324 days, I have only watched my father work on his journals twenty-three times. And not because he hasn't been doing it. He keeps a full stock at all times. But because *I* haven't been paying enough attention. Or rather, I must have been doing something else, noticing something else, while he was working. Twenty-three seems too small of a number, and my throat constricts a little.

When I look up from adding the twenty-fourth mark, Dr. Jenkins is silent and staring at me hard through the screen.

"Want to talk about *that*?" she asks.

I close my journal with one hand, running a finger over the soft brown leather.

"Honestly? Not really, Dr. Jenkins."

"*Julia*," Dr. Jenkins implores.

"Sure."

"Your journal?" she prompts. "We don't have to talk about the noticing pages if you don't want to. What about the poetry? Find anything new lately?"

"The noticing pages" is the name that Dr. Jenkins has given to my tally marks, which is maybe the best thing she's done for me in the—I flip back two pages—forty-four sessions we've had together. Before then, I wasn't sure what I was doing or *why* I was suddenly filled with the need to document how many times I noticed things like Dad working on journals, or the times that we had to change Britomart's tires, or how many essays I've written for school, or the exact number of therapy sessions I've had since Mom died.

But pretty early on, when Dr. Jenkins asked about my ever-present travel journal, I figured I might as well hold it up to the camera and show her. Because unlike the coin, I wasn't sure how she'd respond.

I explained the four individual journals bound within their leather holder: the one with bits of poetry I collect from books and the internet and mass-produced home decor signs at Target, the one I use for keeping up with my online high school assignments, the one for random facts and tidbits that *aren't* poetry but might as well be because of how they make me feel, and the journal of noticings.

Usually, I wouldn't mind talking to Dr. Jenkins about the noticings, but tonight, with the anniversary of Mom's death breathing down my neck, my lingering feelings of guilt about the bard and his unnatural frown, and the coin burning a hole in my consciousness, I don't want to.

She started hinting weeks ago that I needed to start "living my life" and let the noticings fall by the wayside. But I'm tired of letting things go against my will—almost as tired as I am discussing it week after week at Dad's insistence that therapy will "help me cope"—and so I sink gratefully into her suggestion of discussing my poetry journal instead.

It's not totally safe, the poetry, because it reminds me so much of Mom. She's the one who got me hooked on it. She used to read me poems instead of bedtime stories. Mom was a narrator in a previous life *for sure* because her voice could do anything. It could be stormy and dark, light and airy, and everything in between. She made poetry a living, breathing thing that made me want to find more just to hear her read it.

Even when I was too old for bedtime stories, we would sit together on the bottom bunk, my head on her shoulder and her arm around me while she marveled at the poetry I found. She wasn't picky or pretentious or whatever. She didn't care if it was a Shakespeare sonnet or something I read on the back of a coffee cup. Mom read everything in the same reverent, smooth voice.

So yeah, talking poetry feels like a stab, but it's better than the noticings.

"Emily Dickinson," I tell Dr. Jenkins, a canned answer that's almost as good as avoiding her questioning all together. "'That it will never come again is what makes life so sweet.'"

We talk a little about Dickinson, which I use as a segue to talk about how I turned in the last English paper of my junior year two nights ago, which Dr. Jenkins tries to re-segue into talking about my feelings and the "changes coming on the horizon of my life." Somehow I manage to bounce this back to the particular strangeness of online schooling, a necessity in the faire circuit life, which is a topic I find endlessly fascinating and blessedly free of too many emotions.

Because the truth of it is, I *like* online school. I like getting a list of assignments at the beginning of the semester that I can finish at whatever time of day I want, and that the curriculum is looser than in-person public school. I like that I don't have to worry about wearing the right clothes or saying the right things in front of boys like my friend Fatima does. She said it was the weirdest part about quitting the circuit: not living in a house without wheels, not having an entire room to herself that she could fill with treasures or junk or nothing at all, but having to talk with other kids our age on a daily basis.

Dr. Jenkins is not fooled by my enthusiasm at the topic change, though, and she must be able to tell that my mind is elsewhere, because like every Thursday, she finishes off our talk with a short sigh she thinks I can't hear and a slight frown she thinks I can't see. "Well, Madeline. Same time next week work for you?"

"Sure." And just like every Thursday, I tease, "Thanks, Dr. Julia Jenkins."

But this is where she goes off script, where she's *supposed* to smile and say, *Okay, Madeline. See you next Thursday.*

Instead, she peers into the camera like we're together in the same room, then shakes her head ever so slightly, like she was about to say something but changed her mind.

"What?" I ask. "What is it?"

"Nothing," she says, her voice more hesitant than I've ever heard. "I just . . . I think you're going to have a good week, Madeline. I really do."

And maybe it's because I *desperately* hope she's right and that this particular faire, this particular month, won't turn into a pit of quicksand that tries to drag me down and suffocate me, but I want to believe her.

"Thanks, Julia," I whisper.

Her smile is warm, all soft eyes and gentle lips.

"Have a good night, Madeline."

When she disconnects from our video call, my torso fills the entire screen, and instead of shutting my laptop immediately like I usually do, I lean in and examine my face.

It's round, like the rest of me. It's the cruelest of cruelties to have a mother like mine who was beautiful and lithe and fairy-esque but to have all of my genes line up with my father's. Words like "sturdy" and "hefty" and "solid" are fine when applied to a kitchen table or an RV but not to a seventeen-year-old girl who spends an inordinate amount of time dressed in medieval garb.

But there are still bits of my mother embedded in my features. The eyes, for one, the color green in some lights and blue in others, like whoever is in charge of eye color flipped their own coin to decide but still couldn't settle on a choice.

The hair, too—though it lacks my mother's natural fairy-tale ringlets in favor of saddish waves—is the same shade of blond, like *blond* blond. The kind that makes the women at the Southern faires always ask who my colorist is, and makes them look disbelieving when I say it's natural.

The freckle on my bottom lip is entirely my own, even if the lips themselves are fuller like Dad's. Mom used to say I was the perfect sandwich of her and Dad: a little of both of them, but a whole lot of me in the middle.

"But *which parts?*" I would ask when I was younger. "Which parts are just Madeline?"

"You'll find out." She would smile. "And I can't wait to watch when you do."

I wonder if my globe necklace is just Madeline. I *know* the way I snapped at the bard and then at Dad is just Madeline, because neither of my parents would have behaved that way, no matter how irritated they were.

But like it or not, *this* is me now. I'm Madeline Hathaway: Seventeen, fat, motherless, and smart. Smart enough to know that I never, ever want to experience the white-hot grief of losing someone I love again. There's nothing I can do about already loving Dad and Fatima—hence the noticings—but if I close up shop, it'll just be them I have to worry about.

Fate can't take away what you don't have.

I close my laptop as Dad comes in through Britomart's door. An echo of thunder, closer now, chases behind him as I slither down my bunk ladder to help him bring his journals inside.

"Ready for tomorrow?" I ask him.

"Sure, sure," he says, setting the box on the overcrowded dinette table. "You?"

He purposefully doesn't mention my session with Dr. Jenkins, like always.

"Big day," I say. "I bet the crowds will double."

"Surely," he says. "Is your inventory ready for the next couple of weeks?"

"Yeah, we didn't sell as much on closing weekend in Wisconsin, so stock is good."

I don't tell him that the stock is *more* than good, probably for the rest of the summer, though I suspect he knows since there are so many jewelry boxes that they're taking over Britomart. Or maybe he overheard me explaining to Dr. Jenkins numerous Thursdays ago that creating Mom's jewelry—with her patterns and her carefully chosen beads and stones— makes me feel both comforted and confronted, a delicate balancing act of reminding myself of her presence and lack thereof.

When Mom found out she was sick, Dad made her a special journal to fill with illustrations of her designs. At the front are lists of her favorite jewel pairings, charm wholesale dealers, clasp types. There are notes about which metals are for sensitive ears and which of her designs sell fast, price margins, and average construction time.

In the closet beside the front door and under my bed are dozens of boxes of carefully wrapped necklaces and bracelets and earrings, more than enough for the summer. More than enough for the rest of the year. To say nothing of the ones stacking up on the bottom bunk that I mostly use for storage.

But I can't stop making them. I don't know what will happen if I do, and I'm not keen on finding out. When I can't sleep, which is often, I'll sit beneath the single-bulb green lamp that is nailed to the table and string bead after bead, gem after gem, until I am nothing but a pair of hands working in the night.

"What's for dinner?" I ask. We haven't had a chance to hit the grocery store since arriving from Wisconsin, which usually means takeout or fast food.

Dad shrugs. "There's a staff party tonight, if you're interested. Potluck. We have a few bags of chips in the pantry we could contribute."

I turn away so he can't see me wrinkle my nose. I *hate* the faire parties. They're usually too loud and too boring and—oftentimes—too drunken and greasy for me to ever let down my guard, especially with Dad watching my every move and every move of anyone who comes within five feet of me.

It's exhausting.

Stormsworth is different, though, or at least it has been in the past. These parties tend to be a bunch of people like Mom and Dad: old-timers who want to shoot the breeze on past escapades rather than create new ones. But the fact that all the not-aunts and not-uncles—that I call aunt and uncle all the same—will be there with their sympathetic pats on the shoulders and their downturned mouths makes the thought of going even *more* exhausting.

"Why don't you go, Dad?" I say. "I need to work on an assignment anyway."

"I thought you were done with school," Dad says. He's turned away from me and digging around in the pantry for bags of chips.

"Yeah, but I have a summer reading project for senior AP English. I'll just eat some ramen, work a little, hang out, you know? I'm already in pajamas."

I'm not, actually, but if Dad notices, he doesn't say anything. He closes the pantry door and leans forward to kiss me on the forehead, something he only started doing with any frequency after Mom died, and for that reason alone, I kind of hate it. I mentally remind myself to put a tally for it in the noticings.

"I'll see you in the morning," he says. "You'll probably be asleep before I'm back."

"Bright and early," I say, and if my voice is brittle around the edges, Dad pretends not to notice that, too.

And then he's gone, Britomart's door thumping closed behind him as he walks toward the RV parked nearest us—Aunt Jackie and Uncle Stewart's new, shiny Winnebago—where I guess the dinner is being held.

It feels like all the breath leaves my body at once and echoes around Britomart in Dad's wake. It's rare, when your home is less than four hundred square feet and your privacy consists of a single closed door—Dad's—and a red curtain—mine—to feel like you can truly let your guard down, like you can let yourself feel whatever it is you want to feel or think without having . . . input.

It's not Dad's fault; he lost Mom, too. I have to remind myself of this over and over again when he alternates between benign neglect and attention so intense and focused that I want to scream. It's not his fault that instead of jotting down every little noticing in a journal, he tries to absorb it through his eyes, often becoming teary if he looks at me too long.

You look like your mother. You look like your mother. You look like your mother. He says this, now and again, when I'm hunched over the jewelry table or when I'm combing my fingers through my hair as we walk to the faire. That's when I tap the freckle on my lip to remind myself that it's not true—Dad is just grieving, and I have entirely too much of him flowing through my veins.

But his words haunt me all the same, echoing around the empty RV until I decide that even though it's much too early, I'll go ahead and start getting ready for bed.

My routine is the same every night and has been since I can remember. It's a centering thing, Dr. Jenkins once explained. Totally healthy, she said, if I don't let my routine become so rigid that I would suffer without it.

I always nod, like I agree, but I haven't missed a single night since Mom died, and I don't plan to.

As far as bedtime routines go, it's not very complicated:

There's the nightly rinse-off in the tiny triangular RV shower, followed by hair-moisturizing cream wrapped up in a micro-fiber towel Mom always insisted made my hair shinier. While the cream sits, there's teeth brushing, face washing, and—if I'm feeling particularly self-indulgent—a stupid amount of lotion that fills the entire bathroom with its vanilla scent.

The crucial part though, ranking higher in my esteem than personal hygiene, is my nightly cup of herbal tea and my favorite web comic, *The Falconer's Gauntlet*.

The comic only updates on Wednesdays, but every night I reread some of the two hundred episodes, scrolling through the story of a magical falconer, Adelina, and her beloved bird, Cornelius. Their adventures are always intense, but never scary—fantastical, but always rooted in something human enough, real enough, that I could almost *be* Adelina.

It doesn't matter that I've read each episode roughly three billion times. It doesn't matter that I could draw entire scenes from memory. All that matters is that everything—the characters, the color palettes, the weekly upload time—stays bless-edly the same. I think the routine is my small way of trying to shrink the world, to make it tamer for my own self.

Tonight, though, my brain is humming too quickly, too loudly with my worry over Stormsworth's changes, to properly focus. My tea grows cold. The comic blurs before my eyes as I mindlessly thumb through episode after episode, barely registering Cornelius's antics, Adelina's exasperation.

How could they change *everything* about the faire?

I set my tablet aside and flip to my journal of noticings

to place another tally beneath the *cups of hot tea consumed* heading. My eye catches on a page of my poetry journal, this one from a poet named Tor Barnes:

I grow tired
So tired of ever-changing, always moving, never resting.
Even birds must perch, dwell, nest.
If birds that fly over rainbows must land,
Why can't I?

Something in the poem makes my eyes tinge with tears.

Whatever feeling it is, it jerks me out of bed, crams shoes on my feet beneath old sweatpants, and pushes me out of Britomart's door toward the faire.

I don't care that the grounds will be empty. I don't care that it's pitch-black and lightly raining. I need to go see if there is anything, anything at all, that reminds me of the old Stormsworth.

I need to see if there is still a place for me to land.

CHAPTER THREE

I T'S NEARLY MIDNIGHT WHEN I ARRIVE to gawk at the gates of Stormsworth, my chest rising and falling with the effort of having half walked, half jogged through the trees. Hours of sitting while making jewelry is not conducive to athleticism, and my too-long sweatpants keep trapping themselves beneath the heels of my sneakers.

Everything is just as unrecognizable and wrong as I left it a few hours ago, but now I can take it in slowly, unencumbered by boxes of jewelry and journals and the little wagon I use to haul stock from Britomart to our stall.

The entrance, with its new, unfamiliar gilded monstrosities, soars at least five feet above my head. Where once there was a rusting chain-link fence, there are now ornate metal doors bearing a large cursive S that seems to glow menacingly in the darkness. To my left, illuminated by the single lamppost, there is a ticket booth that looks more like a guardhouse than a humble Ren faire entrance.

It's absurd, overwrought, *expensive*.

Maybe it's the statuesque gates, but as I stand at the mouth of Stormsworth with my neck craned upward, I think of the Hyperion tree, the tallest tree in the world. I remember stumbling across a paragraph about it in my science book, mostly boring, mostly talking about how redwoods grow, but at the very end, a sentence that gave me pause. *For fear of vandalism, the Hyperion tree's location, among many other gentle redwood giants, is kept secret.*

I remember writing it down in my journal of facts. I remember thinking how awful, how terrible a species humans must be if something so grand must be kept secret because of senseless destruction.

The solidness of these gates makes me think going out here was a terrible idea. Maybe I should go back to Britomart. And yet I find myself too curious to leave, too curious to stop myself from tugging on the gate, which, to my surprise, budges just the slightest bit. It takes some doing, but I manage to scrape it open enough to squeeze inside when I push with all my weight, the metal cold on my skin when my tee bunches against the gate.

Mom always loved the entrance to Stormsworth, because beyond the chain link, beyond the humble ticket booth, there were trees, redbuds that tangled in and around each other to form a thicket that blocked your view of the faire itself as you entered.

"It transports you," Mom would say. "It's the only faire that gives you time to adjust, a chance to walk from the twenty-first century to the seventeenth."

The trees are still here, at least, but the dirt path has been replaced with a stone walkway and matching walls that come up nearly to my shoulder. My rubber soles give off an echo. So much for stealth.

But there's no one here, and even if there were, I could come up with some excuse of going to check on our stall or whatever. It's not like anyone explicitly told me I *couldn't* be here. But these new owners, whoever they are, must be filthy rich. Rich enough to afford Jurassic Park–ing some dire wolves back into existence for security purposes, or, at the very least, very good alarm systems.

Oddly, the thought isn't enough to deter me.

I'm not sure what it is: the fact that the torches aren't lit and the moon is my only lamp, or if it's the illicit nature of having snuck away, or maybe it's that for a blessed second I forget *why* I came here to begin with. Whatever the reason, when the path widens and the trees sweep back like curtains on a stage, I feel like I've stepped into a fairy tale.

The new Stormsworth is not a medieval village. It's just not. I've been lectured by enough faire-going historians—the ones who always explain that funnel cakes are *not* medieval, as if anyone thought otherwise—to know what is real and what is part of the collective imagination of the Middle Ages. But it's . . . charming. Almost sickeningly so.

I will myself to keep hating it for replacing the Stormsworth of my memory, even as I admire the well-kept flower beds beside each permanent stall, the expensive-looking flags and tapestries hung along the stone walls and buildings.

A closer examination of a flag shows a crest: two identical crowns atop a lion and a hound, a songbird between them. *Ad astra per aspera* is scrawled around the edges, and I resist rolling my eyes. I have no idea what it means, but I can guess it's pretentious.

My brain is madly trying to grip on to what was while my eyes take in what is. Stormsworth used to feel like a beloved, well-worn roadside attraction, one of those places in the middle of nowhere that advertise on peeling billboards, counting down the miles until weary travelers arrive and pay far too much money for plastic toys and corny T-shirts. It was just on the lacking side of luster, a little cheesy even for a Ren faire, but it was a fixture in the circuit, in my world, the one stop a year I looked forward to, the one I clung to as Mom slowly slipped out of reach.

I come to stand beside our shop, where this morning Dad hung our sign: Faerie Queene Gifts. Just like he does every time he finishes setting up, he dusts off his perfectly clean hands and says, "Another day at the salt mines." I mentally put another tally in my journal.

Thinking of my journal again makes my skin feel itchy. The point of the journal was to document the things that stay the same. To remember, remember, remember the little things that make up the everyday-ness of my life, of Dad's life, so that someday, if need be, I will have noticed so much that I won't have to miss Dad at all.

Because it's been nearly a year and I'm forgetting what *her* voice sounded like, the particular way she shaped her vowels and consonants, the way she tucked her hair behind her ear, which way she stirred a pot of soup. I'm forgetting how her smile would start—if it started at the corners and pulled up, or if it started at her cupid's bow and grew outward.

I won't make that mistake again. If I remember to write it all down, I'll have less to forget. Because whether fate is real or not, I'm not risking the chance of not being prepared if I lose someone again.

The tears start to flow a little, and I'm actually wondering what I must look like—a girl in old sweatpants with damp hair standing in front of an empty Ren faire stall, crying— when a sound comes from behind me.

"You there," a man says. "Halt in the name of the kings!"

He stands a few feet away from me, his flickering flashlight pointed square in my face so that it makes it harder, but not impossible, to see the patch proclaiming *security* on his . . . is that chain mail hanging over his shirt and jeans?

"This is private property," the man says before I have a chance to speak. "You shouldn't be here."

My voice is stuck in my throat, my brain stopping any

words from escaping—*I'm so sorry, I'm with the faire. I'm so sorry, I'm harmless*—and though it's hard to make out his facial expression with the light still shining in my eyes, he looks supremely irritated.

"You kids think it's okay to go traipsing around private property and I'm sick of it. The police are on their way, I'll have you know. You just come sit over here on this bench and wait for them to get here."

"But wait," I finally manage, "I'm with the faire. This— this is our stall. My dad and me . . ." I trail off as the security guard finally lowers the flashlight to his side.

"Even if that's true," he says, "you shouldn't be sneaking around. I'm gonna have to call your parents. Let them know what's going on."

The Stormsworth map ought to have a big red X on the spot where I am standing now labeled *a rock and a hard place*. Because the obvious option is to let him call Dad. But I *can't* let Dad know I snuck out. He'll flip in that overprotective, your-mother-is-dead-and-you're-all-I-have-left way, just like when he grounded me for a week last December when I forgot to tell him I was going to be out late studying at the library and he came home to find me missing.

I'm thinking the answer to my problem might be to make a break for the gates—because apparently my fight or flight response has forgotten how much effort it took just to walk here—when a low whistle comes from the direction of the castle. A boy, hands in Scooby-Doo pajama pockets, strolls toward us.

And of course, because this night is already a disaster, he's the *bard*.

"Good morrow, Jacob," he says to the security guard, then turns to me. "Gwen, dear. Didn't I tell you to use the private gate? Jacob here was probably about to call the police."

Jacob rubs his hands through his close-cropped hair, the chain mail clanking merrily against the flashlight that he has blessedly shut off. "Arthur," he says in short greeting. "And I already called them. I didn't know she was one of your friends." He turns to me, eyebrows raised. "She didn't say."

"I'm . . . sorry?" I say, and it comes out a question, but neither the bard—Arthur—nor Jacob the security guard who wears chain mail over jeans seems to notice.

"Your folks didn't mention you were expecting a visitor during our phone call this afternoon," Jacob says.

Arthur's easy smile is now accompanied by a comically large eyebrow wiggle as he slings an arm around my neck, his fingers brushing my collarbone, my necklace. "Jacob, my good man, have you ever been in love? Head-over-heels, weak-in-the-knees love? Can we keep this between you and me, just for now?"

It's hard to tell who is blushing more: me or Jacob.

"Understood, young master Arthur."

"Thanks, Jacob. Stormsworth could have no finer defender than you, my friend."

The security man ambles off, apparently satisfied to leave a potential trespasser in a bard's care.

"Hi," Arthur says, but he might as well have said *I've come to murder you and throw your body in the moat* for as high as I jump.

"I was just leaving," I say.

"Funny, I was just walking around aimlessly."

"Swell," I deadpan. "I'm going to go now."

Before my dad realizes I'm gone and I'm grounded for life. Before I can think about how different this place is and cry about it in front of you.

Arthur starts to close the distance between us, and I turn away, not because I'm afraid—I've felt more threatened by Fatima's twelve-year-old house cat—but because I'm frustrated and done and . . . ashamed. I treated him so poorly this afternoon, and yet he still has the ready smile, the eager-to-please eyes. Everything about him screams *please like me*, and it's making me irritable.

"Wait," he says. "You want to see more of the grounds? I can show you around, if you want."

"Thanks," I say, still walking toward the gates, "but I'm not in love with you and I'm sure I can manage on my own tomorrow."

"That was a joke," he laughs. "To stop Jacob from calling down the cops. Come on, you didn't sneak in just to leave, did you? Don't you want to see the castle at night?"

I don't stop walking but point over my shoulder. I *had* hoped to get a closer look, because the spires are the only thing I can see clearly from vendor's row, thanks to all the stone walls and trees.

"Castle. Saw it. Thanks."

Arthur laughs, undeterred. "Okay, but did you see the moat *at night*?"

I pause. He makes it sound like it's going to be a fundamentally different experience or something.

"What does it matter?" I ask. "It's just darker."

I don't have to look at him to know his grin has widened. I can *hear* it when he says "Nope." He pops the P. "I shit you not: it's enchanted at night by a kind wizard."

Before I can roll my eyes, he makes his voice smooth like honey. "There are dragons," he promises. "Fairies, too."

"There are *not*."

We're facing each other now, so I get a clear view of his hand as he holds it out to me, palm up, still grinning. "Wanna see?"

"Don't you hate me?" I blurt.

Arthur's smile falls a little, confused. "Come again?"

"Well, because of earlier," I say. "I . . . I was rude. Really rude."

"The mark of maturity isn't perfection," he intones, pitching his voice an octave deeper, "but rather the ability to right your wrongs."

"Who said that?"

His eyes crinkle. "Me," he says. He raises his hand a little in my direction. "*Come see*."

I'm thinking of two things at once as I stare at Arthur the bard in an after-hours faire that looks like it fell out of a fairy tale: I think of Mom, dragging Dad and me somewhere, saying, *Come look, come see*, with us forever trailing behind, shaking our heads in exasperation but loving it all the same. And I remember part of a poem I have scrawled in my journal, found on some corner of the internet on some nondescript night when I couldn't sleep:

Some will say they prefer the holy Psalms,
But as for me and my soul,
Our church is where clasp human palms.

I instinctively lean forward and take the hand of the strange boy in pajama pants whom I barely know, but I silently curse both the memory and the stanza for their part in this.

Because *this* is the opposite of my new life plan. The less people I tangle into my heart, the less I'll have to worry about.

"I don't hold hands with strangers," I tell him as he hauls me toward the castle.

"We met today!" Arthur says, his tone as outraged as if we had met five years ago.

"I don't hold hands with *anyone*," I amend.

"You should try it more often," he says. "You have very holdable hands. Probably in the top ten hands I've held."

He says it in a way that makes me hate myself for asking but finding it impossible to hold back. I try to sound as disinterested as possible. "How many hands have you held?"

He snorts. "Like I could keep count. Stop dragging your feet. I feel like Hades dragging Persephone to hell."

"I thought Persephone went willingly," I say, and he snorts again.

"Depends which version you subscribe to. Every story has two sides," Arthur says, "like a coin."

I balk at that, thinking of *the* coin, but he just tugs on my arm a little harder, and then we're standing at the base of the castle.

It somehow looks larger at night. I'm not a great judge of size, but it *must* be three stories, and that's not including the spires. Almost all of the windows are filled with flickering light. It's rather ostentatious to have lights lit from within the facade (because they are almost always facades), but even I can admit it makes the stone look a little warmer to have buttery yellow pouring from the windows.

Most castles at faires, if the faire even *has* a castle, are either temporary structures that disappear the week after the faire ends or are small, empty things with open roofs and windows. The very few permanent fixtures I've seen are much, much smaller than this one. And they *certainly* don't have a moat of moving water with fireflies bobbing at the edges.

"Those are not fairies," I say.

"Says who?"

"Um, science?"

"Don't know him," Arthur says.

"And there aren't any dragons."

Arthur points silently to our right with his free hand, his other still gently clasped around mine. Where the moat curves around the castle, in a nest of shrubs, are three small green dragons lit from within. They look like they're made out of the same stuff as pipe cleaners and Christmas lights.

"They're tiny," I say critically. "Why would someone bother putting them there if they are too tiny to notice during the day and only visible at night after everyone has gone home?"

Arthur shrugs. "Why not?"

I cut my eyes over to him. "I'm willing to bet the new owners are wacky, right?"

"Nope." He laughs, and pops the *P* again, something that I would usually abhor but sounds perfectly natural coming from him. "Well, not entirely, anyway. They occasionally know what they're doing. I mean, you like the moat, right?"

Now seems as good a time as any to drop his hand. He lets go with no resistance.

"It's . . . another change," I say, running my palms over the stone of the moat wall.

He turns to me, folding his arms loosely.

"Not a fan?"

"Of what?"

"Change."

I turn to dangle my arms over the side of the moat. "Who is?"

I can feel him staring at me, but I still refuse to meet his eyes. Instead, I stand on my tiptoes, peering down into the dark, unmoving water.

"So your parents are the new owners," I tell the water.

Arthur straightens. "How did you know?"

I gesture at his pajama bottoms.

"Unless I missed the memo about loungewear being in

style for breaking and entering, you must live nearby. Plus, Jacob said he talked to your dad, right?"

"For someone who looks so lost, you pick up on a lot," he says. "Yes, my dads own the faire."

"Dads? As in plural?"

His voice is careful. "As in plural."

"Cool," I say, fiddling with my necklace. "Just making sure."

He cuts his eyes to my fidgeting fingers and breathes out, slapping me on the back. "Good. I knew I liked you, Gwen."

"Where do you live, anyway?" I ask. I mean for it to come out harsh and accusatory, to wipe the overly pleasant look from his face, but it comes out curious. "Is your house behind the faire?"

Arthur rubs the back of his neck. "In a manner of speaking."

Now it truly is curiosity, not angry-at-the-world-so-let's-make-it-angry-too pettiness that colors my tone. "Okay . . . so what were you doing walking around an empty faire at night?"

His laugh sounds mocking. "Gwen, my love, one as beautiful as you can't possibly imagine the trials of us poor sods who are nothing but a few pounds of oddly proportioned bone and sinew."

"What?"

Arthur's grin is rueful. "I mean that you couldn't possibly understand what it's like to be burdened with unattractiveness."

I bristle. I haven't managed to identify how exactly my body is too much, but I know it is. I know because when Mom would take me shopping every fall, it got harder and harder to find clothes that fit my hips, my thighs, my torso, my butt. My body felt like a remix of "Goldilocks and the Three Bears": A conglomeration of too big and too small and just right all at once, depending on what outfit I was wearing. The shirt might fit in the bust and the arms, but too baggy in the middle. Or it might fit in the waist but leave angry red rings around my arms from the too-tight sleeves.

It's not like it's a *thing*, my size, but sometimes it's hard to be reminded every weekend of my life—on faire flyers and advertisements and vendor signs that all feature thin royalty and fairies and mermaids—that my body is not ideal.

Ideally, I wouldn't think about this at all, but then there are the sideways comments from boys in Scooby-Doo pajamas, and I go on the defensive. Which *then* makes me feel worse, because shouldn't I be strong in myself and above other people's opinions or whatever?

But it's been a long day, and I'm too tired to self-evaluate my reaction. "I'm going home," I say, and my tone is unmistakably pissed as I turn once more to walk away.

Arthur, smart boy that I can already tell he is, picks up on it immediately.

"Wait, what did I say?"

I speed up. "Figure it out."

I hate myself for how much it hurts to have him point

out my weight, even indirectly. I hate how much I care what this boy, this *stranger*, thinks of me. Not even *of me* but *of my appearance.*

Years of telling myself not to care, not to place inherent value on outward appearances, has only made me feel ashamed when I do. But most of all, I hate that Arthur was obviously mocking me when he called me beautiful.

"Gwen, I really was talking about *me*."

I don't stop, but he's keeping pace easily.

"Really. Look, please stop? I didn't mean to . . . Oh, for fuck's sake. I was talking about *me* because I got stood up, okay? Just yesterday. Like, less than twenty-four hours ago."

I stop, the iron gates just a few yards ahead of us.

"Stood up?"

He breathes out, like he's relieved I'm listening. "*Yes*. If you require gritty details, I'm afraid you're out of luck. She was supposed to meet me at the restaurant. She didn't show. I texted her and she said that she got busy, and now she doesn't know if she has time to reschedule. But of course, it's a lie, because no more than ten minutes later she posted a pic of her shopping with the theater dreamboat guy who has been making eyes at her since the homecoming dance."

Oh. It wasn't about me at all.

"Sorry," I say. "That sucks."

Not that I would know. I've never asked or been asked for a date to begin with.

But this boy with the mouth made for smiling and stupid

pajama pants is clearly sad, and somehow, even though I don't really know him, this seems wrong, a glitch in the matrix of his personality.

I decide to let myself care about his downturned mouth, just for a few minutes. It won't violate the no-caring rule if I put a time limit on it.

"Her loss," I tell him. "You seem nice in that overly attentive sort of way."

He smiles, but it's small. "It's not like she owes me anything," he says, "but a text saying she wasn't coming would have been nice. Or maybe a 'Hey, the Greek god that is Noah Leos finally asked me out after he heard I was going to meet up with you. Sorry.'"

"Not to question you in your time of distress or anything, but that doesn't exactly answer why you're walking around *here* at midnight in your pajamas."

His smile shrinks even more, almost slipping into a grimace when he answers. "My dads are . . . well, they're hopelessly in love. *Hopelessly.* Usually it's great, but it's not exactly conducive to the brooding, stood-up-for-a-date environment I was looking for. Besides, what better place to have melancholic feelings than in a medieval village by moonlight?"

The last part comes out a bit like a question, like he's asking *me* what I'm running away from.

"I get that," I whisper. And because he's being honest and the time limit isn't up yet, I add, "My mom died last year."

"Shit," he says. "I know it doesn't help to say it, but I'm sorry."

"Yeah," I say. "It's . . . been not great. I guess I came here to see what changed because it's our favorite and it was the last faire she attended. Last year, I mean. I came because . . . Because I wanted to see if there was anything left that she would recognize if she were here, you know?"

He's rubbing the back of his neck again. "Yeah, they kind of overhauled everything."

"I can see that," I say with a sigh. "Whatever. It's not like it's"—I raise both of my hands to gesture at everything around us—"hideous or something."

"No," Arthur says, "and it can't be all bad if fate used it to bring us both here at the same time, right?"

I drop my hand from where it was just unconsciously fiddling with the globe necklace. "I don't believe in fate," I say.

Somewhere, in the distant past where Mom was still alive and I was even less of who I would be than what I am now, I hear the same words echoed back to me from the Wizened Old Wizard's stall.

But I didn't. *I don't.* Not today, and if I ever do, it *certainly* won't be because of meeting Arthur.

"Believe in it or not, it still exists," Arthur says. He leans forward and taps a single finger on my globe. "Just as surely as the world keeps turning—which is a *great* song by Fleetwood Mac, by the way—fate will keep fating."

"I don't think 'fating' is a word," I say.

"It is."

My sigh of exasperation quickly turns into a traitorous yawn, which is just as well because we are far over the deadline of my allotted time for caring. Arthur straightens and takes a small step forward.

"You're tired. Let me walk you home," he says, the energy from our argument on fate seeping out of his voice as quickly as it has mine. "Please?"

"I'm good," I say, because letting him come to Britomart would absolutely violate the time limit. "I'm perfectly capable of walking back on my own."

"I would hate for you to run into Jacob again without me there to save you," Arthur says. "You might need a fearless protector in the night. What if you come across a feral cat? A rabid racoon?"

"Got a lot of those hanging around, do you?"

Arthur steps around me and bows ridiculously low. "It would be a great honor if my lady would allow me to escort her home."

I find that I'm too weary to argue, so I groan and nod my assent. "Fine, but that's it."

He practically skips beside me as we walk toward the gates, trying once, twice, and then a third time to link arms with me. I give in on the third attempt, mostly because I'm afraid if I don't, I'll laugh aloud and it will only encourage his antics.

Even through the arm-linking, we walk in a not-entirely-uncomfortable silence as we make our way out the lavish front gates and to the RV park and camping grounds. The walk seems both shorter and longer with Arthur by my side, in part because he keeps dragging me forward with his longer stride before realizing and adjusting again to match my shorter one.

"I really am sorry about your mom," he says when I thump Britomart's bumper to indicate we've arrived.

"I really am sorry about your date," I say.

Arthur smiles. "It's nice of you to say that, but they are *obviously* very different."

His ten minutes are up, I know, but I can't help but say, "Yes, but no one else ever lost my mom like I did and no one ever got stood up for this particular date like *you* did."

"That's . . . an extraordinarily generous outlook."

I shrug, blushing even though I'm not sure why. "My therapist sometimes says smart things. She says grief isn't a contest because there are no winners, so we might as well all help each other toward healing or something."

"I don't know if I would say I'm *grieving*," he says.

My hand is on Britomart's door when I respond. Somewhere, an invisible clock hand is ticking, reminding me to sever this conversation, to not care. "I don't think grief has to mean death. I think there are lots of different types of grief. You're grieving what could have been with that girl and that night and that date. It doesn't mean you won't feel better tomorrow, but it doesn't take away from your feelings tonight, either."

Arthur's eyes are luminous in the starlight as he looks up at me.

"Gwen, I don't know what it is you sell, but you shouldn't be a vendor. With speeches like that, you should be a princess. No, it's your *fate* to be a princess."

I can't help but smile, even as I tell myself not to. "I don't think the dress would fit," I say. And then I stop the clock, opening the door. "Okay, bye."

Not *see you later* or *see you around* or even a hopeful *thanks for walking me home*. Just "goodbye," definitive and final.

But Arthur is oblivious to the ticking clock. His half wave is careless, even if his eyes are still scrutinizing mine when he smiles. "Good night, Gwen," he says. "I'll see you tomorrow."

The door is nearly closed, but I open it enough to say, "No, you won't."

His smile widens. No matter how big he's smiling, I can already tell he can be *more* enthusiastic. It's like watching a puppy with a tongue lolling cheerfully out of its mouth.

"You will," he says. "It's a promise."

"It's *not*," I say. "Not from me anyway."

"From me it is, Princess."

"Don't call me that, either," I say. "Because I'm not. And my name isn't Gwen."

"We'll see," he singsongs. Before I can argue again, he turns on his heel, puts his hands in his pockets, and whistles as he walks back toward the faire.

CHAPTER FOUR

I'S ONE IN THE MORNING WHEN I slide back into my bunk, but Dad is still gone, so I pick up my phone.

Fatima answers on the first ring.

"Nice of you to remember I exist," she chirps.

I rub my eyes. "You sound . . . awake."

"Well, it's only . . . Shit, is it really two?" I can hear muffled shouting followed by Fatima's, "Sorry, Baba." She says to me, "Now look what you made me do. Mama keeps threatening me with extra cousin babysitting if I can't 'moderate my language.' The little pests."

She sounds irritated, but I know she loves her cousins

more than anything and is thrilled to live near them instead of running the circuit and performing sword dances with her parents and little brother.

"Sorry to call so late," I say. I take a deep breath and squeeze my eyes shut before saying, "I . . . I met a boy?"

There is a beat of silence and then a high-pitched squeal that makes me flinch, followed by "*Sorry*, Baba. Sorry!" Fatima lowers her voice. "A *boy*, boy? Like, our-age boy?"

"I think so," I say. "We didn't exchange drivers licenses or anything, but he looks it."

"What's he like? Where'd you meet him? Is he with the circuit? Is he dreamy?"

Her tone pulls a laugh from my throat.

"'Dreamy'? What is this, 1952?"

Another change I wasn't ready for: learning how to miss Fatima in the same year I learned how to miss my mother. Her voice is too quick, too loud, too *wonderful*, and it makes my stomach ache in almost a good way but not quite. It's not the same kind of missing as Mom, of course, not as sharp, but sometimes the dull repetitive thud of a paper cut is more noticeable than a greater injury.

Thank god for technology and video chats and texting.

"I called to ask *you* questions, you know," I say. "Not to be interrogated."

"How can I possibly be of help if I don't have all the details? Now spill."

It takes at least five minutes to explain what I was doing sneaking around the faire and the almost-arrested incident, but somehow I manage to convey how I ended up beside a castle alone with a lopsided-smile boy on a Thursday night.

"So you like him." Fatima says, a statement, not a question.

"No. I mean, no. How could I? We just met. And besides, you know I can't."

"I know no such thing. Why can't you like the boy that appeared *mysteriously beside a castle during an illicit midnight excursion*? Too romantic for you? Too perfect?"

"Too *different*," I say. "I've got enough going on without piling a crush on top of everything else."

Which is good enough explanation without going into the real reason of not letting anyone get close enough to care about ever again.

"It's *summer*," Fatima says. "You know? Summer loving? Kiss 'em and leave 'em? Make out in the pool for a couple months and then shake hands and go your separate ways? It doesn't have to be, like, a permanent thing, Maddie. And also—"

I hear the thin sound of a door opening over the phone followed by the low, exasperated tones of Fatima's father.

"It's Maddie, Baba." A pause. "Yes, *Madeline*." Another pause and then a sigh. "Baba says to tell you he misses you, and also could you make something for Mama's birthday? He wants something to match the earrings you gave her last year." Another pause. Another sigh. "*Aaand* he wants me to ask if your dad is doing well and if *you're* doing well and to tell you that we pray for you every day."

"Tell him yes to all of it." I laugh. "And thanks."

"Just *try*, Madeline," Fatima says after her bedroom door clicks closed again. "What's the harm?"

I think about how after I hang up, I'll need to update my journal before I sleep and forget the day's events and about how there is not enough *time*: for recording all my noticings, for running through memories over and over again in hopes of pulling something new to write about Mom, for reading comics, and drinking tea, and making jewelry, and reading poetry online and wondering what Mom would say about the poems if she were here.

"The harm is," I say to Fatima, "that I don't want to. I'm too busy; that's the harm."

As I talk, I take the coin—*the* coin—from beneath my pillow and dump it from its pouch into my hand.

I consider flipping it: heads, I let myself think more about this bard than I know I should; tails, I listen to reason and go back to my not-caring plan. My palms sweat just thinking about flipping it, because fate or no fate, I know I wouldn't be able to ignore the coin's verdict.

Fatima's voice is even, cool, oblivious to the weight of the coin in my hand. "Bullshit, Hathaway. He hardly sounds like the kind of boy who is going to bring about the destruction of the world. Give it a shot. All of this angst just to let yourself *crush* on a boy? I swear, Mama and Baba would trade us in a minute. Mama's still peeved about the Avengers poster I put on the wall because she knows I fancy Loki and 'I'm not allowed to date until I've graduated from college.' As if Tom

Hiddleston is just waiting for me to take our relationship from poster-on-wall to the next level."

If Fatima were here, she would take the coin and plunk it down heads up without flipping and call it good. Fatima has one of those annoyingly healthy relationships with fate where she believes that everything is ordained by God and he guides her path and choices. I envy her.

"Okay, but *this* guy might actually talk to me for an extended period of time, whereas the chances of you talking to Tom Hiddleston *ever* are . . . slimmer."

"First of all," Fatima says, "*rude.* And secondly, you don't need my help to talk to anyone. You just need to be you and be true to your heart and all that other bullshit."

I hear the distant sound of muffled parental outrage. "*Sorry, sorry,*" Fatima says. "Gotta run. Loki won't be able to save me from the wrath of Mama."

And I know she doesn't mean it to, but it stings a little bit to know she still has a mother who can be mad that she's up too late and using "dirty, filthy" language on the phone.

"I'll talk to you later," I say.

"I must away," Fatima says in her frighteningly good faire accent.

And then the line is dead, and my tea is colder than cold.

With the last of my energy, I open the journal of noticings and scratch a new, sloppily written heading at the bottom of an already-crowded page: *Times I've talked to the bard.* I tell myself I won't need any more room. I tell myself that it's just for posterity, the noticing and the documentation. It doesn't mean I *care*.

I take longer than usual dragging my pen to form the two tallies beneath it.

I've almost drifted off to sleep when my travel-weary brain makes a connection: Gwen, *Guinevere*. Like the legend of King Arthur and his true love.

I tell myself it's a coincidence, that it doesn't matter *anyway*, because I am not, not, *not* going to talk to him again.

* * *

There aren't enough hours between my late-night debrief with Fatima and the opening of the first official day of faire. My eyes are still puffy from lack of sleep, but I manage to squint through them long enough to trudge alongside Dad to our stall.

In the light of day and with the blessed separation of sleep, Arthur seems like a distant memory, and the heady, time-limited caring seems a nonconcern. I don't know why I bothered calling Fatima about it. It's very obviously nothing, an accidental meeting of two same-ish-aged people that won't happen again, no matter what he said last night. He was grieving, I remind myself. He was pining for the date that never was, and I just happened to be there to hear him out. Nothing more.

Dad and I walk to the faire in silence. It's not uncomfortable or awkward. It just is. This is how it is between us since Mom died. We're too alike, both too *unlike* Mom, too unwilling to risk breaking the safety of the quiet with words that may or may not make sense if we don't have enough time to think them through.

But it's familiar, the way Dad unlocks the door to our stall, the way I take the feather duster that is older than I am and run it over the jewelry stands, the stacks of journals, the displays, the counter where the blue zippered bank bag of cash and Dad's phone with the credit card attachment will serve as our cash register, the wooden sign beneath it that says WE ACCEPT MASTER OF THE CARD, LADY VISA, NEW WORLD EXPRESS, AND COIN OF THE REALM.

If online school were in session, I would set up my laptop in the corner and work on assignments and projects until Dad needed my help. But since it's summer, I instead haul myself to my stool and workbench at the front of our stall, shaking my fingers out before rubbing my damp palms over my forest-green skirts.

I probably have about half an hour before the faire opens and patrons pour in. I should use it to work on the matching earrings for Fatima's mother.

I don't like to deviate from my mom's designs . . . much. Mostly because I get a low-level headache when I even *think* about doing something differently than she did, but also because the few designs I've made myself have done . . . not well. When I finally got the courage to display them late last year, tucking them behind Mom's prettiest designs, they flopped *spectacularly*, not selling faire after faire after faire until I finally slipped them into a small box beneath my bunk bed.

I should have known. Mom was always so put together. Even her costumes—which she always bought from dressmakers and modified with hand-sewn beads and details— were the envy of both patrons and faire staff.

But Fatima's dad wants me to make a necklace to match the earrings. The ones *I* made. I don't have to look up a photo or struggle to remember what they looked like because to me, if no one else, they were perfect: the lightest jade beads dangling at the end of delicate rose gold links, the contrast balanced by tiny cubic zirconia diamonds that glitter in the light. My favorite, which is why I gave them to Mrs. Noori.

A headache pulses behind my eyelids, but I remind it that Fatima's father *asked me* to make a matching necklace, so it's really not a betrayal of Mom and her memory, is it?

I know what Mom would say: *Of course not. You are entirely your own, Madeline.* And yet my heart throbs and my head pounds thinking of changing *another* thing that Mom has not lived to see.

This is why caring is dangerous: it causes something as simple as jewelry-making to be a monumental pain in the ass.

I'm thinking of how the beads in the tray will see more of the world than Mom ever will when my elbow knocks the worktable and a wooden bead drops to the floor and rolls toward the door. I scramble after it, holding my skirts to the side and exposing my not-faire-compliant tennis shoes.

I'm so focused on trailing the bead with my eyes as it rolls over the doorframe and into the path, I don't notice.

I don't notice the fanfare, the entrance of the faire's court, the kings. And I *certainly* don't notice the bard until he stops the bead with the toe of his leather shoe just as I've bent to grab it.

Arthur's grin is wicked when I look up and meet his eyes.

"Princess." He smiles.

"*Maiden*," I hiss, glancing up to see his fathers, the kings, only a few steps behind. I take advantage of my bead-fetching stance to bob a curtsy. "A pleasure, your highnesses."

His dads are, for lack of a better word, striking. The taller of the two, with a dark brown complexion and even darker eyes and hair, has teeth that came straight from a toothpaste commercial. He smiles broadly, easily, and I can already tell Arthur got a great deal of his personality from him. The crown atop his head is adorned with emeralds and twists of gold that look like ivy.

The other king, the other father, is significantly shorter, thinner, but no less attractive. Something about his eyes and the way they crinkle at the corners, the sharp angle of his jaw that seems to tilt up just the slightest bit in defiance as if the world itself needs putting in its place, and the pale skin and floppy hair make it easy to see where Arthur got *his* looks. His crown manages to be impossibly grander with rubies and diamonds stretched across a landscape of silver.

Almost all of the jewelry Mom made, that I make, is

high-quality costume jewelry, but I know something of real gems that we would occasionally see at craft shows and jewelry stores.

Either those crowns are real or they are very, *very* good fakes.

"Rise," the taller king says. "And tell us your name, young maiden, if you please."

"Madeline, your majesty," I say, and I'm sure to put on the vaguely British lilt I use for official faire speak.

A small crowd of patrons fresh from the ticket booth and vendors is gathering at the spectacle of the halted royal entourage. Little kids wrestle excitedly to stand in front of each other. One darts forward to touch the fur cape that hangs from the shorter king's shoulders before running back to her mother's side. Another looks wide-eyed at the pair of trumpeters that flank the kings.

Arthur grins at me from behind his dads, and it is an effort to keep my eyes from narrowing.

"We seek a maiden to rule at our side as princess for the entirety of our fair faire." The tall king smiles. "We would be honored if you would join our merry court." His eyes are warm, kind, and it's almost enough to make me agree to whatever he asks on the spot, but of course I can't. For *so many reasons*, I can't.

I shoot a glare at Arthur. "A kind offer, your majesty, but my father requires my assistance in our shop. I am afraid I must decline."

And of course, Dad chooses now to come out from the

little storage area at the back of the shop, his hands splotchy with leather stains. He bows at the waist to the kings before turning to me.

"What's all this, then?"

"Madeline has been chosen to be the princess of faire, sir," Arthur says. "We will, of course, supply you with an assistant for your shop while she attends to her royal duties."

I shoot him another look that I don't care if his fathers see. This is beyond ridiculous.

"I didn't agree to anything," I say quietly to Dad. "I know you need my—"

"Oh, nonsense," Dad interrupts, his voice grumbly and slow. "You know I can manage just fine without you for a spell. Go with your friend."

"But, *Dad*—"

And then, dropping the faire speak and revealing a Midwestern accent that sounds like what chocolate chip cookies taste like, the shorter king says, "You don't have to, dear, but Arthur was very persistent."

I'm about to say no, once and for all, to find a diplomatic but firm way to say *absolutely not*, when I absentmindedly adjust my skirts and hear a light *clink* against the wooden floor of the shop.

There, sitting just to the right of my shoe, is the coin. *The coin.* I must have fallen asleep without putting it back in its pouch and it somehow came along for the ride to the faire today.

My stomach turns a little at the thought of almost losing

the coin. It could have fallen out on the way to the faire this morning and been lost forever, this family heirloom that has been passed down for literal generations.

But even as my stomach turns, I can't help but notice the way the coin has landed: heads up, the letting-myself-care option, the keep-talking-to-Arthur option, the dangerous option.

I bend to collect it, hoping Dad doesn't notice it for what it is, but also trying to buy myself time to make sense of the whirling thoughts in my head.

Of all the thoughts, the one I keep pinging against is the most ridiculous one of all: *Maybe this is a sign from Mom.*

Which, again, is stupid. *So stupid.*

I meet Arthur's eager gaze from where he still stands beside his fathers and narrow my eyes. The coin—whatever it says—doesn't change the fact that I'm pissed at him for putting me in this situation.

"Can I have the day to think about it?" I hear myself ask.

"Of course, of course. I suppose you know where to find us." The taller king laughs, pointing at the castle. "We look forward to hearing your answer."

When they leave in a flurry of trumpeters and cape-swishing—they walk hand in hand while the taller king swings their arms and the shorter rolls his eyes—I expect Arthur to go with them. Instead, he comes to stand beside me when I sit back on my bench. Dad mumbles something about checking stock and talking to me later and heads back to the storage room. I can't tell what he's thinking. I can't tell if he knew the coin was *the* coin or if he doesn't actually want me to go play pretend and leave him with the shop.

"They *love* you," Arthur says, interrupting my thoughts and nodding toward his retreating fathers. "I knew they would."

"You know no such thing," I say, placing the wooden bead back on the table. It seems like hours ago that I dropped it. "They are being nice to me because you made them be nice to me."

Arthur snorts. "You're too modest. But yes, I may or may not have influenced their choice in adding to the royal party."

I plunk another bead down with more force than necessary.

"*Why,* though? Why did you choose me, and why did somebody have to be chosen at all? I don't even know you."

Arthur stills a little, his hands back to cradling the lute that he has now pulled to the front of his body. His eyes are serious, solemn.

"I don't know, Gwen. It just seemed . . . right."

He won't meet my gaze.

"I'm not agreeing to anything until you tell me what's going on," I say. "And I might not be agreeing at all."

Arthur's sigh is long and low.

"I have a thing in, like, ten minutes. I told the puppeteer I'd do the music for their kids' show this afternoon. There's not enough time to explain. Meet me at the castle after lunch, okay?"

"Fine," I say. "But this *isn't* me agreeing to anything, you know."

"Yet," Arthur says, and the grin is back and infectious. And annoying.

"Yet," I mutter, and I tell myself it's just to make him go away.

When he leaves, presumably going off to entertain children that will no doubt find him charming and fun, I retrieve my journal from beneath the bench, cross out the *Times I've talked to the bard* heading, and move it to its own page.

I have a feeling that, like it or not, I'm going to need more room.

In the ensuing quiet, I try my best to sink into my own head, to blot out the world by ignoring it for a while, but Dad clearly has other plans.

"Princess, huh?" he asks after a customer buys one of the medium-size journals. "That's something."

"Yeah," I say offhandedly. "But I don't know. What about you? And the store?"

"We'll get by," Dad says. He pretends to straighten a stack of perfectly neat journals to avoid making eye contact when he adds, "You *know* I'll be fine, no matter what you choose."

It sounds like a double meaning, but I don't have time to find a way of asking him about it because a group of people dressed as Lord of the Rings characters comes in. Dad's attention is captured immediately, and they all fall into a deep conversation about *The Silmarillion* that I have no prayer of following.

Just as well. Dad and I have a comfortable truce since Mom died: We don't pester. We don't pry. And despite Dr.

Jenkins's insistence that we should "talk out our feelings," we're mostly happy to remain in our separate grief corners.

It's better that way. I *know* it's better for us this way.

And yet, for a second, when I watch Dad laugh in his grumbling way as the cosplayers, eager to share their costume-creation processes, chatter around him, I wonder what he *would* say if I asked his opinion on the whole princess thing. What does he think *Mom* would say if she were here?

I try to parse out my own feelings, but it reminds me of the time I helped my parents decorate our stall for Christmas and all the lights were tangled in a box. It took longer to untangle them than it did to put them on our sign. There are far too many things spinning around in my head to examine them individually. It's a clump of fears, mostly: that I'm too quiet, too socially awkward, too busy with the shop, too preoccupied with making sure Dad is okay, too busy caring about the people left in my life to incorporate new ones, too fat.

That last one comes out of nowhere, and I quickly stuff it down, *determined* not to let it influence my decision. *Of all the stupid things to be worried about*, I chide myself, while simultaneously sweating a little at the thought of everyone staring at me in a princess costume and silently judging.

For all my determination, when I kiss Dad on the cheek and head to the castle, I inhale a little bit inside of my corset top, trying to practice keeping my stomach sucked in tight, just in case I say yes.

CHAPTER FIVE

THERE ARE NOT ENOUGH WORDS IN the English language, not enough travel journals in the world, to describe what it's like to enter a castle in the middle of Oklahoma while Arthur the bard impatiently tugs on my arm when I slow to gawk.

There's a lot to gawk at: the stone walls, the *literal stone fireplace* that I could easily walk into without bending, and the electric torches attached along the nave. A *nave*. A real one, as grand as anything I've seen on TV and certainly grander than I've seen at a Ren faire.

"This is ridiculous," I say.

"You've said that," Arthur points out. "Twice."

"But it *is*," I insist. "It's ridiculous."

"Which part, exactly?"

"Um." I gesture at our surroundings.

"The castle? That's all?" He stops, turning me to face him with gentle hands. "Look, Gwen: It's a house. Lots of people have houses. This one just happens to be made of stone and have a weird choice of decor."

"You live *inside* a Renaissance faire."

"I live in a house, just like lots of other people. Next?"

I raise my eyebrows to show I do not concede his point, but I move on anyway. "The part where you want me to be a princess? Ridiculous."

He doesn't pause in his dragging as we approach a huge staircase, but his hand tightens on mine quickly. It's an unconscious pulse, one that a polite person would ignore, but a person in a loose-fitting vaguely Renaissance, vaguely modern peasant dress with a habit of noticing things cannot.

Arthur is hiding something. It's written all over the tightening of his hand and the tick I can just see along his jawline.

"Out with it," I say.

His foot catches on a stone step, but he quickly rights himself.

"It's nothing," he says.

"It's something enough that you are hell-bent on making me a princess instead of picking from the dozens of girls who probably *want* the job."

He turns his head, just enough that I can see his eyes.

"That part is easy. I already told you: You talk like royalty. You look like royalty. It's fate. What's the problem?"

I scoff.

"Hey," he says, stopping as we come to the top of the stairs. The long hallway stretches on either side of us, lined with hand-painted portraits in gilded frames. I'm looking at the farthest one my eye can see—whose subject looks suspiciously like the boy in front of me—when Arthur steps into my line of vision.

"Hey," he repeats. "I already told you. You'll be perfect. You're eloquent and beautiful and I *know* you're benevolent because you haven't shoved me into the moat in the last twenty-four hours."

"Doesn't mean I haven't thought about it," I mutter.

He might not be conventionally hot, might still be random Teenager #3 in a movie, but when Arthur smiles, I can see how he could be the natural conclusion of his attractive fathers.

It's almost enough to make me consider going along with whatever this is—to make me consider letting myself care—but not quite. Something still seems off.

"There's another reason," I say. "One you're not telling me."

Arthur's smile falters. "Maybe," he says, "but that doesn't make the other reasons any less true, does it?"

"God, you have an answer for everything, don't you?"

"Words are the weapons of us bards, Gwen. You didn't expect me to go toe to toe with royalty unarmed, did you?"

I *expected* to have a summer of figuring out how to live

another year without my mom, of reading comics and noticing and maintaining the routine that gives me an ounce of sanity. *Not* throwing all sense of continuity out the window on my second day in Stormsworth. *Not* agreeing to a plan where everyone will look at me when I don't even want to look at myself too closely.

But I recall what Dr. Jenkins said, about having a good week, whatever that means, and I wonder if this is the thing she had a premonition about. I wonder if Mom is trying to communicate from the great beyond or whatever with the coin. I wonder a lot of things, but there's only one way to get my answers, even if it makes my heart race in my chest, even if I already doubt my decision.

I'm about to ask Arthur why *he* isn't a prince, why his dads specifically want a princess to complete their court, when the aforementioned kings enter the hallway from large, double wooden doors with iron details.

"No, Martin," the shorter one is saying.

Martin, the dark and handsome and taller of the two, trails behind, arms outstretched. His crown tilts to the side of his head as he stalks after his husband, pleading.

"Tim, my love, my dearest, you can't possibly expect me to sit *outside* in this godforsaken Oklahoma heat without *air-conditioning*."

"We'll discuss this later," Tim says, coming to stand before us. His smile isn't as wide or as ready as Martin's or Arthur's, but it's kind. "I see you've decided to be our princess, Madeline. We're so pleased."

"Well, actually—"

"Yes, isn't that lovely!" Martin interrupts, clasping his hands together loudly. "And wouldn't it be a pity to have such a pretty maiden faint, or worse, *sweat*, while watching jousting matches from the royal un-air-conditioned box."

Tim blinks slowly, like he's internally counting to ten. "For the last time, we are not paying to install fans in the box. You can do what every king has done for centuries and—"

"Hire fan wavers?" Martin interrupts again, his voice hopeful.

"*Suck it up.*"

"Um, Dad? Pops? Can we maybe do this later?" Arthur points a thumb at me. "Madeline has some questions about princess duties."

"Of *course* we can do this later," Tim says. "Yes, thank you for agreeing to be our princess, Madeline. Arthur told us just this morning he is quite convinced you are the woman for the job."

"Well, I don't—" I start.

"She is," Arthur says. "Undoubtedly."

"Yes, many thanks," Martin says. "We really can't go another week of faire without a woman in the court of Stormsworth. It's just not right. And Arthur was so heartbroken when—"

"*Dad,*" Arthur says. "Just get her to agree so we can start alterations, okay?"

"Alterations?" I ask. Trying to add *anything* to this conversation feels like trying to cram another piece into an already-finished puzzle.

"We have some costumes made that should suit," Tim tells me. "We'll just need a few tweaks to fit them to your measurements, and you'll have a wardrobe fit for a princess."

"Pity about the sweat," Martin says. "It'll soak right through your dress and then you'll regret agreeing to help us, Arthur will be humiliated, and Stormsworth will crumble as the royal family turns against one and other. Then, of course, there will have to be a war of some kind."

"I'm *not* picking sides, Dad," Arthur reminds him. And then, turning to Tim and grinning, he says, "Nobody will be able to see into the box, Pops. Let him have a fan in the corner or something. *Literally* nobody cares, even if they can see it."

"Arthur, I have conceded and conceded and conceded on points of historical inaccuracy, but the line must be drawn *somewhere*."

"And that line wasn't the flat screen in our room that looks like a mirror when it's turned off?" Martin asks.

Tim inhales slowly. "*That* is in our *home*. Not out for all of Stormsworth to see."

"Can't say the same for the historically questionable camel jousting, can you, Pops?" Arthur asks.

Tim shoots him a glare. "And *that* was also your father's doing, as you well know, young bard."

Arthur leans toward me and talks from the side of his mouth. "I'm 'young bard' when I'm in trouble at Ren faire, I guess. Usually it's 'young man,' but Pops has been—forgive my pun—harping on my refusal to be prince of faire."

"You don't play a harp," Tim points out. Even though he is the shorter of the two kings, he is clearly the one in charge. "And it's not your princely refusal that's irking me."

"Yeah," Martin chimes in. "It's that it's already the opening week of faire and your girlfriend caused such a hiccup in our plans for the royal court, all the official royal festivities and coronations had to be postponed from opening day."

I watch as Arthur's face reddens at the word "girlfriend." "For the millionth time, she is not—*was not*—my girlfriend, okay? She just wanted to be princess and now she doesn't and—"

"I *distinctly* remember you saying at least a dozen times, 'My girlfriend, Breanna. Breanna, my girlfriend. Can Breanna of girlfriend status please be princess of faire?'" Tim says.

Arthur's eyes dart toward mine and then quickly away. "Yes, but—"

"Okay," Martin interrupts, clapping his hands again. I notice for the first time that his gloves are embroidered with gold thread. "We've been standing in the hall for a millennium and we have far too much work to do." He turns to me, hands clasped in front of him like he's praying. "Madeline: Would you do us the honor of being Princess of Stormsworth? We'll of course have someone help your father in the shop, we'll pay you a salary, and it's not as if you need to spend *all* your time as a princess if you don't wish to."

"But most of it, to be fair," Tim adds. He begins ticking a list off with his fingers. "You'll be helping with daily parades, knighting ceremonies, the fairy garden, overseeing the tournaments from our historically accurate box."

Martin either doesn't hear or ignores the jab. "Precisely. It's your choice, but we really should get going. There's much to be done, and it would be *lovely* to have a Saturday coronation, don't you think?"

"Coronation? *Tomorrow?*" I ask, glaring at Arthur. "He didn't mention a coronation."

"He probably didn't mention a royal Renaissance makeover, either," Martin says, his tone apologetic. "But that's about to happen, too."

I look to Tim, who I can already tell is the voice of reason, the *normal* one of this family, but when he meets my eyes, he sadly nods.

"Sorry, Princess. But these"—he nudges my skirts aside with a leather boot to expose my sneakers hidden beneath the fabric—"are not fit for Stormsworth royalty."

"Neither are electric fans, but Dad is still getting those," Arthur snickers. "Don't lose hope."

* * *

Apparently, the one-day delay in the assembly of the royal court means that Martin and Tim have *nothing* to do besides make me over. What follows is what feels like *hours* of poking and prodding and tape measures and safety pins and fabric so decadently colorful, it makes my eyes water.

As Tim flutters around with pins sticking from the corners

of his mouth, Martin follows close at his heels, an inconceivable number of makeup pallets and brushes appearing in his hands like magic.

"Less bronzer," Tim says from where he kneels, pinning the hem at my feet. "We're going for sun-kissed, not sun-accosted."

"If you would have chosen a color other than that shade of blue for her bodice, we wouldn't have this problem."

We are in another room of the castle dedicated entirely to fabric and costumes and burlap-covered mannequins. His dads, Arthur explains in between my disappearances behind a changing screen, are the costume designers for the local schools and community theater groups, including Arthur's high school. Silently, I wonder how costume designers—even gifted ones—can make enough money to buy all of *this*, all of Stormsworth. The fabric in here alone must cost the ransom of two kings, if not more.

Arthur is casually leaning against the doorframe. He looks annoyingly smug each time I come out from behind the ruby-red hanging screen in a new outfit. I glare at him as Tim immediately sets to adjusting and Martin begins color matching.

Stupid coin. Stupid *me* for thinking it falling out of my skirts counted as a flip. I blame the sleep deprivation—and Fatima's excitement discussing the bard on the phone last night—for my current plight.

At some point a lunch of chicken and rice bowls is produced, along with a visit from Dad, who has been *summoned* to the castle.

"Maddie," he breathes when he steps into the room. "You look—"

"Ridiculous," I finish. I pull on the absurd golden skirt and petticoats of what Tim keeps calling my "grand finale" ball gown. "I know."

"No," Dad says. "You look just like your mother."

I glance at the threefold mirror behind me. Even with the yards of fabric and jewelry and different swipes of makeup on my cheeks and eyes, all I see is the girl in the blank laptop screen. The one who looks much too much like her father and not at all like her mother.

In the fairy tales, there are wicked stepmothers and ugly stepsisters, and the princess is always, always, always this beautiful creature of sunlight and kindness. It wasn't enough to be wicked: the villains had to be *ugly*, too, as if their looks had to reflect what was on the inside.

So what does that mean for me, I wonder, if I am neither ugly nor beautiful? What does it mean about my insides?

Plain, I think. *Remarkably plain*. And *remarkably stupid if you think another change, another thing that will be different this summer is going to make your life any easier.*

As if he can hear my thoughts, Dad steps forward and gives me a gentle, slightly awkward hug.

"*Enjoy* yourself, Maddie. What was that quote you had me stamp on the front of your journal in middle school? 'Tame the world'?"

Tim, who has been ignoring our conversation as he hovers

at my feet holding different styles of slippers near my hem, pauses his movement. "Tame the world, you say?"

Martin looks up with a smile from where he is trying to open another package of makeup wipes. "That sounds hopeful."

Tim snorts. "Sounds lofty."

"It sounds like advice you could take to heart, too, my love," Martin says. "*Good* advice."

Another snort from Tim, this one much louder than the last. "Every time I try to tame just the world of Stormsworth, I'm thwarted by you and our son."

Something has shifted in Arthur's eyes, something that makes his gaze soften and warm as he takes in me and his dads and *my* dad as we're all standing amid costumes and half-eaten stir-fries arguing about taming the world.

Arthur's gaze reminds me of the light coming out of the castle. It reminds me, weirdly, of being in my bed in Britomart, snuggled beneath my quilt with a mug of tea and a new episode of *The Falconer's Gauntlet*.

Over the chaos, our eyes meet, and his smile, impossible as always, widens.

"So what will it be, Gwen? Will you tame the world?"

"Of course she will," Martin says, finally having opened the wipes. "The world should bend to the princess, not the other way around."

I consider all the many, many ways I haven't been able to bend the world to my will: no permanent address, Fatima leaving the circuit, the body I was born with, the body my *mom* was born with and the cancer that came for it. I think about how my list is a reflection of the unkindness and cruelty of the world that the Wizened Old Wizard warned me was inevitable.

It's stupid, the heady feeling of coming full circle, of finally being able to heed the stupid wizard's stupid advice, but I smile at Arthur, even if it feels a little wobbly on my lips.

"Why not?" I say. "What do I have to lose?"

CHAPTER SIX

I HAVE *A LOT* TO LOSE.

All my fears—the changes that take me so many steps farther away from the memory of Mom and the faire we both held dear, leaving Dad alone in the shop to bear her memory without me while I parade around pretending to be something I'm not, and the nearly debilitating thought of everyone staring at me and judging me as princess of faire—come clanging back into my chest when I finally leave the castle that evening.

Arthur offers to walk me home, which I refuse. I like walking alone, or that's what I tell him, but actually my ears are ringing from the constant banter of Arthur and his dads and I just want a moment of peace. And the lute-strumming bard with his puffy sleeves is the exact opposite of peace.

I feel like I've been run over by a truck and all I want is a shower, my bed, my comics, and tea. My head is spinning. I want to have words with Dad about leaving me to the well-meaning but persistent wolves that are Arthur's parents and Arthur himself, but *all* of this can wait until after I swab off the last round of makeup and get out of this dress, the one the kings insisted I just go ahead and wear home so I could put it back on for my coronation first thing in the morning. The eye shadow and blush and lipstick Martin chose to go with the dress are all stuffed into a Stormsworth Faire tote on my arm, along with my original outfit.

The dress turns out to be the biggest hurdle in a literal sense when I yank open Britomart's door, put my foot over the threshold, and then . . . stop.

Damn. It. All. To. Hell.

The *stupid* petticoats won't fit through the narrow doorframe.

"You've *got* to be kidding me," I say aloud, and then, "Dad! Dad? Hello?"

Nothing. He must be out visiting or still packing up the shop for the night, which instantly makes me feel guilty.

I shouldn't have agreed to this. For *so many reasons*, I shouldn't have agreed to this. *This* is what I get for giving into a bard's puppy eyes and a wayward definitely-not-magic coin.

I try to backpedal, to extricate the dress from the door-frame, but something has snagged on the door hinges and I am stuck. I can feel every single square inch of fabric start to rub against my overheated skin as the panic sets in. The strap of the tote pulls at my shoulder, also jammed among my skirts.

"Shoot," I mutter. "Shit. Shoot shit. Stupid kings. Stupid faire. Stupid, meddling, egotistical bar—"

A lute strums behind me, stopping me midword.

"I wouldn't advise shooting shit. Sounds messy."

I manage to crane my neck around just enough to glare at him from the corner of my eyes. "What are you doing here? I told you I could walk myself home."

"Speak of the devil, and he will appear," Arthur says from behind me. "Unless the devil happened to go down to Georgia, in which case—"

"If you *dare* breathe a single *note* of that song, so help me, I will . . . I'll rip this dress in two."

Over the sound of my heart beating in my ears, there's a half-hearted strum and a breath of a laughter.

"Is that a threat or a promise?"

My face heats. "Stop that."

"Stop what?" Another strum, this one suspiciously sounding a bit like the opening chord to the song I just forbade him to play.

"Teasing me. I don't like it."

The strumming stops. "It's called flirting, Gwen." His

voice has lost all bravado, is almost gentle, and something about it makes my shoulders slump and the fire in my cheeks blaze hotter.

"Well, I don't like that, either."

The strings hum as he releases the neck of the lute. "Then I'll stop," he says simply. "I'm sorry."

I say nothing, and I don't know why, but my eyes are prickling and my nose suddenly feels clogged.

"Do you want my help?" he asks, his voice gentling further, and he sounds more like the boy I met at midnight instead of the bard. "I can go find somebody else if you don't want it to be me, but please don't rip the dress in two. Dad will kill me and then Pops will be mad about it and then they will divorce after my inevitably well-attended funeral and *then* I'll have to split my time between haunting them, and I'm not ready for that kind of time commitment in the afterlife."

"Are you *ever* serious?" I ask. "For a second?"

"Oh, I'm deadly serious," he says. "*Deadly.* Which is why you should let me help you dislodge yourself before something tears. My neck is on the line."

I hang my head. "Fine," I mutter, "but make it quick."

We stand in silence, not so much awkward as tired on my part, concentrated on his task. Maybe I grew used to the constant chatter of the afternoon, though, because I only manage to count to twenty before I ask, "You're eventually going to explain why you suddenly backed out of being prince of faire and why your would-be-princess friend abandoned ship, right?"

Arthur's quiet laugh comes from the vicinity of my hips, and I feel a bit of the fabric come free. His voice is muffled by skirts when he says, "Is that an order, then, your highness?"

"Oh, drop the faire thing," I say. "Tell the truth."

There's a second of hesitation, so brief that if I were doing anything other than actively being stuck in a doorframe in a monstrosity of a dress, I would miss it. But it's there.

"How do you know I *suddenly* turned it down?"

He can't see it, but I roll my eyes.

"Oh, I don't know. Probably the biggest hint was the six mannequins shoved in the corner with royal-looking outfits that blended both of your dads' signature colors."

"You don't know they were royal," Arthur points out. "My bard costumes are pretty elaborate."

"There was a matching *crown*, Arthur."

I expect a witty comeback, to hear a smile in his voice, but instead, when Arthur finally replies, his voice sounds small.

"Oh, nobody wants these jelly-beans-for-muscles arms to be the ones battling off a dragon, do they?"

He tries to sound cavalier, which is the main identifier for his bard voice, I realize. But there's something buried underneath, so I say, "Oh, but you think the people want the Plump Princess?"

He can't turn me around to face him, of course, because the dress is still lodged in the frame, but he reaches up and turns my chin toward him sharply.

"Has somebody called you that?"

I roll my eyes, my chin burning in his hand. I tell myself it's the warm summer air.

"What?" I laugh. "Are you going to defend my honor? Hit everyone that's ever called me a name with your lute? Best of luck. And they haven't called me names, but that's because they haven't seen me yet."

Arthur's eyes search mine before letting go of my chin and turning his head downward to address the fabric again.

"And *I* won't mean anything by it when they find themselves on the business end of a horse."

We're quiet for a bit, with the cicadas roaring and the sound of RVs humming.

"Arthur?"

"Yeah?"

"Why . . ." I hesitate.

"Why what?"

"I'm afraid if I ask you, you'll lie, and . . . well, I want the truth."

With a final gentle tug, Arthur releases the dress and me from the frame.

"Not a single snag," he says proudly. And then, more earnestly, "Ask me. I won't lie to you."

I turn to face him, looking down at him from my perch atop the stairs, my skirts rustling around my ankles. "Why do you want me to be princess so badly?"

His laugh is careful. "I already told you, didn't I? You're beautiful. Aren't fairy-tale princesses always beautiful?"

"Yes, but—"

"No buts. You look like a princess. You should be a princess. I was in the fortunate position to make that happen. It's just good ol'-fashioned nepotism, Gwen."

He's hiding something. I can see it in the way he rubs the back of his neck, the way he unconsciously shifts from foot to foot, the way his hand flutters to his tunic just below the collarbone and away again. But I don't think he's hiding it from me; he's hiding it from himself. There's no sense in asking him again why he made me princess, because I don't know if *he* knows the real answer.

"I should be going," he says, and the showmanship he usually wears like a shield is conspicuously missing.

I don't want to invite the bard inside, but I'll invite Arthur, even if he *is* still wearing the outfit with the ludicrously puffed sleeves and every cell in my body is flashing a red warning light: *Warning, warning, warning! Danger of caring dead ahead!*

Because even if I've decided—or Mom or the coin or whoever has decided—that I should give the whole princess thing a go, I still can't quite make myself *care*. It's just too risky.

"Look," I say, already regretting my words, "it's not a castle, but if you want to come in, I have some leftover kettle corn."

Arthur's eyes are careful, more careful than I've ever seen them. "I'll have to call and ask Pops," he says, confirming my suspicions that Tim is indeed the one in charge. "Will *your* dad mind?"

"He probably won't care," I say. "But I'll double-check as soon as he gets back."

"I can wait outside," Arthur says, "for you to shower and stuff. Or until your dad gets back. Like, if it would make you more comfortable."

I can feel the tectonic plates of whatever this is—acquaintanceship? Friendship?—shift beneath our feet. Arthur is extroverted and bright and *alive* in a way that grates against my nerves. But, I'm realizing, he is also watchful and considerate and unsure.

For someone so loud, he is awfully careful to be quiet when needed.

"You can come in," I repeat, beginning to extricate myself from the skirts. "And before you think to comment on the outdoor wardrobe change, you know very well that I have shorts under these."

"Wouldn't dream of it, Gwen."

* * *

Arthur is still sitting at the table where I left him when I come out of the bathroom, his phone in front of him. I've forgone the shower—for now—and put on my sweatpants. I wonder if he can see my discomfort in having the routine off-kilter, the way my brain feels itchy at having skipped a step, even if I know I'll redo everything after he leaves. I hope not.

"I have to be home by ten," Arthur says. "But I can stay if it's still okay with you."

I grab the bag of kettle corn and a couple sodas from the

kitchen and sit across from him, my sweatpants sticking to my slightly sweaty legs as I do. The costumes are beautiful, but Oklahoma heat and full skirts don't mix without consequences.

"It's okay with me," I say, pushing the off-brand cola toward Arthur.

"So this is where you live all the time?"

"Yeah," I say, trying to remember the last time I had to explain such obvious parts of my life to anyone. "We used to have a house, but we had to sell it to help with medical bills and stuff."

Arthur's face looks like he is about to apologize or give some platitude, so I hold my hand up to save him the trouble. "It's okay," I say. "We were only ever there for like a month out of the year anyway. We've always traveled around."

"Do you only do Renaissance faires?"

I watch as his eyes wander from mine to what he can see of Britomart from our seats. I can almost see him trying to imagine it, trying to shrink his life from a *literal castle* to a home on wheels.

"Yeah," I say, and his eyes snap back to mine. "I mean, mostly. There are a couple weeks a year we end up at bigger flea markets and that kind of thing."

"Huh."

"Huh," I echo, watching his long fingers pick at the label on the cola bottle. "So . . . are you going to tell me?"

"Tell you what?"

I raise an eyebrow and gesture at my coronation dress that is now taking up the entirety of the bottom bunk.

Arthur leans back in his chair. "I already told you everything."

"You absolutely didn't."

"Did too."

I roll my eyes. "Sure, you did. So, who's Breanna?"

He has the grace to look embarrassed before looking down to play with his bottle cap. "She's the one who stood me up for our date."

I snort. "Figured that much out, thanks. But what's the story? Like, your dads seemed pissed about it."

Arthur must be constantly fidgeting. He moves on from the bottle and its various accessories to running a nail along the table's rounded corners.

"How much do you want to know?" he asks.

"None of it," I say. "I *want* to be left alone and not be princess at all, but that doesn't seem to be an option, so you might as well spill the why part of it."

Arthur's hand stills. "You know you don't have to be princess," he says. "Really."

I make a disbelieving noise. "Yeah, after all the work your dads put in today? Not likely."

"They'd understand. Don't worry about them," Arthur says. He's looking at me intently again, and I feel antsy beneath his stare. "If you really, really, *really* don't want to do it, I get it."

I open my mouth, but he barrels on.

"However, I really, really, really, *really* think you should. Be princess, I mean. You'll be perfect."

I swallow what I was going to say. "Tell me about Breanna."

Arthur sighs and begins spinning the cap. "We go to school together."

"Sure." I wave for him to continue as I get up from the table and walk the two steps to my bunk.

"She's in theater. I'm not technically a theater kid, but I'm kind of an honorary member since Dad and Pops do their costumes every year. Anyway, I was helping with the sound equipment for their spring show when we, like, actually met. We hung out. I mentioned that Dad and Pops wanted me to 'bring a friend' so we could have a girl in the court. Bre agreed to do it, and then she un-agreed."

I sit back across from him, plopping one of my weirder jewelry creations in front of him, a necklace that can turn in and over itself. Arthur immediately begins to twist it between his fingers. I tell myself the flash of satisfaction I get from correctly identifying his fiddling tendencies and—at least momentarily—solving them is not the same as caring about someone. He's annoying. I just concentrated his annoying-ness to get him to put the bottle cap down.

"So you liked her but she didn't like you?" I ask bluntly.

He coughs. "Well, I wouldn't say that, exactly. I mean, I thought she liked me? Maybe? We hung out a lot. She seemed really interested in the castle and the faire and stuff, but not in a using-me-to-get-to-it kind of way, you know?"

There's something about his expression that tells me he is

trying to convince himself that the last part is true, that she wasn't using him as a means to an end.

"But," he says, his voice returning to its overly chipper cadence, "what's done is done." The necklace makes a sharp sound as he accidentally drops it against the table. He immediately picks it back up. "She wanted to date Noah, I guess, so she did that instead of being princess of faire."

"And that's where I come in," I say.

"Precisely," Arthur says. "Because it was fated that *you* would be Princess of Stormsworth, not her."

"Sure," I say, and my eye strays to the tote bag, where my coin waits to be returned to its pouch. "*Fate.*"

Arthur raises his eyebrows at my tone. "You say it like it's a bad word."

"Isn't it?"

"It can't be if it brought us together, right?"

"Ugh," I say. "The only thing that brought us together was my stupidity and your angst. Fate had nothing to do with it."

"I think you're wrong," he says. "And I hope I'm there someday to say 'I told you so.'"

"Doubtful."

Arthur nods sharply once, like a decision has been made. He holds up a piece of kettle corn. "To fate," he says, "whatever it may bring."

I don't want to toast to that, because I've seen what so-called fate can do, but I don't want to keep talking about it, so instead I hold up my own kernel and echo, "To fate."

We clink kernels and I can't help but laugh at how serious Arthur looks, as if we've just toasted with wine goblets to agree to start or stop a war. But underneath my laughter is the sudden, deep-set understanding: *Oh.* I'm a replacement. For Breanna and for the princess he wanted. I'm a fill-in. That's what he is seeing as fate.

In some ways, it makes me feel better, like some of the pressure has been lifted because I can't possibly be this almost-girlfriend person anyway. In other ways, it makes my insides feel inky and weird, like low-level nausea, because fate or not, it wasn't a part made for me. I'm just the only available peg—a round one, at that—that can be shoved into the square hole.

"I like you, Gwen," Arthur says, oblivious to my inner dialogue. "I think this is going to be a *great* summer."

His words so strongly echo Dr. Jenkins's promise of a good week, I can't help but look toward the coin again. This time Arthur catches my glance.

"What are *you* hiding?"

"Nothing," I say, but it's too quick, too sharp, and he smiles.

"Gwen, I'm not sure if you know this, but I can be annoyingly persistent when I want to be."

"*Literally* no one would doubt that," I say.

Maybe it's because it's late and I've tried on one too many dresses and had one too many makeup brushes poked at my face. Maybe it's because he is careful—so careful—to make sure I'm not being forced into something I don't want to do, but I don't even bother arguing with him.

I scoot my chair back, reach around him to the bag, and bring out the coin, wrapped in a bit of fabric I swiped from the scrap pile at the castle.

I hope if I drop it unceremoniously before Arthur, he'll be fooled into thinking it's nothing, but of course he chooses now to be serious.

"May I open it?" His voice is a little reverent, a little hushed, as if he impossibly knows how much this coin means to me, what it means *for* me.

"I gave it to you, didn't I?"

With what I am beginning to understand is a signature trait, Arthur pauses with his fingers hovering over the bunched folds of the fabric.

"You don't have—"

"I know that," I interrupt. "I know. Just open it."

Arthur's way to tame the world, it seems, is to check and recheck and then check again for good measure that no one is being forced to do something against their will.

Or maybe he's just self-conscious and doubts himself.

Whatever the case, he dumps the coin into his palm and stares at it for a while.

"Not what you expected?" I ask.

He nudges it with his index finger. "It's a pirate cob," he says. "Spanish. Probably from the sixteenth century, by the looks of that lion crest."

When he glances up and sees my stunned expression—because he's completely correct—Arthur shrugs. "Pops collected old coins for a while."

He slips the coin back into the makeshift pouch and scoots it across the table to me, watching me. Waiting.

"My great-great-grandparents bought it at a Ren faire," I say. "The very first one they went to. They loved the faire so much they decided to quit their jobs and join the circuit."

"Like running away to join the circus?" Arthur smiles.

I can't help but smile back. "Yeah, pretty much."

"Were they the grandparents from your dad's side?"

"God, no. Dad comes from one of those traditional get-a-job-in-an-office, marry, have-a-picket-fence, stay-in-one-place kind of families. They basically disowned him when he married Mom and they did the Ren faire thing."

"That seems . . . harsh," Arthur ventures.

I glance toward the door, certain that Dad will walk in and hear us discussing his family, which, while not forbidden, makes the vein on his forehead bulge.

"They weren't exactly a warm, fuzzy kind of family."

"I get that," Arthur says. "So the Ren faire coin-flippers were your mom's family, then?"

I smile. "Yeah. They were . . . eccentric, to say the least. Mom was raised in the faire just like her mother and her mother's mother, and now I'm the next link in the chain."

I don't think my voice sounds anything but matter-of-fact, but my tone must have slipped because Arthur places the coin on top of its pouch and leans forward, suddenly very still. His eyes run over and over my face, like if he looks hard enough, he'll get an answer to the question he won't ask.

"What?" I ask.

He leans back and folds his arms, but I can hear his foot tapping beneath the table. "Nothing."

"That was something," I say. "That wasn't a nothing look."

Arthur's smile is the teeniest bit lopsided. "What kind of look was it, then, Gwen?"

Something about *his* tone makes my ears redden. "I don't know," I say. And then, to change the subject, "But it doesn't matter. What matters is I'm the Breanna replacement of faire."

"No, you're the original Gwen of faire."

I take the coin back, placing it in its pouch. "Whatever," I say. "The point is I have to reconfigure my entire summer."

"Why?" Arthur asks. "What was your summer supposed to look like before fate herself danced in and declared you to be royalty?"

I was *supposed* to spend the summer figuring out a way to acknowledge Mom's anniversary. I was *supposed* to help Dad in the shop, come home to Britomart, read my comics, drink my tea, and go over and over my journal until the tightness in my chest eased. I was supposed to *notice things*: Dad and the faire and the Stormsworth of my memory, the Stormsworth that Mom so loved. I was supposed to remember, because every day that passes feels like forgetting and one step closer to losing something else.

I definitely wasn't supposed to already feel my insides warming around a stupid bard and his stupid way of being painfully earnest.

Arthur doesn't react at first when I say, "I was supposed to be Madeline," but he must understand what I mean, because when he answers, his tone is the gentlest I've heard it yet.

"You can be Madeline," he says, "but it's okay if you're a different Madeline than the one that came before, too."

"Is this different Madeline's alter ego named Gwen?" I ask archly.

His smile is bright and I briefly—*briefly*, and then I stuff the thought back down in the lagoon of my subconscious, where it belongs—wonder how this Breanna or anyone could be on the receiving end of such radiant attention, such careful glee, without sort of . . . swooning?

Because he's annoying as hell, my brain suggests helpfully.

And it's true, but I forget it a little when Arthur says, "Only one way to find out, isn't there?"

"Carry on as close to normal as possible?" I ask hopefully.

"Nope. It's to try Gwen on for size. See if she fits." He pauses, and when he speaks again, his eyes are somehow brighter. "Hey," he says. "You should come with me. I have these road trips planned. They're only day trips, but I made a list of places I want to see nearby this summer, and I want you to come."

"I don't know . . ."

Arthur shrugs, cutting me off. "Neither do I. That's the beauty of it, Gwen: nobody does."

"What does that even *mean*?" I ask. "Where are we going? What kind of trips are they? Why on earth would I go with you when—"

He looks at me for a long moment and then his gaze drops to the pouch with the coin in front of me.

"Flip it," he says, cutting off my line of questioning.

"What?"

He points at the coin. "You say you don't believe in fate, but you believe in that coin, right?"

My neck feels clammy. "No," I say. "Absolutely not."

I don't need to tell him that the coin has already flipped *itself* today. I'm not about to flip the damn thing on purpose.

Because what if it says yes? Then what?

"Heads, you spend the summer with me as part of the Gwen Discovery Program. Tails, you can tell me to go to hell."

I stand up, too jittery to sit. "Even if it's heads, you'll tell me I can back out," I say. "So what's the point of flipping it if you're just going to puppy-dog-eye guilt me into whatever you've got planned anyway?"

Arthur stands, too, setting down the twisty necklace and rapping the table with his knuckles. "My thought exactly. We'll start Monday. That is, if you don't have plans?"

It feels like standing on a precipice, for some reason, even though *technically* nothing needs to change. I can let Arthur drag me around during the weekdays and still hang out with Dad and update my journal and read my comics at night. Going with him doesn't mean I implicitly *care* about him or anyone else.

It's just a distraction. Just something to do in the long summer weekdays.

Maybe I can be both: Madeline and Gwen, whoever she is.

"Okay," I tell Arthur.

His entire face lights up like a firework. "Okay?"

"Yes, okay." I sigh. "So long as my dad is okay with it, which he probably won't be, by the way. Where are you taking me?"

Just as I wonder if he's going to immediately whisk me away to some room in the castle with a whiteboard and a perfectly drawn-out plan with maps and itineraries, his phone alarm goes off, an aggressive, loud clang of cymbals that makes me jump.

"It's ten," he says, silencing and pocketing his phone. "I gotta go."

"Okay," I say again. *"But where are we going?"*

"You'll see on Monday," he says, his voice annoyingly bordering on singing again. He shifts his weight from foot to foot by the door and is still grinning like an idiot. "But I'll see you tomorrow? At the coronation?"

"I should think so," I say. "What is a ceremony without the court jester?"

"Bard."

"Whatever you say."

He narrows his eyes, searching my face before breaking into one last grin.

"I like Gwen. And I think you're going to like her, too."

"Where is Gwen going on Monday?" I try one more time.

"You need to learn to be surprised," Arthur grins. "*And* I bet you'll come to like it."

He knocks his knuckles on the doorframe and waves with one hand as he grabs the lute with the other. I tell myself I'm imagining the extra jaunt in his step as I watch him disappear into the darkness.

CHAPTER SEVEN

WHEN HE'S GONE. IT TAKES ME a full minute of standing frozen in the two feet of space that passes as a hallway between the door and the kitchen to remember what it is I'm supposed to be *doing*.

My brain is sluggish, turning over the idea of there being parts of myself I haven't discovered, new parts that have either developed since Mom left, or maybe they were always there and I'm only just now ready to find them. Then there's Arthur and whatever it is he has planned for the Gwen Discovery Program—which *really* needs a new name, or better yet, no name at all because *it shouldn't be happening*.

Even though I've only been wearing them for an hour, I put the sweatpants in the nearly full hamper Dad and I share while the shower water heats up. Then comes the hair mask, the towel, the teeth brushing and the face scrubbing that takes extra long thanks to the makeup, and because I'm *still* preoccupied with thoughts of Arthur and summer and Mom and the coin and everything, I stand in the steamy bathroom and put vanilla lotion on every square inch of my legs and arms and stomach.

Before I go to sleep—but after Dad comes home and cheerfully informs me that a guy named Neil has been reassigned from security to assistant shopkeeper in my absence—I take the coin from its pouch once more and let myself feel the weight of it in my palm.

I consider flipping it.

To see what it says about the Gwen Discovery Program and road trips.

To see what it says about the *bard*.

It would be so much easier, my life, if I had clear directions. When Mom was alive, I could talk through anything with her, because she had this great way of making the final answer feel both right and yours, like it was something you knew all along and she just pointed it out for you.

All I have left is the coin. I'm not stupid. I know it's not actually magical . . . probably. But it's been such a focal point of family lore for as long as I can remember and even before I existed, it's hard not to think it *knows* what it's doing, inanimate or not.

The questions start piling up as it warms in my hand, and I find myself using my other hand to turn to the last page of noticings. In the dim light coming from around the curtains beside my bed, I write my questions out in an ugly scrawl: *What if I make the wrong choice? Am I supposed to be princess of faire, or does it not count because I didn't* actually *flip the coin? And what if Arthur is bad news? What if he's just using me to feel better about the whole Breanna-sort-of-dumping-him thing?*

I'm still holding the coin when I call Fatima.

"Two calls in two days? And at such indecent hours, too. To what do I owe the pleasure?"

"Life is hard," I say. "Why is it so hard?"

"Oh." Fatima's disappointment is palpable through the phone.

"What?"

"I thought you were calling to give me an update about the boy."

"I mean, he's part of why life is hard."

I actually have to pull the phone back when she squeals, "*Oh!*"

"*Ima.*"

She must hear my exasperation, because her voice is minutely calmer when she says, "I mean, *oh.* Yes, musician boys and midnight rendezvous are just awful. Terrible. What did lover boy do this time?"

"He is *not* a lover boy."

Fatima mutters something that sounds a lot like *not yet,* but I let it go.

"Hey," I say. "Do you think I'm . . . stuck?"

I wait for the *of course not* or *what would make you say that*, but I'm met with silence.

"*Fatima*, really?"

"Shush! I'm thinking."

"You're never that quiet," I say. "Especially when you're thinking."

She sighs, and her voice loses all playfulness. "I think you're still grieving."

"Yeah, but that's not the same as stuck, is it?"

Silence again.

"*Fatima*."

"It doesn't have to be the same thing," she says. "Maybe think about it in a different way. Like, what would your mom be most excited for you to do? Spend the summer flirting with the cute boy or moping around Stormsworth wishing she were there?"

"I do not *mope*. And she doesn't get to decide," I say. "Because she's not here. *And* I'm not going to flirt with him, no matter what I decide."

"You're right," Fatima replies. "Your mom can't decide. But if you're so concerned with what she would want, I can tell you right now which option she would pick."

I sigh. "He's *a lot* to handle."

I can practically hear Fatima grin. "I like him already."

"I'm glad someone does," I mutter. "But how am I supposed to know what Mom would want if she's not here to ask?"

And maybe it's because it's Fatima and we've been friends

since third grade, but it's like she knows I'm asking about more than Arthur. She sounds just as uncertain as I feel when she says, "I don't know. If I did, I would tell you."

I'm not sure why my eyes are watering, but I can't stop them from making my voice wet when I say, "Yeah."

"You'll figure it out, though," she says. "You always do."

"Because I have to," I say. "Not because I want to."

We spend another hour on the phone. I fill her in on being dragged into the princess of faire role, which she is *way* too excited about. We talk about Fatima's plans for summer break— going to the beach with her friends, trying to drop hints to the boy she likes without being *too* obvious, taking her cousins to the local water park.

"Do you miss it?" I ask for the first time. "The faire, I mean."

Fatima's answer is quick, ready. "I miss *you*. But no, I don't think so. I like having my own room, and Mama and Baba are happier, which makes my life easier. Did I tell you about the flowers they bought for the front yard? We spent half of last weekend outside planting, and it looks kind of terrible, but every evening Mama makes us come outside and look at the beds and the new blooms."

I laugh. "I love your mom."

I can hear Fatima's smile. "Yeah, she's okay."

After she makes me promise at least a dozen times to send her pictures of the coronation, we hang up. The silence sounds much bigger without Fatima's voice ringing in my ear, but even though my stomach is in knots thinking about to-morrow, reading *The Falconer's Gauntlet* eventually makes my eyes grow heavy and my mind slow down enough to—temporarily—forget about princesses and coins and bards.

* * *

At first, the coronation is not nearly as stressful as I imagined. Partly because I wake to a text from Arthur saying they've made me my own changing room in the castle so that I don't have to worry about lodging my dress in Britomart's doorframe again, but also because Martin and Tim are clearly the stars of the show.

But even though it's not as terrifying as I thought it would be, my sweat glands don't get the memo, and I worry that all anyone is going to see is a bucket of perspiration held together by a corset and concealer that I'm worried I've applied too thickly.

We hold the ceremony at the mouth of the drawbridge with the day's first lazy river occupants entering the cool water and yelping with glee below. For all of Tim's Latin reading and Martin's pomp and circumstance and booming voice, it feels more than a little silly, even though there is a sizable group of people that have come to watch the proceedings.

Arthur stands to the side, his puffed sleeves and lute back in place along with his fixed lazy bard grin. I barely have time to make eye contact with him, forget talk to him, before I am swept up onto a temporary throne that has been set on the bridge for the ceremony. It looks disturbingly real, but it's actually a chair that has had impressively crafted Styrofoam built up around it to make it look grand.

For half a second before sitting, I worry. It's an old worry, a constant one that I carry in the back of my head when I see tables in restaurants that are put close together or the couple times I've ridden on an airplane and looked at the seats. I worry that the seat won't hold me. I worry that beneath the Styrofoam that makes it look wooden and sturdy, the chair will creak too loudly when I sit, or worse, break entirely.

It does creak when I sit, but it's not too bad, and I tell myself that what sound there is should be muffled by the layers and layers of skirt beneath me. For once I'm thankful that the arms dig into my sides a little; I need them to keep me balanced atop my mountain of a dress.

Martin, who is standing on my left, leans down and whispers in my ear, "You're doing great." From my other side, Tim smiles down at me in agreement. In the audience, as if he, too, can hear, Dad smiles up at me, giving a very small wave before returning his hand to the pocket of his apron.

"Hear ye, hear ye," a crier in the Stormsworth colors yells to the crowd. "On this day, the seventeenth of June in the year of our lord 1560, we declare Lady Madeline Hathaway henceforth be known as Princess of Stormsworth. God save our kings. God save our princess."

I have a heading in the journal of noticings—*Times I've felt mom's presence*—but instead of tallies, I write a short sentence so I can remember the specifics, so I never, never forget.

There is only one right now, but I know when I get back home tonight, I will add another. Because as the crier bows with a grand flourish and the audience follows suit, as I sit between Arthur's dads and the crowd dips their heads in my direction, I swear I feel Mom beside me. It feels like she's right there, standing beside Dad and grinning from ear to ear.

Enjoy it, baby, she whispers in my head.

And stupidly, even though it *is* all in my head, I feel myself tearing up. Because she would love this. She would love seeing me in makeup and in a dress other than my usual peasant gowns. She would lean against Dad's side and he would have a hard time deciding whether to smile down at her or look up at me on my Styrofoam throne. And later, she would smile and say, A *princess, just like I was.* A *family legacy,* as she helped me take the pins from my hair and washed the makeup from my face.

In a flash, she's gone, and just as quickly, as the crowd senses the short ceremony has concluded, people meander off toward shops and food and the faire at large.

With their departure comes Arthur's hand on my elbow.

"You did great," he says.

"I should hope so," I say. "My job was to literally sit there."

"Yeah," he says. "But it was a *royal* sitting. Very different from us poor commoners."

"Yes, you did quite well, Madeline. Thank you for indulging these old kings," Tim says.

"Speak for yourself, my love. I'm young and vibrant," Martin mutters before turning to Arthur. "Speaking of young and vibrant, you two pretty things are free until the first joust in an hour. Madeline, Arthur has agreed to see you to all your events for the remainder of the weekend until you know your princess schedule."

"Oh," I say. "No. I mean, I can find my own way."

"Nonsense," Martin says, clapping a hand to my shoulder. "He begged to be the one to help you. Tim and I wanted to get you a lady-in-waiting, but Arthur *insisted*."

"Repeatedly," Tim adds.

"*Thank you*," Arthur says, coming forward to push them away. "Thank you *so* much for making me sound desperate. I hate you both."

Martin leans down to kiss Arthur on the head, his crown tilting forward as he does.

"Hate you, too, son."

"*Goodbye*, fathers."

"Have a good day, Madeline," Tim says over his shoulder. "We'll see you at the jousts."

As the kings walk away arm in arm, Arthur strums his lute and smiles at me. "A whole hour," he says. "What would you like to do, Princess? What's your favorite thing to do at faire?"

When I try to articulate to people that aren't faire vendors what a typical weekend looks like, I find myself at a loss to account for how tired I am when it's over. There's making sure the stock is replenished as people buy journals and jewelry, there's talking to the patrons who have questions about this necklace or that bracelet, and also the customers who want to know when Dad will be doing another journal-making demonstration at the front of our shop, and can they take pictures? Can they buy the journal he's actually working on?

It's exhausting enough that there isn't often time to look around the faires other than passing glances at vendors on the way to get food or refill our water bottles.

"I'm not sure," I say honestly.

"We'll have to fix that." Arthur grins. "But not today. Not in an hour. And not when you're looking *dreadfully* uncomfortable to be seen in that dress. You look beautiful, by the way, Your Highness."

"How do you know I'm uncomfortable?" I ask, choosing to ignore the compliment.

Arthur leans forward and for a heartbeat, I wonder if he's going to kiss me, which is ludicrous on *so* many levels, they're not even worth listing. He doesn't, of course. He's a flirt with words, but a careful one. He wouldn't kiss someone unless he was absolutely a million percent certain they wanted to be.

And I don't. Not by him. Not by anyone.

Not that he's interested anyway, no matter how much he teases.

He's in love with Bre, I remind myself. Even his dads said so. Besides, I don't *like* him. Not like that. Probably not at all. Because no matter that my stomach does a strange little lurch when I see him, I am resolved—*totally resolved*—not to care about anyone else.

Instead of kissing me—which, again, *duh*—Arthur's hand rests lightly on my shoulder and pushes downward. I don't know when they jammed up next to my ears, but now that he's pointed it out, I can feel the tension in my shoulder blades, my back. My middle hurts from inhaling so much, from sucking in my stomach. I don't know why I bother; the corset for the dresses, though not *actually* confining, is sturdy enough that I doubt anyone can tell the difference by looking at me.

But I do it anyway. I can't help it with so many eyes on me.

"So, only an hour," he says. "And no people, so you can give those shoulders a break. I have just the thing."

Just the thing is a video game on handheld consoles in the castle's basement media room, which seems very like something you would do with a friend and not someone you're interested in. I'm feeling increasingly stupid for thinking I needed to worry about Arthur's flirtations. It's obvious he wants me as just a buddy, a pal. There's no reason for me to have my guard up.

Which is fine. More than fine. It's what I want.

"We're just . . . acquaintances, right?" I check twenty minutes into being destroyed by ink blasters at every turn. It's going to be a necessity to put a name to us, I realize, and I figure I better get the jump on it before he does.

Arthur—who is a level 53 to my 1—doesn't look away from the screen where he has just taken out the other team's paint sniper.

"I think so," he says. He flicks his eyes up to me, but then quickly back down to the controller he has balanced on his bent knees. "Can't we be acquaintances inching our way down the road to eventual friendship, though?"

"Probably not," I say. "But acquaintances I can live with."

Arthur glances at me again and nods once. "Acquaintances," he agrees.

"Good," I say. "So acquaintances can tell acquaintances when their games are stupid, right?"

It's the most indignant I've seen him. "*Splatterbomb* is *not* stupid. You're just new at it. Give it some time."

"It's been half an hour," I point out.

"*More* time. We have all summer."

Against my better judgment, his words make my skin flush with something that, if I look too closely, might resemble happiness.

I resign myself to adding a *Video games with Arthur* heading to my journal—to account for the ridiculousness of a girl in full medieval princess garb and a boy dressed as a bard sitting side by side playing a twenty-first century game—just as I am taken out by the other team once more.

* * *

In all my years at faire, I've probably seen collectively an hour of jousting, which is more than fine by me. It's the same every time: Knights pump up the crowd from their horses. Knights hit each other with pointy lances. Knights hit each other with swords in overly choreographed fight sequences.

But just when I take my place in the box next to Arthur's parents and resign myself to looking politely enthused about the show, a man in full armor runs into the sandy arena beneath us, cups his hands around his mouth, and yells something unintelligible.

"Oh, for Christ's sake," Tim mutters. And then, turning to Martin, "This was *your* idea. You deal with him."

"What was I supposed to do, love? They needed their big break and you and I agreed that Stormsworth is a place for all."

"*I* thought we agreed that their act was a good idea for a smaller, less sophisticated faire," Tim says under his breath, but his words are lost to everyone but me as Martin yells down, "What is it, fine fellow?"

"The camels," the knight stresses. "There's a small problem."

Camels? I thought this was the joust.

Tim taps his fingers irritably against the arm of his throne, looking every inch the impatient royal. "Out with it, then," he shouts.

"The camels," the knight says again. "They're . . . Well, they don't like the lances."

Martin turns to Tim, who is looking murderously down at the knight. "Didn't the brochures they sent us show them jousting with lances?"

"*Yes*," Tim grits out. "And for the last time, I'm *telling you* those were photoshopped."

Arthur, who is standing in the back of the box, darts his eyes between his dads and then to me. He must see the confusion on my face because he says, "Camel jousting. An act made by a company called HACK. Dad voted yes. Pops voted no. So naturally here they are."

I turn in my seat. "HACK?"

"Horse-Adverse Chivalrous Knights," Arthur says just as Tim interjects, "They're hacks, all right."

"Camels were used for centuries in battle," Martin argues. "*You* told me that, oh great scholar. You went on and on about how Napoleon used them in battle on our first date."

"I did *not*."

Arthur steps forward and stage-whispers to me, "No, he saved that for the second date."

Tim is about to argue again, but Arthur holds up a hand. "No, no. I can fix this. Just give me ten minutes. Madeline? Can you stall the crowd?"

The sound I make—something between a squeak and a growl—is decidedly not princess-like.

"Stall?"

"Just"—Arthur waves vaguely—"make a royal proclamation or something. Give me ten. Five, even."

Before I have a chance to refuse, because of course that's what I want to do, Arthur is gone, and his dads are looking at me expectantly.

"Well, Princess? Would you like to address your loyal subjects?" Tim asks.

I glance at Martin, hoping he'll provide an out, but he is staring fixedly out at the crowd.

It is maybe the least changed part of Stormsworth, the jousting ring and the surrounding wooden bleachers, another cluster of redbuds bordering one elongated side. Both the stands and the fence surrounding the sanded ring have gotten new coats of paint, but otherwise they look as I remember.

For a moment, I try to remember if Mom and I ever came here together, and if we did, I wonder if there's still a bit of her—maybe a strand of hair or sloughed-off skin cells—trapped somewhere beneath the sand.

As implausible as it is, I let the idea of it lift me from my seat and carry me to the large open window of the box before I can think better of it. If I cannot be brave on my own, maybe I can borrow from Mom and whatever parts of her linger here.

"Hello—" I start quietly.

"*Good morrow.*"

"*Speak up.*"

There are smiles in both Tim's and Martin's voices from behind me, and I know they probably see this as a character-building exercise or something that their parent brains think is for my own good, but it's actually torture.

I clear my throat. "Good morrow, Stormsworth."

A cheer rises from the stands. It makes me want to shrink beneath the window and hide until Arthur comes back, but I think of Mom, clear my throat, and continue.

"We're experiencing, um, a slight delay."

The crowd is quiet, waiting for more, but I don't have more to say.

My palms are sweating.

My back is sweating.

Every part of me is sweating, and it's not just from the heat of the unforgiving Oklahoma sun.

"So . . ."

Whatever I was going to say—which is just as much a mystery to me as the crowd before me—dies on my lips when I notice two boys, probably nine or ten, in the front row of the stands to my left. One of them points at me with his index finger, before turning to his friend and drawing a circle in the air. A large one.

If I was a different kind of person, I wouldn't let it bother me. They're little kids. What do they know? But it's enough, that circle that I can practically see hanging in the air, to make me take a step back from the window.

"You're okay," Martin whispers to me, coming to stand beside me. "You did good, honey."

I didn't, though.

There's a type of fungus, the *Ophiocordyceps unilateralis*, that I wrote down in my facts journal. When it spores, the fungus can work its way into certain ant species in rainforests and literally control their brains, which is why scientists call it the zombie fungus.

That's not why I wrote it down, though. I wrote it down because the other ants recognize the signs of the spore taking root in the brain. If they catch it soon enough—before the fungus grows and kills the ant and spreads spores to the rest of the colony—the other ants will carry their infected brethren away from the colony and kill them.

Those boys are looking at me like I'm the infected ant in a colony of glowing, ideal ants.

Beside me, Martin's smooth, loud voice assures the crowd

that they will soon witness a joust of unparalleled delight and awe. He begs their patience, promises rich rewards in the form of kingly appreciation to the section that cheers the loudest, and just as he launches into what I suspect is an entirely fictionalized account of the many uses of camels throughout history, Arthur runs to the side of the fence, waving foam swords—still dripping slightly from their time in the castle moat—at one of the HACK knights.

The crowd goes wild as the camels enter the arena, their knights each catching a foam pool sword from where Arthur throws them over the fence as they pass.

One of the knights misses his catch and it falls in front of the boy who drew the circle in the air. He picks it up, his face glowing with delight, but the second he sees the little girl who raced forward hoping to collect it, he hands it to her without hesitation.

When Arthur rejoins us in the box, he is sweaty from the run to the moat and back, but triumphant.

"Foam doesn't shine in the light," he says in greeting, his voice lost to the cheers as the camels begin to race toward each other at a surprising clip from opposite sides of the ring.

"Knights afraid of horses and camels afraid of lances," Tim sighs deeply. "This is a farce."

Arthur leans down to kiss his cheek. "Come on, Pops. Look, the crowd *loves* it. Let Dad have his fun."

Martin doesn't hear them. He is leaning forward with his hands sprawled on the open window, cheering on the blue knight atop the smallest camel.

"Thanks for stalling for me," Arthur says, settling into a chair beside me.

"I didn't, really," I say. I hesitate under Arthur's overly attentive stare. "I . . . clammed up."

I don't like how Arthur seems to see right through me. I don't like the understanding gaze under the scrunched, confused eyebrows.

And I don't like change, so I don't like how natural it feels when he takes my hand in his.

"There's always next time, Gwen," he whispers. "Now pick your champion. My money is on the green knight."

CHAPTER EIGHT

IN THE UPHEAVAL OF PACKING UP and leaving the last faire, traveling to this one, and then the sudden princess thing once we got here, it feels like it has been years since Dad and I sat across from each other at the table to eat a meal.

"Thanks, kid," he says when I plunk the chicken tenders and fries in front of him. "You look beat."

"I kind of am," I say, squirting ketchup on the corner of my paper plate. "This whole princess thing . . ." I trail off. "It's been a lot."

And it has been. Since the first camel joust, there have been real jousts with real horses, two outfit changes (one of which was Arthur's fault for spilling soda on my skirt), and a litany of photos with passersby who urge their kids, their significant others, their friends to get a photo with the royal family after we ride in the parade or just happen to be walking by.

I'm zonked, and usually I would have the summer weekdays to lounge around and nap and recuperate, but Arthur is still insisting that I go on road trips with him starting tomorrow.

Joy.

Dad and I don't really have conversations. Not because we don't want to talk or we aren't interested in the other's day, but because without Mom it's like we've forgotten how to make words flow like a river. We're more of a puddle these days, something you're already out of by the time you realized you've stepped in it. Which, right now, with my exhausted brain, is fine by me.

So it's highly unusual for Dad to clear his throat and say, "Arthur came to visit me at the shop today."

I put down my paper napkin.

"What?"

"He said you wanted to take some road trips with him this summer."

Dad watches me, and this particular silence is expectant as he waits for me to confirm or deny.

"It's okay," I sigh, then quickly add, "I understand why you're saying no and that it would cause too much anxiety and that you need help during the week with shop stuff and—"

"Madeline." He raises his hand, like he can physically block my water hose of words. "It's okay. You should go."

"Dad, I—"

"No," he interrupts again. "Your mom . . ." He pauses. When he starts over, I can tell he's trying to keep his voice from shaking. "Your mom and me, when we decided you would have a different childhood, there were things we hoped you would still have. This is one of those things."

I scoff to hide the feelings making my own throat sound watery. "Sure," I say. "Because all those years ago you imagined me getting in a car with a deranged bard and riding off into the sunset of god knows where."

"No," Dad says. "Not exactly. But we did want you to have friendships and relationships and—"

"*Dad*, ew. Can we please not talk about relationships?"

It's impossible to say who looks more uncomfortable, me or Dad.

"Maddie, I need you to know you can talk to me," he says, and it sounds like he's swallowed a bag of rocks but is making himself power through it. "If you need to. I'm here if you need to talk about crushes or sex or—"

"*DAD*. Please, I have Fatima. I have Dr. Jenkins. I'm good."

He looks relieved. "Good, good. But if you ever do need to talk—"

I am not going to let him finish a single one of these sentences, for his sake and mine.

"I can ask you," I say for him. "I know. Thanks."

His smile is soft, still embarrassed. "But no thanks?"

"Precisely," I laugh.

We finish dinner looking down at our plates and not

talking, and I suspect both of us hope our cheeks fade from bright red to their usual pink. I assume that's all the conversation we'll have for the night, but when I get up to clear our plates, Dad gently folds his hand around my wrist until I look at him.

"Your mom would be proud of you," he says. "About the princess stuff. She'd be tickled pink."

I inhale deeply. "I hope so."

"She would. *Is.* I am, too."

"Thanks, Dad," I say.

He hugs my waist. "Love you, kiddo."

"Love you, too."

* * *

Dad showers first, so I update my journal while I wait for my turn. It takes some flipping, but I find the heading of *Chats with Dad* and add a mark, surprised at the number of tallies I find there.

It's just enough to make me panic, the surprise. Because I can remember one or two of our bigger talks—and I'll *definitely* remember the awkwardness of this one—but what about the other sixteen? Why did I think tallies would be enough?

I'm not paying enough attention. I need more detail, more focus, more time.

After all the work Tim and Martin have already put into it, I can't back out of the princess thing without feeling like a complete jerk, but I can turn down the rest. I can't let my pseudo-friendship-whatever-it-is with Arthur get in the way of time with Dad.

Before I can change my mind, I shoot a text to Arthur. **Sorry, but I can't do the road trip stuff.**

Of course he has his read receipts on, and *of course* he ignores all social protocol about initiating phone calls. My phone lights up with his number and I'm about to reject it when a text bubble pops up on the top of the screen: **I'll just call again.**

I answer, sighing loudly.

"Gwen, dear. Thank you so much for accepting a call from a mere peasant."

"Why are you calling me?"

His laugh sounds the same over the phone, but somehow it *feels* warmer and deeper pressed up against my ear like this. I hunt around for my headphones as he begins to talk.

"No road trip?" he asks.

"No road trip." My headphone case has fallen between Britomart's wall and my bed and my arm is too fat to squeeze between.

"Tomorrow or ever?"

"Ever," I grit out as I attempt to scrape the case up the side of the wall with a spatula I've borrowed from the kitchen.

"Are you okay? It sounds like you're in distress."

"Headphones fell," I say. "Is there something else? I'm not road-tripping. I can't."

"Why? Did your dad say you couldn't go?"

I consider lying, but don't. "No, he said I could."

"So what's the problem? Afraid it's gonna be too awesome?"

The headphones, mere inches from recovery, slide off the spatula with a soft *thunk*. Somehow this seems like the bard's fault.

"Damn it," I say.

"Do princesses curse?" Arthur is smiling. I can hear it.

"This one does," I say.

"I believe a cursing princess would very much enjoy the delights of . . . drum roll, if you please, Your Highness."

"Absolutely not."

Arthur, as per usual, is undeterred by my complete lack of enthusiasm. *"The zoo!"*

I finally manage to drag the headphone case onto my bed and pop one into my ear. "We have to road trip to a zoo? Really? I'm pretty sure we passed one, like, an hour away from here when we came into town."

"It's the *Fort Worth Zoo*." He says it like he's just announced we're going to Disney World.

"Okay . . ." I match his tone.

"It's like one of the top five zoos in the country."

"I've been to the San Diego Zoo," I say. "And they had pandas. And polar bears."

There's a great deal of rustling on Arthur's side of the call to the point that I worry we are about to be disconnected.

"Hello?"

"Sorry," he says. "I was grabbing a penny."

"What for?"

"Fate. Heads, you go to the zoo with me. Tails, you don't. Agreed?"

"No."

"Flipping," he says. I hear the clink of the penny, the slap of his hands.

He doesn't say anything.

I try not to ask, but I can't help it. I'm curious. "What is it?"

Arthur doesn't lie. "Tails," he says. And it's the most morose I've ever heard him.

Maybe it's because of what Dad was saying—about how Mom would want me to have relationships and adventures and whatever—or maybe it's because he sounds so, so sad, but I pop the other headphone into my ear and then reach up to dig for the coin pouch.

"What are you doing?" he asks over my rustling.

"It's the coin," I say, when I have it in my hand. "The *real* one. Same rules. Heads means yes, tails means no."

I can't tell over the phone if Arthur understands what a big deal this is, how I haven't flipped the coin for fear of what it would say, but it sounds like he's holding his breath, so maybe he does.

"Agreed?" I ask, echoing him.

"Yes, Gwen. Flip it."

I do, and for the split second the coin is the air, when I don't have time to parse out my feelings and only have time to feel them, I find myself praying it's heads.

When I raise my hand and see the age-worn profile instead of the lion crest, the smile escapes onto my lips before I have time to stop it.

"It's heads."

Arthur's whoop is loud enough that it makes me flinch, but I laugh anyway.

"You won't regret it," he says.

"This better be one hell of a zoo."

"On the morrow, Gwen, dear."

"On the morrow."

Just before I hang up, I can hear Arthur beginning to sing "Rewrite the Stars."

When Dad is out of the shower, I start the process: shower, hair cream, towel. Then the teeth brushing, face washing, and the Olympic sport that is applying lotion to my legs in the nearly nonexistent space between toilet and shower.

After the electric kettle rumbles to life and I pour my tea, I cue up my tablet with the web comic app. I have to go to my saved comics to find *The Falconer's Gauntlet*, because it's almost never featured on the main page, which is ridiculous. It's got the best artwork, the best storyline, the best characters.

It's not Wednesday, so there's not a new episode, but I'm on episode 49 of my current reread, which is one of my favorites where Adelina and Cornelius must navigate the forbidden forest to find the lost prince. Cornelius continually soars above the trees to find a path forward for Adelina, using their set of signals to let her know which way to go, which mostly feels like an excuse for the artist to show off how amazingly she can paint big double-paneled landscapes.

Beyond the art, the last panel is what makes it one of the episodes I revisit most often, because it's just so badass. Adelina is *gorgeous* and brown-skinned with super-long black hair that always makes me think of Fatima's, but best of all, she's not super thin like so many of the other main characters in web comics.

This last panel is zoomed in on her entire body as Cornelius comes to perch on her outstretched arm. Her legs are slightly spread apart, her thighs are touching, her waist is a smooth curve rather than a sharp angle, and her head is held up in triumph as she and Cornelius look down at the valley where the lost prince is hidden.

Nobody could look at her and think she looks anything but capable and confident and athletic, even if her thighs touch and her chin isn't super defined from her neck.

When I fall asleep, not for the first time, I hope I dream of Adelina and Cornelius and can go with them on their adventures.

But for the first time, in the split second before sleep, I think it would be nice to dream of my own adventures, too. Maybe ones that include bards and zoos.

★ ★ ★

Monday comes with a wide-open blue sky that stretches in every direction when I walk out of Britomart to find Arthur's beat-up Ford monstrosity from the 1970s with a long, extended trunk that looks like it probably could hide two or three bodies.

I don't remember my dreams from last night, but I know they didn't include this.

"Here she is," Arthur announces proudly, opening his door. "Your chariot."

"I didn't know cars could come in an avocado color," I say.

"Don't hate," Arthur says, patting the hood. "She's a classic."

"Right up there with those meals that are mostly made of Jell-O. Some classics should stay in the past where they belong." I make my voice a bit lighter, lest I *actually* offend him. "Why do you have this piece of junk anyway? Don't tell me it's the best your parents could afford."

Arthur rolls his eyes. "It's the best *I* could afford. Pops and Dad have this annoying thing about buying my own first car because it's a 'rite of passage' or something."

I laugh. "You'd think they would have bent the rules to avoid this disaster."

Arthur—who is dressed in shorts that are somehow both too long and too short and a T-shirt that says hard to be the bard—stretches himself across the top of the car, his cheek pressed into the hood.

"She didn't mean it, baby. Daddy won't let the princess be rude to one of her oldest subjects again."

"If I was actually royalty, I wouldn't let that thing within a football field's distance of my kingdom."

Arthur straightens and grins. "You would for me, wouldn't you?"

"*Especially* not for you," I say.

His grin widens at my tone. "You would," he says. "I can be *very* convincing."

"Well, convince yourself to get in the car, then," I say, opening the passenger door. "Did you know this stupid zoo is like three hours away? You *do* know there are zoos in this state, right?"

"Yeah, but this zoo is one of the best in the country. *And* they have a new baby hippo."

"I could just find you a video of a baby hippo online and save us the trouble," I mutter as we both sink into the ancient, cracked leather seats (also avocado-colored).

"Where's the fun in that?" Arthur asks. He buckles his seat belt before handing me a pair of cheap, fire truck–red plastic sunglasses off the dashboard. "Here."

"What are these?"

Arthur lowers his matching blue ones to glance at me dramatically over the rims.

"Sunglasses, Gwen. *Road-tripping* sunglasses. Keep up."

"I'm not wearing those."

He turns the car on—the engine sounds like it's been pulled from retirement for this trip—and says, his voice a little louder, "No road-tripping sunglasses, no road-tripping Tootsie Pops. Those are the rules."

I think he's kidding, but then he reaches into the back seat and pulls out a plastic megatub full of blue, brown, red, and orange suckers all standing upright on their sticks like little sugar soldiers.

"Did my dad tell you these are my favorite?" I ask, sliding the glasses onto my nose and grabbing a brown Tootsie Pop.

"Are they really?"

His grin is too genuine to be teasing.

"You didn't know?"

Arthur honks the horn twice in glee before backing away from Britomart. He does that thing people do when they have no rearview camera, bracing his hand on my headrest and twisting his entire torso to look out the back window.

"It's fate, Gwen. Pure, unadulterated, sugary fate. Hand me an orange one, will you?"

"It's not fate," I say, handing him a sucker. "It's coincidence." I tap the clearance sticker on the side of the plastic tub.

"I don't know," he says, pausing to unwrap the sucker with his teeth. "Someone somewhere decided that these perfectly delicious suckers weren't selling quickly enough and put them on clearance at the exact right time so that when I walked into the store, they were front and center. And *then* they turn out to be your favorite? Too many things are lining up, Gwen. It's. *Fate.* The coin even said so."

"*Or,*" I say, "it was just a grand coincidence that happened to work in my favor." I try to keep my voice serious even though it's hard not to laugh at the ridiculousness of sitting next to a boy with plastic costume sunglasses and a sucker in a truly hideous car.

"Suit yourself, Princess."

"We're not at faire," I say. "Don't call me that."

Arthur lowers the glasses again to glance over me. I'm

worried I'm going to have to add a new heading for it in my journal if he keeps this up.

"You're still my princess," he says. "Stormsworth or not."

I make a loud gagging sound. "Oh my god, really?"

He laughs, but it's one of those *I'm not sure why we're laughing* laughs.

"Um, that's the *cheesiest* pickup line," I clarify.

"It's not a pickup line," Arthur says, popping the sucker back into his mouth. "It can't be, because this isn't a pickup; it's a Ford Truckster."

"Stop talking," I moan. "It's just getting worse."

"Don't worry," he says as we turn onto the highway. "Only three hours to go."

"And back again," I mutter, like it's a burden.

He pats my knee so quickly, I barely register it. "And back again," he says, like it's a gift.

* * *

Three hours go by surprisingly fast when the Tootsie Pops are flowing and Arthur is in charge of the music. For all my worry that he would want to ask me endless questions about myself and talk about feelings and futures and whatever else his overly earnest, fate-loving self likes to do with a captive audience, I actually have . . . fun.

His car is too ancient to have Bluetooth or even an aux cord, so he has a tiny wireless speaker that sits on the bench between us, blaring everything from indie songwriters I've never heard of to Taylor Swift to Simon and Garfunkel. Each song, shuffled from his extensive library, is punctuated by him saying, "*Oh!* This is a great one," and then him launching into why it works musically and why it's "criminally underrated."

"You *cannot* say that Queen is criminally underrated," I tell him when his phone chirps that we are one right turn away from the zoo. "They are *widely* considered one of the best bands of all time."

"Yes, but 'Liar' is one of their best songs and no one talks about it."

"Okay, but you said the same thing about Beyoncé's *Lemonade* album, and that's just . . . also incorrect."

Arthur leans out the window to pay the five dollars to park. The attendant eyes the car as we pass like she considered charging double for the eyesore. "Do you think Beyoncé and her work are as appreciated as they should be?"

"She's *Beyoncé,*" I stress. "Everyone appreciates her."

"Yeah, but do you think she deserves *more* recognition?"

"Sure, but—"

"Aha! See?" Arthur crows triumphantly, putting the car in park and turning to me. "She deserves more recognition than she has, therefore she's underrated."

I sigh. "You're impossible to argue with, you know that?"

"Good to hear," Arthur says, coming to walk beside me as we head toward the entrance. "Because I'm going to *insist* that you wear your road trip sunglasses for the entirety of our visit."

"You're kidding."

"Sun exposure is never a joke, Gwen."

* * *

Road-tripping sunglasses or not, after spending hours wandering the zoo in the bright sun, the indoor lighting feels dim and weak. The gift shop is an overwhelming jumble of plush giraffes and penguins, plastic elephants, T-shirts, and crappy personal fans that will almost surely break as soon as they're used. Arthur and I wander the aisles, our cheeks red and sweaty from hours walking in the sun between exhibits.

"Not to be dramatic or anything," he says, coming to stand beside me, "but I'm going to find the air-conditioning unit in this place and marry it."

"I know I said I don't believe in fate," I reply, "but I've decided my true destiny is to live in this gift shop until I die because I literally can't stand the thought of leaving it to walk to the car."

Arthur pauses in his examination of a pink plastic tumbler with a sticker on its side that promises all proceeds go to refurbishing the flamingo habitat. "I'll bring the car to the entrance for you," he says. "No problem."

Most things for Arthur, I'm finding, are *no problem.* When I needed to take a break—because the heat and the surprisingly hilly pathways conspired to kill me—it was no problem for him to sit me on a bench in front of a bunch of tropical birds. It was also no problem for him to go to the bathroom and return having also stopped to purchase two frozen lemonades. It was no problem for him to stop and refill the water bottle he bought for me at every fountain even when it wasn't empty, because *I want you stay hydrated so you can enjoy yourself.*

It was no problem for him to ignore my protestations of *I'm fine,* when we sat down in a booth for lunch and my stomach felt jammed and confined against the table. Even though I didn't say anything, he saw I was uncomfortable and insisted we sit at an outside table beneath an umbrella. I think he would have preferred sitting inside—who wouldn't, in the heat?—but you would have thought it was his idea of perfection with how he carried on, singing love songs to the squirrels that inched closer and closer for a bite of food.

He is ridiculously accommodating, endlessly aware, and careful to not offend, to have no problem with the world and for the world to, in turn, have no problem with him.

It kind of makes me mad. Not him, exactly, but the unfairness that I've had a good day, a *really* good day, like probably the best day I've had in over a year, and I can't tell Mom about it.

There's not a heading in my journal for this feeling of a sunset tinged with rain. I don't know how to document it, so I force my head to recenter, to be in the present in the gift shop instead of reviewing the day or leaping ahead. Dr. Jenkins would be so proud.

"We should start going back," I tell Arthur. He's at a turnstile full of postcards, a card in each hand. "What are you doing?"

"One for you, one for me," he says. "Do you want the baby hippo one that says 'Hip hip hooray' or the baby hippo one that says 'Hip hop to the zoo'?"

"Neither," I say. "What do you even do with postcards?"

"Tape them to the wall so that at the end of the summer you can behold our grand quest for adventure all at once."

"I'm not going to do that," I say.

But Arthur buys them anyway, handing them to me in their small plastic zoo bag with a flourish.

"Hold these," he says. "I'm going to grab the car."

"I was kidding. I can walk to the car, Arthur."

"I know you can, *Gwen*," he says, mimicking my exasperation. "But there's no need for us both to suffer. I'll be right back. Listen for my honk!"

When he's gone, I pull the journal out of my tiny backpack, quickly marking tallies beneath the Arthur heading, and one beneath the new heading I wrote last night: *Adventures*.

I'm wondering if it would be cheating to go ahead and mark Arthur's promised Wednesday trip since I know without flipping the coin that it's going to happen, when I feel a tap on my shoulder. I jump hard enough to drop my pen.

"Sorry," Arthur says, bending to pick it up. "It's just I found a spot right at the very front, so I figured I'd come and get you."

"You said you would honk," I say, and my voice is sharp

with embarrassment. Did he catch a glimpse of the tallies? What must he think?

"Sorry," he says again. He spins his car key around his finger, watching me closely. "Next time I'll honk."

We walk in silence the short distance to the car. The quiet extends to the gas station stop, to the on-ramp to the highway, to the first twenty minutes of the drive.

Arthur, of course, is the one to break it.

"I didn't mean to startle you," he says.

I look out the window. I can still see his reflection in the light of the setting sun, but it's easier than looking directly at him with his lazy hand on the wheel and his ridiculous shirt.

"I know," I say. After a minute, I add, "Sorry for freaking out."

"Do you want to talk about it?"

I've told him about the coin. I've told him about Mom. Why does this feel so much harder?

"It's just a journal," I say, and he doesn't make it worse by pretending he doesn't know what I'm talking about. "It has a few different parts to it, but I mostly use it to notice things. That's what my therapist calls them: noticings."

"What kind of things do you notice?"

He doesn't sound weirded out, just curious. I try to tell myself this is a normal conversation, nothing to be embarrassed about, but saying it all aloud makes it feel stupid in my brain in a way that I hate.

"Everything," I say. "Mostly stuff about my dad, about my schedule, that kind of thing."

When I glance at him from the corner of my eye, Arthur is smiling. "Am *I* in there?"

My face warms beneath the already-forming sunburn.

"Stop," I say. "You shouldn't ask those things."

"Am I?"

"I don't want to tell you."

"Then you don't have to," he says in his understanding way. We're silent again, except for his fingers dancing on the wheel, but this time it feels like one of Dad's silences: comfortable.

Comfortable or not, Arthur is—of course—the one to ruin it again.

"So now that you've basically admitted I'm in there, what do you notice about me?"

I want to blow him off. He makes it so easy to do, and I think it's mostly a kindness—how cautious he is—but the more time I spend with him, the more I wonder if it's also born of insecurity.

It's not that kind of noticing, but I *do* notice Arthur.

I noticed when we leaned against the lion exhibit railing and a very muscular guy in a tight T-shirt stood next to us and Arthur looked down at his own loose bard shirt and grimaced. I noticed each time he tugged his shorts down, each time he ran his fingers through his hair like a tick, each time his constant fidgeting turned to clothes-straightening.

Arthur, for all his bluster and charm, is woefully self-conscious, constantly aware of the eyes of the world.

If I was braver, I might tell Arthur the things I've noticed about him, but it feels too intimate. So does telling him the real purpose of the journal, but of the two options, somehow the truth seems less embarrassing than admitting I've been watching him as closely as I suspect he's watching me.

"You *are* in there," I say, "But everyone is . . . sort of. I started it after Mom died as a way to remember things."

"What kind of things?" he asks again.

I sigh. "Um, mostly boring stuff. I keep track of how many times I notice a sunset, how many times I've gone to Target, that kind of thing."

Arthur's face is becoming shadowy in the setting sun. It makes him look more angular than he actually is, his chin a point in the light when he says, "That sounds . . ."

"Boring," I supply. "I told you that."

"No, I wasn't going to say boring. I was going to say . . . Well, I was going to say tedious, but I don't mean it as a criticism. I just mean it sounds like a lot of work."

I haven't even told him about how it feels compulsory now, like something I *have* to do.

"It kind of is."

I'm beginning to learn how to read Arthur's silences. It's almost like I can see the questions he isn't asking.

"Do it," I tell him. "Ask."

He doesn't hesitate. "Why do it?"

"Because if I notice everything, maybe it won't be so bad if I lose something else."

He hesitates. "You mean someone else."

This boy is entirely too perceptive.

"Yes," I say. "Exactly."

Arthur picks at a snag in his shorts hem without taking his eyes from the road. "Do you really think it will help, keeping track of everything you notice?"

Because it's dark, because the air-conditioning is puffing with all its might and I'm exhausted from walking, but mostly because while I find the bard kind of irritating, I'm beginning to really like Arthur, I answer truthfully—more truthfully than I've answered Dr. Jenkins, even.

"I'm forgetting her voice," I say, and it feels like a confession. "I mean, I remember . . . sort of. But it's like looking at a sandcastle on the beach that has been hit with waves. Like, you *know* what it probably looked like before it was hit? Maybe? But you can't be really sure. You're more working off the idea of a castle instead of an actual memory. The tide washed too much away. I can look at videos on my phone and remember, but I can't *remember remember.*"

"Was your mom like a castle?"

"She was the *best* castle."

Arthur's smile matches my own. "Do you want to tell me about her?"

I mean to say something obvious—how she was always full of light, how she dragged Dad and me from place to place—but I find that once I start talking about her, I can't stop.

"She liked tiny things," I tell him. "I got that from her. That's part of why she was particularly well suited for life on the road. She didn't want to keep much, and what she did keep was so small it didn't matter."

"Like the coin?"

I nod in the darkness. "Yeah, but that's more of a family heirloom. She also had a whole shoebox full of tiny souvenirs and gifts and stuff she kept. I used to love when she would bring it out and go through them."

"What was your favorite thing in the box?" Arthur asks.

"She gave it to me," I say. "It's a blown glass elephant, smaller than a penny. Dad bought her a handful of animals from a glass blower at the faire where they met on their first date. The elephant was her favorite, though, so she gave it to me before she died. Dad has the others."

Even though neither of us have moved on the car bench, Arthur feels closer than when we started. In the intermittent flashes of streetlights, I can see the hairs—so much lighter than his mop of brunette strands—on his arms, his chipped nails, a freckle next to his right ear.

And suddenly, I'm terrified.

Because I am noticing things about him.

Because I only have the two headings in my journal for him and I don't want to make any more.

Because if I have another person that I have to take notes on, I'm going to scream.

But I can't *not* take notes on him, because what if he leaves, too? What if he has to go away like Fatima did? Or like Mom?

There are no winners in grief.

"We're not friends," I insist suddenly, panicked. "Like, video games and road trips don't make you friends." And if Arthur is jolted by my pronouncement, he doesn't show it.

"Of course not," he says sardonically. "I'm a mere subject of her majesty's court. We're acquaintances at best."

"I'm not kidding."

His eyes flick to me. "Neither am I. If you don't want to be friends, we don't have to be friends."

"Good," I say.

He waits all of two seconds.

"Madeline?"

I blink at my real name coming from his lips. "Yeah?"

"You'll let me know if you change your mind, right?" And there's the uncertainty again, the vulnerable interior that hides beneath his armor of endless singing and cheer.

"I will," I say, "but I probably won't." And because it's all I can give him, I add, "It's for the best."

"We'll see, Gwen," he says. I thought he'd be sad, but it sounds like he's trying not to smile. "We'll see."

The safety of the darkness makes me ask him again, "Why do you call me Gwen, really?"

I feel like most boys would hesitate. Not that I have experience with "most boys," but it seems like something they would dance around or shrug off as a joke. But not Arthur. Arthur smiles and says, "There was a beautiful lady called Guinevere in a picture book Pops used to read me with hair so blond, it shined like the sun. I remember asking Pops if the color was real and he said it was, but it was rare. We played a game for years when I was little, as a joke, of 'is that Gwen hair,' and we never found someone with hair close enough to earn the title of being close to the picture book. But when I saw you leaning on the moat, the very first thing I thought of was Guinevere and her shining hair."

The air between us still smells like sweat and zoo. I get a mouthful of it when I slowly inhale. "You think I look like a princess from a fairy-tale book?"

Arthur nods. "Yes. It was one of the big, neon arrows fate had pointing at you when we met."

"What were the other arrows?"

He taps the side of his nose and smiles before returning his hand to the wheel to drum his fingers along the cracked leather.

"Ah, that's only a secret for a good friend, Gwen. A very good friend, at that."

I slump down in my seat and groan. "Not. Friends," I say.

"Under. Stood," he echoes.

I'm tired, both from walking around the zoo and from being constantly under Arthur's intense scrutiny for an entire day, and yet when he puts his car into park beside Britomart, I don't leap from the car like I thought I would.

For some reason, I don't want him to go. I don't want to say goodnight.

Arthur must feel the same way, because he says, "We could go to my house. Play *Splatterbomb*, if you want."

"I don't think so," I say. "Dad doesn't like it when I stay out late."

I wonder about what Fatima or Adelina would do, what my Mom would want me to do, but before I can give it too much thought, I reach for his hand.

I should start a new list to tack onto the noticings: *Things that do not mean I care.* Beneath it, I could already write *hand holding, road trips,* and *inside jokes about hippos and air conditioners.*

We don't look at each other—me, because I'm afraid doing so will cause my already-red face to explode; him, because I suspect he is afraid of scaring me off—but Arthur's fingers curl ever so gently atop mine in the loosest of clasps.

"Top five," he says after an indeterminate amount of time has passed. "Easily."

"What?"

He looks at me now, his whole face smiling. "Holdable hands, Gwen. The more I hold your hand, the higher you rank."

I want so badly to surprise him, to be carefree and have something to tell Fatima on our inevitable phone call debrief, but more than anything, I want to *tease* him.

"You should hold it more often," I say, allowing myself a second of insanity. "I'd like to get first place."

His laugh has an edge to it. "That honor is also reserved for friends, I'm afraid. We'll have to see where 'yet' gets us."

Did he just move his thumb over my knuckles, or did I imagine it?

"I need to go inside," I say, but I don't drop his hand.

"So go, then."

I do, even though it feels like there is still something—or some *things*—left to say. Arthur waits until I'm inside Britomart before he crunches over the gravel in his hideous

Truckster. He can't see me from where I stand by the kitchen window, but I, too, watch him until he's out of sight.

I look at my left hand in the dim nightlight that Dad constantly leaves on beneath the microwave. It's always looked too round to me, my hand, with its babyish wrist dimples and wide palms.

But now, with the fresh memory of Arthur the bard's fingers wrapped around mine, my hand looks soft. Still not delicate, but *normal*. Maybe even holdable.

I'm so tired that after my shower, with my legs weary from walking miles around the zoo, I decide to skip the tea and comics tonight. Just for one night. I'm too exhausted to notice if the break in routine makes my skin prickle.

CHAPTER NINE

I DON'T CHANGE MY MIND ABOUT BEING friends, though. I *don't*.

Even when we go to the Route 66 Pops Soda Shop and Arthur buys me every weird soda flavor I so much as glance at.

Even when we leave at the crack of dawn and drive to the middle of nowhere just to see the Texas Stonehenge replica for ten minutes and head home.

Even when we're not road-tripping and he follows me around at faire, always making sure that I'm comfortable, that I've got an ice-cold water bottle and a battery-operated fan, that I have a good view of the HACKs, with their foam swords and obstinate camels that participate in the joust only half the time.

Never mind that for the first time since Mom died, I have a new part of my nightly routine. After the shower, but before *The Falconer,* I take the coin out and hold it in my hand, wondering if I should flip it and what I should ask if I do.

The obvious answer is starting to take up more brain space than I care to admit, no matter how much I insist—both to Arthur and myself—that we aren't friends. Because even though I know I shouldn't, sometimes I think about asking the coin if I should give in to Arthur and, as Fatima calls it, his "very-obviously-actually-interested-in-you flirting, Maddie. Get a grip."

I'm not so sure it's obvious, though, because as much as I know Arthur wants to be friends, I can't get the thought out of my head that it would be *another* person to care (and therefore worry) about. It helps, in moments of weakness, to remind myself of the facts: It was supposed to be Princess Bre instead of Princess Madeline, and Arthur was very, very recently in love with her, not me.

It's easier to tell myself I don't care if I can convince my brain that Arthur, too, is better off without me.

"What are you thinking about?" Arthur asks me, and even though we haven't spoken for the last five minutes, I don't startle when he speaks. It has only been three weeks, but I've gotten disturbingly used to having him at my elbow. There have been maybe three days in the last twenty-one that we haven't spent at least some time together.

"How annoying you are," I joke.

"Ah, but you *are* thinking of me, so I'll take it."

It's a rare cool day at faire. The sky is overcast and low with gray clouds that might open on us at any minute. Arthur was a little too eager to buy a leather sword sheath and an umbrella with a sword hilt as a handle. It is slung across his back, his lute conspicuously missing because of the possibility of rain.

"What's a bard without a lute?" I asked him this morning.

His grin *looked* normal, but it felt flirtatious all the same when he said, "A guy with nothing to do but be your humble servant for the entire day, your highness."

"Isn't that what you do every day?" I asked.

The smugness was gone when he answered, "Yes, actually."

Thinking of it now makes me blush as we wander the vendors aisles. (Not that you can tell. Even with the cooler weather, my face instantly turns red the second I step out of Britomart and her trusty air-conditioning.)

It's been happening more and more lately, the blushing thing. God, I hope he doesn't notice, the smug bastard. For someone who clearly lacks a certain level of self-esteem, he's awfully sure of himself around me.

I don't want to stop and think of why that is.

Arthur and I are supposed to be heading back to the castle to get ready for the one o'clock parade, but he is on his own mission to take me to every single stall today when it's cool enough to be outside in my princess getup for more than ten minutes.

"We should go," I say as he tries to drag me by the elbow into a shop that sells custom medieval-style maps. I don't recognize the middle-aged woman behind the counter. That's been happening a lot at the new Stormsworth, even though most of the usual crowd seems to be here, too. Arthur says his dads expanded to be able to include more local merchants who aren't usually able to take part in the Ren faire circuit.

"But she has a map of *The Princess Bride*, Gwen."

"It'll have to wait. Your pops will have us drawn and quartered by camel if we're late *again*."

"Those camels aren't coordinated enough for that," he scoffs. "We would probably just get dragged *slowly* until they found another patch of grass to destroy."

"Not worth the risk either way."

He groans loudly. *"Fine."*

For the parade, I sit in an open-air carriage with Arthur and his dads, waving with our gloved hands at the end of a long line of trumpeters, vendors walking with signs advertising their shops, and some of the character actors that wander the faire aisles.

I don't mind this spectacle as much as some of the others that come with being princess of faire. At least in the carriage, you can only really see my head, my crown, and my hand. I don't feel like people stare at me as much when I'm next to bold Martin and commanding Tim.

They do stare, though, at the fairy garden party, which happens once a weekend. Little kids can sign up to be taught how to fly by Ren faire employees dressed up as pixies. At the end of the half-hour lesson that mostly involves letting the participants wear fairy wings and jump inside a bouncy castle, I come out as princess of faire to give them a special sticker and declare them royal pixies in Her Highness's enchanted gardens.

The kids love it, and they're usually too enamored with the fairies to pay me much mind, but their guardians are another story. More than one woman—and so often it is women, which feels particularly awful—in straight-size tights and sneakers has given me the once-over, her eyes wavering between confusion and superiority. I can practically see her shining the crown to place atop her own head.

But this, the parade, isn't so bad. It's fun, even, with Arthur verbally sparring with his dads through smiling lips as we all wave at the little crowd. Martin and Arthur take turns trying to be the most ridiculous to make Tim break and laugh aloud, which almost never works on him but always works on me.

Martin is the best at it, much to Arthur's irritation.

Both the game and the parade are cut short today when it finally begins to rain, though. Arthur gleefully whips out his new umbrella and extends his arm to hold it over my head.

"There's room for both of us under here," I tell him as Martin and Tim pull a blanket from their seats to cover their heads, Tim loudly fretting about his stitchwork and how could Martin have forgotten an umbrella again.

"It's okay," Arthur tells me, but the rain is already coming down harder and the mousse he sometimes uses to carefully swoop his hair is already giving up the fight.

"Yes," I say, grabbing his arm and pulling him up against my side. "It *is* okay."

Arthur's dads are staring into each other's eyes and laughing under the cover of their makeshift umbrella-blanket with the kind of stupidly-in-love look that reminds me of Mom and Dad.

They're obsessed enough that I doubt they notice when Arthur bends his head to say in my ear over the increasingly deafening downpour and the happy shouts of people scrambling for cover, "Are we still not friends, then, Gwen?"

When I turn to reply, he hasn't moved, and for a moment, it feels like we're suspended underneath the cherry-red umbrella with the sword hilt, just looking at each other, waiting for the other to break.

But I can't break. I can't. I'm still trying to figure out how to put together all the pieces that broke last year. I'm still desperate to fit all of my Arthur interactions beneath the *Times I've talked to the bard* or *Adventures* headings without making another.

Because if I add another heading, it means he's taking up more room in my journal and my head. And if he takes up too much room in my head I know that, coin or not, he'll bleed over into my heart.

I don't want to risk being that broken ever again.

"I don't think so," I say, still staring. "I'm sorry."

This time, it's not just something I say. I *am* sorry, for him and for me.

There's a poem in my journal by a poet Mom and I love

who uses the pseudonym Lark. I have part of it memorized, and the line I underlined leaps into my head as I watch Arthur carefully pack away the emotions behind his eyes, determined as always to spare me from feeling obligated to him:

Careful, little one, to not cut yourself on the sharp edges of the world. Careful, still, to not become one yourself.

I hadn't realized until now how close it is to the Wizened Old Wizard's edict to tame the world, to make it kinder.

"It's okay," Arthur says. "I'm just happy you're here."

He clearly means it, and I don't know if it's the poem or the thought of the old wizard, but I don't stop my hand from leaping forward and clumsily hitting Arthur's elbow before landing on the hand holding up our umbrella.

"We aren't. Not yet."

Arthur's thumb moves to touch my wrist so lightning quick and petal soft, I can almost pretend it didn't happen.

"*Yet.*" He smiles. "I like 'yet.'"

And because it's raining and we're almost back to the castle, I let myself slip my hand into his.

"Yet," I repeat.

* * *

In bed that night, out of the direct laser gaze of Arthur and the heady feelings of being so near him beneath the umbrella,

I take out the noticings. I only hesitate a little before opening to a brand-new page and writing *Times I've thought about saying yes.*

Thinking of the carriage ride in the rain, I put a tally, but the more I think about it, the more tallies appear.

"Shit," I say quietly to myself. "I'm *so* screwed."

* * *

The binder of Mom's designs is heavy enough that I don't want to drag it to my top bunk to work. Instead, I unfold the full bed beneath, settling in for an Arthur-less, adventure-less day of jewelry-making.

I've been lax in making new pieces, and since Arthur and his dads tell patrons that the princess shops exclusively at our shop (ha), there has been increased foot traffic and more sales.

Dad is too thrilled to see me being princess of faire to bring it up, but when I dropped by to say hello before the rainy parade yesterday, I overheard him telling Neil that they would need to intersperse his leather journals among the jewelry stands to make it look fuller.

My little portable worktable is a glorified lap desk, but with the way my stomach sticks out when I'm sitting with my back against the bunk wall, I can wedge it between my body and my knees to make a sturdy surface for myself. It's comfy, actually, especially if I stick pillows at the opposite end of the bed to brace my feet against.

I flip to the earring section of the binder and—after running my finger through the little tray of beads and jewels I have in a bowl beside me—get to work making a design Mom labeled "drop (dead gorgeous) earrings."

Dad is gone again to visit friends at another RV for dinner. This always happens, his frequent absences from Britomart, but especially with Stormsworth. Especially since Mom died. I wonder if they talk about her when I'm not there? I wonder if *he* talks about her. The wondering of it makes my fingers clumsy, heavy, but I keep sliding string and wire between my hands, holding ends of it in my mouth as I wield the tiny scissors shaped like a bird.

He invited me along, but as usual I declined. This feels like the first calm moment I've had totally to myself since the start of faire. Between Arthur and his Gwen Discovery Program, video game sessions at the castle that are increasing in regularity, princess duties, therapy on Thursdays, phone calls with Fatima about summer bonfires and parties, and the occasional meal with Dad, it feels like I'm constantly around other people.

Even my nighttime routine, usually a time of solitude, has begun to feel rushed and not quite like it was before. Lately, I'm too tired by the end of the day to manage much beyond the tooth brushing and shower, let alone read a single episode of *The Falconer's Gauntlet*.

The finished pair of drop earrings wink up at me from my hand, and I'm setting them on the quilt beside me when I hear a light knock on the door.

I know without getting up to look that it's Arthur. I also

know that his face is full of the possibilities of my "not yet" from a couple days ago, because I can practically feel it radiating through the door.

"Go away," I say.

He comes in, casually leaning against the doorframe.

"You're decent, I take it?" he asks.

"If I wasn't, we'd be in trouble, wouldn't we?" I unwind a bit of wire from my spool and wait for his retort. When it doesn't come, I fold and look up expectantly. "Cat got your tongue?"

"Nope." He pops the P. "It's just I know my status is under review, so I don't want to push my luck by saying 'I like trouble,' or something worse that will make you frown at me and write something bad in your journal."

"Still a strong possibility," I say, but I move my jewelry stuff so he can sit beside me on the bottom bunk.

He's quiet again, for a long enough stretch that I abandon the guise of working entirely.

"What now?" I ask. "Are we going somewhere? Is this a princess-napping?"

Arthur raises his eyebrows. "It would have to be a kidnapping? And here I was thinking you were beginning to tolerate spending time with me."

"You're acting weird," I say. "Like, stuff-Madeline-into-a-bag-and-take-her-to-that-stupid-Prada-store-a-million-miles-away strange."

"Look, I already promised not to take you to Marfa. *Even though* ten hours and seven minutes seems like a small price to pay for the crucial experience of viewing mysterious floating lights and an iconic permanent sculpture installation *all in one trip.*"

"There is no way those lights are a real thing," I say.

"We watched the same YouTube video. They're absolutely real. Why would an entire town lie about the existence of mysterious alien lights?"

"Maybe because there's *literally* no other reason to visit?"

Arthur covers his heart, the picture of great offense. "You just don't appreciate cultural experiences."

"In this case, cultural experience is definitely code for incredibly boring and not at all important or fascinating," I say. "Didn't the video say the lights aren't even always *there*? We're going to drive for literally half a day to look at a bunch of cracked Texas desert, a store with ancient Prada bags you can't touch, and an empty field that only *sometimes* has floating lights? No thank you."

His chuckle is dry. "We're *not* going to Marfa," Arthur says again. "What I have planned isn't nearly as fun. Or cultural."

"What is it?"

He purses his lips, and I see his fingers flutter down like he's looking for the lute that isn't there.

"Well," he says, rapping his knuckles on the wall. "I wondered if you wanted to come to our summer cookout. Dad's family is here, so my cousins are currently tearing through the castle and generally causing a large amount of chaos. Should be a good time if you want to join in. Pops says he's going to do hot dogs and burgers, which means that lunch will eventually be catered when he realizes his super-fancy grill won't make up for his tendency to burn any and all food."

"Sure. Why not?" I say, and I'm surprised at how easy it was to decide, how unbothered I am to leave my journal behind lest it be lost in the chaos.

"*Huzzah.*" Arthur grins. "Grab your suit. Let's go."

I freeze, halfway off the bunk. "Suit?"

"Yeah, for swimming. We've gotta do something to pass the time while we wait for the food Dad will have to order on the sly when Pops isn't looking. Besides, princess duties have kept you from meeting my favorite alligator float. His name is TikTok Croc."

"Like Peter Pan?" I ask, my voice strangled and weird as I try to swallow the frog that's suddenly in my throat.

"Like the app. He has his own account."

Just when I thought that maybe I was getting better, less paranoid, less *stuck*, everything comes crashing back around me.

Being princess of faire and wearing a corset and being in a parade is one thing, one *very big thing* that I still don't feel totally comfortable about.

Wearing a swimsuit in front of complete strangers is another.

I sit back down. "You know what?" I say. "I shouldn't. We've been selling a lot of jewelry, and I don't want to fall behind. And also—"

"Hey," Arthur says, and he leans forward so our faces are level. "Do you want to tell me the real reason?"

Stupidly, my eyes water a little. I'm not going to *cry* in front of him, so I lower my lids so he can't see. "Yeah, no. You already know anyway, if you're asking like *that*."

"Like what?"

"Like you already know, because you do," I say. "The swimsuit thing. The being-on-display-in-front-of-your-family thing."

Arthur looks properly stunned. "Gw—Maddie, no. I thought it was because you didn't want to be friends with *me*. That it was too much to come see the Guevara family ransack a castle. What's this about a swimsuit?"

I hate how he actually sounds confused.

"Oh, don't feed me the bullshit that every body is a beach body," I say, my voice angry. Not so much at him, but that I'm thinking about this *at all*. "You know that if I come, people will stare."

"If by 'people,' you mean the fam, I can assure you, the only thing they'll be staring at is the grill engulfed in flames."

I want to answer him. I want to be anybody but me, somebody who puts on the suit and doesn't give it a second thought. But instead, I'm standing stock-still, my body rigid with frustration.

"Hey," Arthur says, his voice gentle. He inches toward me, then quickly away, like he considered hugging me and thought better of it. "Hey, it's okay, Gwen. We don't have to go if you don't want to, okay? We can stay here. Or we can go and not swim. Whatever you want."

I wipe my eyes, still fighting back traitorous tears. "I'm sorry," I say. "I'm sorry. It's stupid. I'm being stupid."

"You're not being stupid. I get it."

I don't have it in me to beat around the bush or be overly concerned about what is the *right* thing to say in this situation, and for the first time all summer, I have a strong hunch that I would most definitely not like public high school. I can't even handle *one* boy, one pseudo friend, who, for all his bluster, is considerate and kind in a way that I suspect is rare.

"How could you *possibly* get what I'm talking when you look like that?" I ask, gesturing at him.

I can see now that his dark navy shorts are actually swim trunks, and I'm kicking myself for ever thinking he wasn't attractive, for thinking him *plain*. How did I not notice the way his eyebrows are naturally perfectly shaped? How did I not notice the lashes—*god*, the lashes—or the way his arms move with purpose and intent in everything he does? Not quite graceful, but not rushed and clumsy, either.

His jaw isn't the sharp model kind, but it's definitely a boy jaw, angular in a way mine is not. And it's kind of fluid? Like he's constantly moving and fidgeting and all of his limbs including his neck seem like an extension of the same movement, a wave compared to my awkward, stilted motions.

I guess I didn't notice Arthur's looks for the same reason people don't notice me: They glance, they decide, they move on. They don't bother with a second chance. They don't bother at all. I guess everyone does this. It's not like we have time to stop and stare at every person we pass in the street or at the store or wherever. It doesn't work like that.

But Arthur doesn't know what it's like to be looked at and judged in this specific way.

"Disturbingly skinny?" Arthur's answer makes me blink in surprise.

"You're a dude," I say. "You can be whatever. Skinny? Cool. Fat? Great, you're cuddly. But me? I need to eat a salad. I need to exercise. I need to do *something* to fix myself before I'll be worth looking at."

Arthur's laugh is the driest I've ever heard it. "God, I wish that were true. You think guys don't have to deal with the same shit? 'Did you skip leg day, bro?' You think guys don't have social media accounts where they zoom in on the photo where you have terrible acne and send you a rude message about it that they say is a joke? And god forbid you order something with the word 'skinny' in the name at a coffee shop, because then you get the judgy once-over from the barista who thinks you're already *too* skinny."

"It's not the same," I say, second-guessing myself as soon as the words come out.

"How is it any different?"

"Just because people don't think you're conventionally hot doesn't mean that you're socially hideous," I say. "They don't try to *fix* you like they do me."

Our voices have steadily risen to the point that we're pretty much shouting at each other. In the sudden silence, Britomart creaks a little, as if she is having to expand her walls to hold in our anger and my few errant tears.

But I don't think we're angry at each other.

We're angry at the world for making us second-guess, third-guess, fourth-guess ourselves at every turn. We're angry that, in this particular case—for all the talk of body positivity and self-love and whatever—the world doesn't feel any tamer. Not at all.

I know I'm right, because when Arthur says, "You're perfect," and it's laced with bitterness, I know it's not at me.

"So are you," I say.

I expect him to say something glib. It's in his nature, the peacemaker, the appeaser that he is, to try and smooth the wrinkles out of a conversation, an emotion.

Arthur surprises me, though, when he reaches forward, takes my hand, and says quietly, "Grief has no winners, and neither does this. So screw them all. Let's go tame the world, Gwen. Come swimming with me. Please? I swear my family won't think anything of it."

Thinking of the next tally I'll make later, the one where I consider saying yes to friendship and to that glint I can see in Arthur's eyes just now, I take his hand and try not to dwell on how nice it feels when his fingers curl around mine.

CHAPTER TEN

I WISH ARTHUR WOULD HAVE MENTIONED THAT I would have no time, no room in my head, to think about anything other than how avoid being trampled by his large, *very loud* family.

Martin, it turns out, is the youngest of *six* Guevara kids, and all five of his brothers and sisters have come to the castle for a mini summer reunion. Including Arthur, there are—by my count—twelve cousins running about, from the college-aged down to the baby with dimpled wrists and a two-toothed smile.

It's chaos, but in the best way. Absolutely no one pays

attention when I shrug off the oversize T-shirt I'm using as a cover-up, even though I feel exposed and vulnerable in my solid-black one-piece.

I haven't been swimming in so long—since well before Mom died—that I've almost forgotten what it feels like to step from the scorching sun into the cool water. The moat is a lazy river, and the water ripples along at a gentle pace, tickling my legs as I make my way down the steps and submerge myself both in water and in the hubbub of Arthur's family.

"Cousin Arthur has a *girlfriend*," a little boy in swim trunks and water wings says confidently, swimming over to point at me.

Arthur, who is sporting a T-shirt tan that has left his stomach and chest frighteningly white, splashes him. "What Cousin Arthur has is a mighty need for volleyball," he says.

"Volleyball?"

Arthur points to the small straightaway a few yards down the river, at the side of the castle where some of his aunts are setting up a net. "I mean, it's not *exactly* volleyball, because that has rules other than trying your level best to hit someone in the head with the ball, but yeah. It's volleyball."

This poses a new problem: boobs. Like the rest of me, mine are big, which I try not to think about because, while everyone says big boobs are like this huge selling point for being attractive, that's only if you have a small waistline to match.

No, my kind of boobs are just annoying. They make it harder to find corsets and Ren faire outfits that don't make me look like I'm trying to audition for the role of adult bar maiden (ditto with trying to find street clothes). Sleeping on my side is impossible unless I want to smother myself. And—in this instance—playing volleyball without worrying that every single person is going to watch as my breasts bounce above the water is . . . not great.

"I know that face," Arthur says, and he steps in front of me, slightly crowding me to the edge of the water. "What's up?"

I look around him, at the frolicking sea of brown and white and black skin that constitutes his cousins and aunts and uncles.

"I just . . ." I don't mean to, but I look down, and Arthur follows my line of sight.

"Oh," he says. "Gwen, you look wonderful. Come play with us. Nobody thinks anything of it."

I want to hear him say it. "Of what?"

"We'll pick you up a new, less-boring swimsuit on our next adventure. Literally no one will care. I actually don't know if Dad or Pops can do anything with swimsuit material, but we can go ask if you want."

I blink. "You think I don't want to play because my swimsuit is . . . plain?"

Arthur blinks. "Is . . . is that not it?"

"I'm *worried* about having a wardrobe malfunction if I play," I say.

I thought we were being quiet, but we must not be quiet enough. Almost as soon as the words have left my mouth, a woman in a bikini glides next to me in the water.

"Hi, sugar," she says. Even without the little boy on her

hip, I could tell she's a mom by the way she pats the side of my still-dry head. "Look at that color. *To die for.* What's this I hear about a swimsuit problem?"

"I want her to play volleyball, Aunt Judy," Arthur says. "But she's afraid that . . ." He gestures awkwardly.

Judy slides the wiggly little boy into Arthur's arms. "Say no more. Hold Jonathan while I work my magic. You hang tight, sugar. I've got just the thing."

She's out of the water and back again in a flash, armed with a surprisingly large plastic safety pin.

"These things are a *godsend*," she says. "I use them for my own blessings." When she says *blessings*, she gestures at her bikini top. "Can't have the girls tryin' to break free in the middle of our game. May I?"

When I nod, she floats behind me and directs me to hold my hair up. It only takes her a second, but I can feel her draw the arm straps closer together at my back, pinning them in place and turning it into a racerback.

Instantly, my chest is slightly lifted, but held much more firmly in place.

"Whoa," I say. "Thank you."

"My mama taught me that," Aunt Judy says, patting my shoulder. "All the girls in my family are very blessed."

"Probably because Aunt Judy has 'Lord bless this house' signs all over her walls," Arthur says.

Aunt Judy pats me on the shoulder once more before smacking Arthur on his and sliding the boy back into her arms.

"I'll remember that when you beg for mercy in volleyball," she says. "Let's play."

And we do. It's a vicious, fast game that seems to be more focused on light carnage than it does rules or points. Within the first half hour of playing, Arthur has a quickly forming bruise on his arm, his cousin Trey has swallowed a mouthful of water and is *still* coughing five minutes later, and Aunt Cynthia has pegged her husband Marcel square in the nose twice because they requested to be on opposing teams.

I decide I'll half play, maybe stand next to Aunt Judy, but she wasn't kidding about others begging for mercy. Apparently Aunt Judy played volleyball in college and still has a killer spike, even in the five-foot water.

As for the safety pin, it holds up through my few half-hearted attempts to join the fray. But I'm having so much fun just listening to the fake, kid-friendly insults flying between the teams, I mostly fetch the ball when it goes well beyond the reach of Arthur's and my teammates.

Everyone appears to be having a good time, too good of a time to come out of the pool, even when Tim and Martin yell over our screams of victory that we should reapply sunscreen, even when there is a disturbingly loud *bang* from the direction of the outdoor kitchen. We play on, taking turns holding babies and wrangling the younger kids on some of the moat steps away from the action so that their parents can compete, too.

Only when the lunch of freshly ordered pizza arrives do we all pull ourselves from the moat and walk through the garden gate to sit around the ginormous table that can hold us all. I hadn't seen it before in our walks around faire, but I guess I wouldn't. The fence is almost as tall as the gates of Stormsworth, a bit of privacy, an oasis among a very public home.

One of his cousins is now asleep on Arthur's shoulder, so I grab his slices and soda for him.

"Having a good day?" I ask when he smiles his thanks.

"It's not every day the humble bard is served by the beautiful princess," he whispers, rearranging baby Addie's sunhat to cover her eyes. "I'd say it's a good one."

"Don't get used to it," I say. "I hear she gets grumpy when not plied with offerings of Tootsie Pops."

His perpetual smile tilts a little, making it uneven. "Duly noted."

"So, Madeline," Aunt Maya—the oldest Guevara sister—says, sliding into the seat across from me. "You're part of the faire?"

"Yeah, my dad and I sell journals and jewelry as part of the circuit."

Martin comes up behind me then, leaning forward to rustle my hair. "That's what she usually does, but for us she's princess of faire."

"Princess?" one of the cousins pipes up, her face already covered with pizza sauce. "I wanna be princess."

"When you are older, you can come stay the summer and be princess," Martin promises.

"Princess and shopkeeper," Maya smiles. "That seems like

a lot. What are you? Arthur's age? Are you going to be a senior next year, too?" She asks all of this while pouring some ice from her cup and wrapping it in a paper towel to hold against a passing little girl's arm.

"Yeah, I am," I say.

"Oh, which school do you go to? Same as Arthur, I assume?"

Arthur, not wanting to wake baby Addie, whispers, "I thought you were off the clock, Aunt Maya. Writing an article?"

"Sorry," Maya says, and her lip quirks in this weirdly specific way that I've seen Martin's do when Tim attempts (and usually fails) to playfully curtail Martin's enthusiasm. Exuberance must run in the family. "I was just curious. Arthur's never brought a girl to one of our get-togethers before."

"No, it's okay," I tell them both, but I direct my words to Maya even as I feel Arthur carefully watching my profile. "I do online school while I'm on the road with my dad. We do faire stuff all year."

"That must be hard," Maya says. "But how lucky you got here just when they needed a princess! I know Arthur is happy to be at the faire. Beats his last summer job of folding shirts at Old Navy."

Maya's wife leans over and winks at me. "Which he got fired from after exactly one week."

"They didn't appreciate my creative genius," Arthur protests.

"He means he got fired for changing the company-approved

music station to his own personal 'Olivia Rodrigo Is a God-dess' playlist."

"She *is*," Arthur argues.

"*Anyway*," Maya interrupts before they can start arguing, "It's great that you two get to work together for the summer. I know Martin was worried about little Artie being bored." At this, Arthur shoots her a quick death glare, and for a second, I can imagine him as a grumpy five-year-old. Maya ignores him and goes on. "These things have a way of working them-selves out, don't they?"

"Yeah," Arthur says. "It's like fate."

"Or coincidence," I counter.

When Addie wakes up and gets passed to her parents, Arthur and I go sit on a bench beneath a huge tree a little away from his family, paper plates of cinnamon twist bread balanced on our knees.

"So this is part of your family," I say.

"Yeah, most of it, actually."

"Not much family on your pop's side?"

Arthur sighs, the most weary sound I've ever heard from him.

"Do you want the short version or the long version of that answer?"

I bump his shoulder. "You don't have to tell me," I say.

"So the long version, then," he says.

"You don't have to," I repeat. "We can talk about some-thing else."

"No," he says. "I'll tell you. It's just . . . a lot." He pauses. "Do you remember the night we met?"

I tap my chin and pretend to think. "Which time was that? I meet so many strange boys after midnight in deserted Renaissance faires. It's hard to keep up."

"Okay, smartass. Do you specifically remember when I said that my parents are like grossly over-the-top in love?"

"Yeah?"

"I'll tell you their story. It's a bit easier that way." Arthur is quiet for a full minute before he laughs and starts again. "It's dumb. I don't know why the whole thing gives me a bad case of the feels, but it does. I guess I should start by saying that Pops's family sounds a bit like *your* dad's family. They're . . . not supportive."

"Of him?"

"Yes, but more generally they are not supportive of people deviating from their preconceived notions of what kind of love is acceptable."

I blink in the darkness. "Because he's gay."

"Sort of," Arthur says. "But honestly I think they were more offended that he didn't love what they loved. They're rich, you see. Like, *stupid* old-money rich. Like, Taylor Swift–music-video-in-a-mansion-going-around-slashing-Rembrandts-for-fun rich."

"How?" I ask.

"Pops seriously never talks about them—most of this stuff I've gleaned from talking to Dad—but it has something to do with oil, maybe? Whatever it is, it goes way back and apparently Pops grew up with, like, maids and drivers and weekends of 'shooting' with hunting parties. That kind of thing."

"For real?"

Arthur nods, pausing to take a bite of cinnamon twist. "For real."

"So they weren't mad because he was gay. They were mad because . . . Why? Did he not get along with the butler or something?"

"Oh no, they were *definitely* upset that he was gay. But they were *also* mad because he loved the wrong things. He loved reading old history books more than socializing. He loved volunteering at animal rescues more than animal hunts. You get the picture."

"His family sucks," I say. "Got it."

"It's more than that," he says. "This is all important for my family, yes, but also for how the whole faire thing came about. You know how you talked about the coin? How it's like a bit of your family lore?"

"Yeah?"

"This is my family's lore," he says. "And it's important that you know that Pops's family didn't like *him* and he didn't much care for them either."

"Poor Tim," I whisper.

"Yeah, it sucks. Even though it ends happily, it doesn't erase the suckage." He takes another deep breath. "Anyway, so yeah. His family sucked. His school life sucked because he went to a fancy, cutthroat private school in the city and he was shy and quiet and didn't make friends easily. He was bullied, Dad says, and that's how Dad found him: crying in the bathroom during lunch. Some of the jocks had put his blazer in the toilet."

"And they fell in love?" I ask.

Arthur's lips quirk. "Depends which parent you ask."

"Let me guess: Your dad fell in love and your pops was having none of it?"

"I believe Pops's version, actually. He says that Dad was already a little in love with him and didn't know it, but Pops was in no position to love anyone yet. He was still figuring out who he was, which took longer because, well, his family."

"Fair," I say.

"Yeah." Another inhale. "Do you want the adorably sappy bit or do you want me to skip it?"

"Sappy, please," I say, raising my voice to be heard over the shrieks from the moat where some of the younger kids have already piled back in. Most of the adults are still lounging in chairs picking at leftover pizza.

"Good. It's my favorite part. Okay, so, of *course* Pops couldn't just wear the blazer as is. He wore these pins of medieval paintings and maps that he made himself, and one of them had fallen onto the floor when the blazer was put in the toilet. Dad found it—a crown—then found Pops, and knelt down and gave him back the pin and said, 'Someday, we will be kings, and we won't have to ever come back to this place.'"

"Okay," I say. "Our parents have the best love stories ever. And I guess then Tim inherited tons of money from his awful family and used it to buy this place?"

Arthur's mouth tilts. "Basically," he says. "I guess there were some chunks of change that were legally earmarked for Pops that they couldn't touch. The minute he got the money, he cut off contact."

"*Good*," I say.

We both turn our heads to look at his parents. Tim is standing eating a piece of pizza as Martin rubs his hand up and down Tim's back, leaning down to nuzzle Tim's hair. At first, Tim swats at him, but then he takes Martin's hand in his own.

"Does it make him sad?" I ask. "Not having his family?"

"He does have his family," Arthur says. "He has us. But I know what you mean, and no. I think *his* way of taming the world meant cutting out the toxic things that were trying to kill it. Sometimes making the world kinder looks a lot like silence and hard feelings, but it's actually boundaries, you know?"

"I get it," I say. The fireflies are beginning to collect around the edges of the yard, and some of Arthur's cousins begin to chase after them, their feet bare and their swimsuits still glistening wet in the dying light.

"Your dads love you, you know," I say, because for some reason it feels like what Arthur needs to hear.

Arthur kicks at the ground with a pink toe. "I know," he says, his voice tired. "I know."

"My parents were the same way," I say, and I don't like the still-metallic taste of "were" in my mouth, but I continue. "They were obsessed with each other. Like, they still gave each other these long pining looks from across rooms after they'd been married for a gazillion years."

Arthur laughs. "Mine do that, too. I should be used to it by now, but it feels . . ."

"Invasive? Like you're seeing something they didn't mean for you to see?"

"Yeah."

"Yeah," I echo. And even though I would pay anything, anything to see it again, give any token I have, the memories of Mom and Dad being *stupidly* in love in front of me makes me laugh. "And kinda gross."

"*Yes,*" Arthur says. "I'm glad their love overcame all obstacles and whatever, but could they just *not*?"

But when he looks back to Tim and Martin—who are now leaning with their heads against one another, watching the fireflies and the little kids—he smiles.

After much pleading from Arthur, we get back in the water and drape ourselves over alligator floaties and huge yellow innertubes. We drift lazily around the moat past the baby dragons and the fairies as the sun fully sets. It's ridiculous, this feeling of lightness, but it's there, and I'm letting it fill me up while it lasts.

"I'm proud of you," Arthur says, paddling over to grab my alligator's tail.

"Why?"

"You survived my family, which is no small feat, and you played volleyball and not *once* did you try to drown me."

"It's not too late for that last bit," I say, but my eyes are closed, my limbs completely languid.

"True," Arthur says. "There's always tomorrow."

"Sure," I say. "Tomorrow."

Our ensuing quiet is peaceful and not so quiet, filled with the happy screams of kids cupping fireflies between their palms, of crickets chirping in the Ren faire landscaping, of spouses laughing, and of Arthur softly singing Vance Joy's "Riptide" as we float round and round the castle.

* * *

Today, I wore a swimsuit and played in the sun. Today, I sat next to a boy on a bench beside a medieval castle and ate cinnamon twists and pizza. Today, I tamed the world.

After the shower, the tea, the fluffy towel, kissing Dad on the cheek good night, I sit on my top bunk and let my wet hair hang around me and soak my pajamas as I open the journal to the page with *Times I've thought about saying yes*.

I draw careful, overly neat tallies beneath it until I fall asleep.

* * *

We had planned to go somewhere new today—where, Arthur wouldn't tell me—but when I open the door and he sees my sunburned face and the tube top I usually only wear in the house because the thought of putting on bra straps made me want to scream, he goes to turn off the truck's engine.

"We're not going anywhere with you like that," he says. "You'll crumble into red ash."

"Want to go to the castle?" I ask, *completely* relieved not to be in the car with its barely tinted passenger window for any length of time.

"I'm afraid to drive you even that far, to be honest," Arthur says. "Can we stay here?"

"Here, here?" I ask stupidly. "In Britomart?"

"Why not? Your dad won't mind, will he?"

"He's off visiting, as usual," I say. "He already left."

"Cool. You stay here, I'll be right back."

I assume he's gone to fetch the gaming console, but he returns nearly an hour later with a bunch of plastic shopping bags that he carries in all at once through Britomart's door. He starts unpacking them on the kitchen table: aloe lotion, a six-pack of sports drinks, an eye mask that he explains can be put in the fridge and then worn to cool your eyes.

Arthur, once again, knows how to be kinder to me than I know how to be to myself.

When we go on adventures now, he keeps baby powder in the glove compartment for me after I once complained about how my shorts rubbed at my skin. He insists on frequent hydration for us both, which is annoying because it means we have to make more pitstops in gross bathrooms, but also great because, though I end our long days tired, I don't feel quite so much like a crusty kitchen sponge.

"You didn't have to do all this," I say. He leaves one bag unpacked, and when I move to open it, he air-swats at my hand.

"No, no, Gwen. Not until we get that sunburn taken care of."

"It's not *that* bad," I say. "I've had worse."

"Not on my watch, you haven't," he says, pointing to the chair. "Sit."

I do, wincing when my back touches the cool metal.

Something has shifted between us since yesterday. When I debriefed with Fatima, she gasped. *"You met his family?"* Even after explaining that it wasn't a huge deal, that it was more me crashing a cookout, she refused to take it as anything but "a big step." Toward what, she wouldn't say.

But even if she's wrong about that part of it, I can feel that we've stepped closer to something else than what we were before.

Arthur opens the bottle and moves behind me. I can practically feel the cool radiating from the gel on his hands as he holds them a breath from my shoulder blades.

"Okay?" he asks.

Externally, I nod. Internally, I watch as every last defense I had crumbles.

It's the longest we've touched, and maybe the longest we've gone without verbally sparring with each other. Arthur's hands are strong and firm on my shoulders and arms. When he gets to my neck, he unclasps the clip I'm using to hold the small hairs at the nape, fixing it so that it holds all my strands.

He's so careful and cautious and *him*, and I wonder how much of the past month I have cared for him without realizing it. Because against all my better judgment and my best attempts, *I do care*.

It's not just that I can put up with his singing and fidgeting and his biological need to flirt, but I want him to be happy. I *enjoy* when he smiles and worry when he frowns. When I flip through my poetry journal and see stanzas that talk about an easy exhale and an easier inhale being like love, I think of him and breathe.

It's terrifying, how closely caring is linked to losing Mom. It's almost like I can't think of Arthur without thinking of the natural conclusion, of *losing him*, because at some point— probably the end of the summer—I will lose him. I'll move on to the next town, he'll go back to school, and maybe we'll talk for a little while, but it won't be forever.

And even if we do keep in touch, even if he texts me as much as he fidgets and calls me as much as he strums his lute, something will eventually separate us. Time or space or death.

"This is remarkably intimate for someone who's not a friend," Arthur says after a while, bringing an abrupt end to my thought spirals. I'm not sure who's embarrassment he is trying to avoid when he keeps talking without waiting for an answer. "I hope we didn't burn your freckles off yesterday. It would be a pity to see so many constellations disappear at once."

His hands on my neck make me want to make noises that I would rather die than let slip. Borrowing from Arthur's tactic of blurting things out before you can change your mind, I say, "You asked what I noticed about you, that day at the zoo."

I half hope he won't hear me, but of course he does, ever-attentive Arthur.

"Yeah?"

Even now he is careful not to press.

"Do you want me to tell you?" I ask. "What I notice, I mean."

He is quiet for a beat longer than I expected. I thought he would leap at my offer, make a joke about how it would be impossible for me not to notice how attractive he is, how well he plays the lute, whatever.

But his voice is as quiet as mine when he says, "If you want to."

It's easy, I find, to tell Arthur the things I've noticed. Mostly because I can't see his face, but also because he so readily accepts the bad and rejects the good. Not in a way that is meant to be funny, but in a way that makes me wonder what headings he would put in his own journal of noticings: *Times I've messed up, Times I've overstepped, Times I've embarrassed myself.*

I wonder if Arthur is brave because he thinks he isn't actually brave at all. I wonder if he thinks he's pretending.

"You're annoying—" I start, and Arthur's laugh cuts me off.

"Do I need to sit down while you cut me at the knees, Gwen, or shall I remain standing?"

"You didn't let me finish," I say. "You're annoying, but not for any of the reasons you think. You're annoying *because* you think you're annoying, but you're actually not. You're kind and funny and a little chaotic, but in the best way."

Arthur's thumb brushes my ear as he squeezes my shoulder with the perfect amount of force.

"Annoyingly chaotic," he says. "Got it."

"*Not* annoying," I reiterate. "And good. Like genuinely? You try to hide it behind the fun personality because you're afraid of being too good, too vulnerable."

He clears his throat, wiping his hands off a little on my arms in one quick movement before stepping away to the sink.

"Good to know," he says, and his voice is gruff.

"Are you . . . Are you crying?"

He sniffs loudly. He's done washing his hands, but he doesn't turn around. "No."

"It's okay if you are," I say. "As we know, I cry all the time."

When he turns, his eyes are watery and rimmed red, but just barely.

"Gwen, if you keep it up with such grand proclamations, I'm gonna have to withhold this fabulous last bag from you."

It's not a video game. The last shopping bag is full of enough crayons and colored pencils and coloring books and cheap watercolor sets with plastic brushes to entertain an entire kindergarten classroom. Arthur surveys the loot with a grin. "This is today's adventure," he says.

The coloring books aren't the adult kind with tiny, intricate lines and details that take hours to complete. These are like the kind from elementary school, the kind kindergarteners use to learn how to color inside the lines, big and bulky and forgiving.

When Dad comes home and finds us at the kitchen table, he ruffles my hair, and then—with no hesitation—Arthur's.

"Don't get marker on the table, kids," he tells us.

"Yes, sir," Arthur says. He holds up a half-colored dolphin balancing a shell on its nose. "Do you like mine?"

I hold up my circus tent of red and black stripes. "Dad, my circus is better, isn't it? Dad?"

Dad pauses from grabbing chips out of the pantry—his evergreen offering for thrown-together meals with friends—and come to stand beside us. He leans in, pretending to examine each page closely.

"Sorry, Maddie," he tells me. "But the shading on that dolphin is impeccable."

Arthur crows triumphantly, and I have to raise my voice for my mock outrage to be heard.

"Dad!"

And then, impossibly, Dad is laughing, a belly laugh that I haven't heard since Mom. It fills me with a relief so sharp, I can't even pretend to be mad anymore.

"You should see your face," he tells me, wiping his eyes.

"I haven't seen that look since Fatima won that dragon toss game every single time you two played."

"Yeah, because she *cheated*," I say.

"How do you cheat at dragon toss?" Arthur asks.

"*Exactly*," Dad says.

"You don't even know what dragon toss *is*," I say. "The people who ran it haven't been to faire in years. They retired."

"Not much to get," Dad fake-whispers to Arthur. "You throw a tennis ball decorated to look like a dragon into open barrels for points. Not very difficult, unless you're our poor Maddie here."

"*Dad*."

"*Kid*." He smiles. "I'll get out of your hair. Don't mark up that table."

He's off again, to whose RV, I have no idea, but in his wake, Arthur and I are both quiet.

"I like your dad," Arthur says.

"He's okay," I say, but I'm smiling.

When Arthur uses the restroom—and with the thoughts of him laughing with Dad and Tootsie Pops and stupid songs still dancing in my head—I get up from the table and rush over to my pillow, pulling the coin from my top bunk.

Impulsive. Stupid. But I can't stop myself from whispering, "Should I like Arthur?" to the coin.

Heads for yes, tails for no.

With a shuttering breath, as I hear the sink turn on and Arthur washes his hands, I flip the coin, confident—*so* confident—that it will confirm what I already know: that he is a safe, *good* choice for caring. That the now of him is worth the later.

I'm already seated at the table again, the coin jammed back in its pouch beneath my pillow, when the bathroom door opens.

"That soap smells *amazing*," Arthur says. "It was a good call to buy the eucalyptus."

"Yes," I say. "I like it, too."

I thought my tone was careful, but Arthur drums his fingers on the table to get my attention as he slides into his chair. "You okay?"

"Yeah," I say.

"You sure?"

I nod. "Yeah," I repeat, and even I can hear how broken I sound. "Nothing has changed."

If someone didn't know better, they'd maybe almost believe me. *I* almost believe me, telling myself the tails just confirms what I already knew to be true, even though I notice every tiny bit of Arthur for the rest of the day, no journaling necessary.

CHAPTER ELEVEN

WHEN HE SHOWS UP WITH HIS terrible car and the grin I can now admit—to myself, at least—I've *noticed* since the first time I saw him, I consider telling Arthur that I won't come.

"It's a video game museum," he says when I hesitate in the doorway of Britomart. "A *video game museum.*"

"Okay, saying it twice doesn't change anything."

"It has a built-in arcade with vintage games that you can play. Maybe we'll find one you're actually good at since you suck at *Splatterbomb.*"

I choose to ignore his dig. "Don't you have every video game in existence in the castle basement?"

Arthur snorts. "I *wish.*"

It should feel normal, this routine of the Gwen Discovery Program, but the coin's verdict still lingers in the back of my head.

"Come on, Gwen," he says. "I *promise* it'll be fun."

And of course he's right. The ride to the museum is easy and goes by too fast even though the clock says it took us hours to get here. The museum is full of little kids at birthday parties, old people hunched over machines of 8-bit games that look to be about the same age as they are, and bored employees carrying brooms and dustpans.

We're playing with an interactive exhibit that shows how slow dial-up internet was in the '90s when Arthur's phone rings.

"Your dads?" I ask.

"No," he says, and his voice is a little off. "It's Bre."

Something in my stomach twists. This is what happens when you don't listen to coins.

"You should answer it," I say. "She must have a reason if she's calling you."

Arthur is still staring down at the screen when the phone stops ringing and the number fades away.

"You didn't answer," I say, unable to do anything but state the obvious.

Maybe if he looked up at me then and his face was soft and he looked at me like *I* was the reason he didn't answer, it would change things, but at best Arthur looks bemused. At worst, regretful that he didn't answer.

"Nope," he says. He doesn't pop the *P*, but his grin slides back into place between one second and the next. "Let's go kill some pixelated zombies."

Bre doesn't leave a voicemail or text. I know, because even though he tries to hide it, Arthur spends the rest of our time at the museum surreptitiously checking his phone. Each time I see the flash of his screen, it's empty of notifications.

But besides the phone checking, he's annoyingly himself, and I am—more annoyingly—not.

It would be a *good thing*, I tell myself, if he and Bre get together. Great, even, because then I wouldn't have to care about him. Maybe then I could even admit that we were friends, because he would be *her* problem, not mine.

For once, I wish my feelings would line up neatly like the tallies in my journal. I've read a thousand poems about how thoughts are constellations and scattered stars or whatever, but right now all of my emotions are lava, burning liquid coals that can't be distinguished as anything other than dangerous sludge.

If Arthur notices my lava, he doesn't say. When I get home, I'm too burned out to do anything but crawl into bed fully clothed and stare at the ceiling until sleep finds me.

* * *

I am frantically updating the noticings journal when Dr. Jenkins blinks onto my screen.

"You seem busy," she says after our usual pleasantries. "You doing okay?"

"Yes," I say distractedly. "Sorry, I just . . . I haven't had a chance to . . ." I don't want to finish the sentence, because I know what Dr. Jenkins is going to say and I'm not sure if I want to hear it.

She says it anyway.

"It's a good thing, Madeline. Remember how we talked about letting the journal go?"

"Mm-hm," I say, still looking down. How many times have I spoken to Dad? How many adventures have I gone on with Arthur? I glance over my shoulder to count the postcards— one for each stop—taped to my wall. I've managed to count those correctly, at least. But now I'm wondering if I should *also* be keeping track of Arthur's faire-specific shenanigans, even though just the thought of documenting those makes my hand cramp with exhaustion.

And then there's yesterday and the whole Bre-calling-him thing, and do I document *that*? God, I hope I don't need multiple tallies beneath a heading of *Feels like lava flows through my veins*.

It takes me longer than it should to realize that Dr. Jenkins isn't saying anything, and I'm overwhelmed once more with the certainty that I have managed to puzzle a trained therapist with my oddities.

"Sorry," I say, slamming the journal shut. "Sorry," I repeat. "I'm paying attention."

Dr. Jenkins smiles a little. "That's the problem, though,

isn't it? You're so worried about paying attention that it's distracting you from your own life."

I don't answer, but I know that can only last so long. Dr. Jenkins's mouth is set in the way that means I won't be able to distract her or segue the conversation into something not at all emotions-related. She means business, which I guess I knew was coming, but I'm not ready.

I'm not ready.

"How are you feeling about the upcoming anniversary?"

There it is.

I run my finger up and down the leather spine. "It's coming whether I want it to or not," I say.

"That's true." She waits.

"I've had a year to know it's coming," I admit stupidly.

"Also true," Dr. Jenkins says, "but it's okay if your feelings have changed, Madeline."

My finger jumps from journal to keyboard, running my nail along the home row keys. "What do you mean?"

Dr. Jenkins shifts in her seat. "Just that it's okay to have a mixture of feelings." I think of the lava as she continues. "When we lose someone, when we're grieving, it can be hard to imagine leaving any of that sadness behind. But over time, we might find that certain things are easier than we thought, and that's okay."

"Yeah," I say, looking down. My eyes are watering, and I don't know why.

"Sometimes we let go of things before we're ready," Dr. Jenkins says. "And sometimes we hold on to them far longer than we should. Sometimes other things come forward to take up space in our heads and hearts, and that's okay, too."

I don't say anything, and I can't bring myself to look at the screen.

"What are you thinking, Madeline?"

"I'm . . ." I pick at the comforter, and I worry thoughts about Arthur are going to come out, but they don't. The lava has something else in mind. "I'm thinking it sucks. I'm thinking I feel stupid because I knew she was sick for years, but I was still surprised when it happened."

"That's normal," Dr. Jenkins says.

"Yeah, but shouldn't I have learned my lesson?" I ask, meeting her eyes. "Shouldn't *this* part, at least, be easier?"

"You mean the anniversary." It's not a question.

"No," I say. "I mean, yes. I mean, the whole thing of her being *gone*."

Dr. Jenkins tilts her head. "Is there something else you want to talk about this week?"

Again, I stay silent.

"You know, it's okay if there is. It's okay if the anniversary isn't the only thing on your mind. Healthy, even."

"It's all mixed up," I say. "I was supposed to spend the summer remembering *her*, but instead there's this stupid bard and stupid new castle and I'm the stupid princess and—"

Dr. Jenkins holds up her hand. "Madeline, dear, I have the impression that you haven't been completely forthcoming when I've asked if there is anything new you'd like to discuss."

"I don't have to tell you everything," I mumble, but Dr. Jenkins hears me.

"No, you don't. But if you do have something you want to share with me, maybe we can talk it through. Perhaps I could be helpful."

"It's stupid," I say.

She smiles. "Try me."

So I start at the beginning. I tell her about how the summer was supposed to be a time of reflection and introspection, how I was so sure that keeping to my routine would make the one-year mark easier and also reveal the Deep Truth of what I should do for senior year.

I tell her about Arthur, about how—for reasons beyond my understanding—he latched onto me as his summer companion, and how it threw my emotions and my "less humans is more peace" philosophy into the sun.

I even tell her about yesterday, about how my insides went all wrong when Bre—the original object of his desire that caused him to walk morosely around the faire at night, Bre—called.

I expect Dr. Jenkins to stop me at that part, when I reach the end about how Arthur has convoluted everything and now when my brain feels itchy, I'm not sure if it's because I'm grieving my mom or I'm frustrated about Arthur, but instead she nods.

"Love is a risk," she says. "Always."

"Is it worth it?" I ask. "Is it worth it if it takes up so much bandwidth?"

And Dr. Jenkins—the person who is supposed to be my own personal Wizened Old Wizard—shrugs.

"Only you can answer that," she says. "But I tend to think so. The things that can bring us the most pain in life can also bring us the greatest joy."

I'm quiet for a beat. "A wizard from a Ren faire when I was ten told me the same thing," I say. "He said nothing is certain."

"He sounds wise," Dr. Jenkins smiles.

I snort.

"What is it you *want* to do, Madeline? Is there something you feel would make your life better in this instant? Not tomorrow, or the day after, or next year, but *now*?"

There is, but when I see the coin in my head and imagine it saying no, I panic a little. Because the coin said Mom wouldn't get better and it was right. The stupid thing told my parents to have *me*, so how can I go against it and say it doesn't know what it's talking about?

I know it's dumb. I know on some level that it's childish to put so much stock into an inanimate object, but this thing is family lore, and it's *never* been wrong.

It's all I have now that Mom is gone.

I don't want to believe in fate, but maybe I do. Maybe what I want is for someone to *tell me* my fate, so I don't have to keep stumbling around and trying to figure it out on my own, or getting my hopes up that fate has one thing in mind when really it doesn't.

"I can't do it," I tell Dr. Jenkins. "The thing that I want to do."

"Can you tell me why?"

I've never told her about the coin, and I don't really want to explain it, so I say, "Because . . . Because it's not a great idea? It could end badly."

"What makes you say that?"

"Just a gut feeling," I say, which is almost the truth. The coin is its own kind of deep-down feeling, I guess.

"Intuition can be important," Dr. Jenkins agrees, "but so can reason. Can you think of any logical, nonintuitive reasons?"

The thing is . . . I can't. Other than a lingering fear that Arthur is still pining over Bre, there's nothing holding me back from caring.

It's terrifying.

"What are you thinking, Madeline?"

"I'm . . . I need to phone a friend," I say, because suddenly all I want is to hear what Fatima will say. "Is that okay?"

Dr. Jenkins's smile is surprisingly bright. "You know," she says, "that sounds like a great idea. Same time next week work for you?"

"Sure," I say. "Thanks, Dr. Julia Jenkins."

As soon as the screen goes to black, I cue up the videochatting app. Usually, the therapy appointments leave me depleted, but this time I'm energized, practically knocking the laptop over in my eagerness to jump from one call to the next.

I can't tell if the lava is leaving my system, or if it's just moving so quickly it gives the illusion of being cool.

As my computer rings, my nervous energy takes over, and I pull out the box of jewelry I've been working on.

"This better be good," Fatima says in greeting. "You better be calling to say you hooked up with the cute boy, because I'm pausing *just* before the Thanos snap for you."

"You can act out that whole movie from memory," I say.

"Doesn't matter," Fatima says. "Now, what's up?"

Video-chatting with Fatima while evaluating the jewelry I've made over the last month proves to be a challenge for my multitasking abilities, partly because I'm so nervous, my fingers forget how to pick up objects, and partly because Fatima is appropriately enthused about my confession that I might possibly, quite probably, most likely *like-like* Arthur.

And that I might possibly want to *tell him* I do.

"*Mads,*" she says. "Maddie. Madeline. This is huge."

"I'm aware," I say, holding up the earrings for her mom. "Do you think your dad will approve?"

"I mean this with all the love in my heart, but who freakin' cares? You. Like. A. Human."

"Was the species ever in question?"

"You were well on your way to eternally alone cat lady." Fatima says it like it's an inarguable fact.

"Hey, that's still on the table," I say. "Except for the cat allergy."

"Whatever, you know what I mean. I didn't know if you would ever like anybody, which would have been fine except I knew you *wanted* to like someone." She leans forward. "Hold Mama's earrings up again? Yes, perfect. She'll love them. Baba will be thrilled."

"Okay, but what do I say?" I ask, wrapping the earrings in tissue paper. "I can't just go in and be like, 'Hey, I like you,' right?"

Fatima doesn't miss a beat. "Sure you can. What else are you going to say?"

"Something . . . cool?" I offer.

Fatima tilts her head. "Like what?"

"Please don't make me think of something," I groan. "This is why I called you: to tell me how to human."

"What makes you think I'm any more qualified?"

"You go to school with people our age," I say. "And you are now part of the careful social structure that is teenagedom in a way that I'm not."

She rolls her eyes. "God, just go scroll online for a couple hours or something. That's all the education you need. And please don't say 'teenagedom' ever again, thanks."

"If you don't help me think of something, I'm just going to go to the castle tomorrow, knock on the door, and tell him that I like him, that I probably have all summer, and would he please like me back so we can be more than friends."

"Yes," Fatima says. "Do that."

"No."

"*Yes*," she mimics. "It's perfect. Unless you want to sing him a song or something that's related to his bard sensibilities."

"God, no."

"So just tell him how you feel." Fatima pauses, and her smile shifts from teasing to serious, if smiles can be serious. "I'm happy for you, Madeline."

"Thanks," I say. "Is it weird to say I'm happy for me, too?"

"A little. You'll have to fork over your teenagedom card if you say it again, though."

I laugh. "Deal."

* * *

The sun is already too bright when I cross the drawbridge the next morning. I'm jogging a little, trying to outmaneuver the steady thump of my heart that says this confession is a terrible, terrible idea.

Because the coin—*the* coin—has been right every time before, so why would it be wrong now? And how much of an idiot does it make me to think I can go against it and win?

But I can't help it. Through talking with Dr. Jenkins and Fatima and a self-examination of how clouded with *him* my head has been for the past month, I can't imagine not telling Arthur that I like him. Maybe even like him, like him.

With each step, I become more determined. Nothing is going to stop me from telling him how I feel.

I'm a little surprised at how not-winded I am from the jog, how my legs feel strong beneath my secondhand shorts. For a blessed second, I let my brain wander to all the physical activity I've been doing this summer, physical activity that if you had asked me before I did it, I would have said would kill me.

But, to quote an oft-recited Ren faire-esque movie: I'm not dead yet.

Usually, when he knows I'm coming, I meet Arthur at the regular-human-size side door, but that one doesn't have a doorbell, and I was too nervous to text him this morning. I left before I could chicken out.

I'm regretting my outfit choice, though I don't know why it matters. Arthur has seen me red-faced and sweaty from walking around outside, made up and costumed in full princess regalia, and everywhere in between. It's not like it's going to make a difference what I'm wearing *now*, and yet I find myself wishing I had at least bothered to swipe on some mascara or had a particularly cute shirt to throw on.

Now I'm agonizing over if it's too early to show up unannounced, but it turns out to be a moot point. Jacob the security guy opens the door before I can ring, his chain mail shirt shiny in the steadily rising sun filtering through the hall's tall windows.

"Good morning, Your Highness." His bow is deep and long. "I'm here for a uniform refitting and saw you coming up the moat."

"Hey, Jacob," I say. "Just Madeline when we're not at faire, remember?"

I can tell he wants to argue, but he doesn't have a chance. From the top of the grand staircase come the voices of Arthur and his dads, Tim's surprisingly carrying the loudest.

"—and then there is the matter of liability."

And then Martin: "We'll have their parents sign waivers. We can't do *nothing*. I refuse to let all of our work with that blasted green organza go to waste because of something so minor as incompetent public school funding."

Arthur's voice enters the mix, giddy and fast. "Come on, Pops. It's for the *arts*. You love supporting public art initiatives. This is the same."

"These are minors from your school, young man. This isn't quite the same as donating money to nonprofits."

Jacob and I stand frozen in the entryway, both of us dropping our gazes from above to look at each other.

"Kids from his school?" I ask. My voice is a whisper, though I don't know why I bother. It's not as if my voice will carry up the stairs and over the arguing on the second floor.

"First I'm hearing of it, Your Highness," Jacob mumbles.

"It'll be fine, love," Martin says from above, but his voice sounds like it's getting closer. "We know these kids. *And* more hands on deck will make the last month of faire all the more successful."

"*Please* say yes, Pops?"

I don't know what's happening, exactly, but my stomach drops all the same at the enthusiasm in Arthur's voice.

"*Fine*," Tim says, and he sounds like Mom used to when she used her *we'll talk later after Madeline is asleep* voice on Dad. "What's done is done, Martin. You can't very well rescind the offer now."

Arthur crows, a wild whoop of delight that echoes around Jacob and me, still standing unnoticed at the entrance.

"What about the ball idea, guys?" Arthur asks. "Remember? To thank the staff? What if we made it bigger and sold tickets as a final push for the theater group fundraising?"

Martin latches onto this idea with gusto. "We could do pheasant! I've always wanted to try pheasant."

"Oh, and lamb," Arthur adds. "Can we do lamb, Pops? Please?"

As they come to the mouth of the stairs, Jacob and I look up. The three of them are loose-limbed in shorts and tank tops with mismatched expressions of disgruntlement and eagerness. Tim is rubbing his eyes with one hand and massaging his temple with the other. Double stress.

"Madeline!" Arthur's face is wide and joyous. "You're here."

Madeline, I note. Not Gwen.

"I let her in, Your Highnesses," Jacob says.

Martin and Tim wish me a good morning and lead Jacob up to the costuming room. His parents—both still with scrunched mouths from their bickering upstairs—simultaneously raise their eyebrows at Arthur, unmistakably parent-speak for *you need to fill her in.*

They must mean me. They must mean the way I can feel my own mouth twisting as I process that—after talking to Dr. Jenkins and Fatima and hardly sleeping for nervousness of coming to talk to Arthur today—I'm going to do the opposite of what I planned.

A scene flashes through my mind from *The Falconer's Gauntlet* of Adelina and Cornelius trapped in a huge net dangling from a tree. I've always wondered what it must feel like to feel suspended above the ground, helpless. I've wondered if your heart races or slows in fear.

I know now that you can't feel your heart at all. There's not room to feel anything but *away, away. I must get away.*

Stupid. I was so very, very stupid for thinking I could go against the coin, for thinking the phone call from Bre meant nothing. I saw Arthur's face. I *knew* deep down in the depths of lava that he wanted to answer and probably would have if I hadn't been standing right there beside him.

He is clearly *delighted* to have another chance with Bre, to have her and the other theater kids work here for the rest of the season.

It's not Arthur's fault that I assumed he was interested in me beyond friendship. I can feel the higher part of myself, the smarter one, pushing that thought forward again and again, but my jealous, petty, dear-god-Bre-is-going-to-be-at-faire self is not having it.

Arthur opens his mouth.

"I can't be princess anymore," I say.

He blinks. "But—"

"No," I say. "Just don't. Don't."

"Don't what?"

"Don't say this doesn't change anything or that everything can go on like it has been, because we both know it's not true."

"What's changed? Can you pump the brakes for a second? I'm literally *so* lost, here."

"I heard," I say, pointing to the stairs. "The theater kids are coming to work the faire for the rest of the summer, right?"

Arthur nods, his eyes lighting up at my words. "It's gonna be *great*. We can—"

Almost subconsciously, I reach forward to touch his arm and make him stop talking. As soon as I realize, I drop it.

"I'm sorry," I say. "Get someone else to be princess. You'll have plenty of options now."

His mouth moves around a second before words form. "But *why?*"

I look upward at the skylights filtering in the sun from all directions of the castle entrance. Through the toes of my shoes, I can feel my feet sink into the plush red carpet. I know that if I were to speak up, to speak louder than I usually do, my voice would echo slightly in the nave. I subsequently want to scream and hurt both our ears and never speak again.

For all of last night's resolve that I would care about Arthur as long as I was able, that it was worth it even if it was doomed to end as all things are, I never imagined it would be over quite so soon. I never imagined it would be over *the next day*.

"I guess fate just has other plans," I tell Arthur. "Get Bre to do it."

"We won't have time to make the costumes fit her," Arthur says. His words are quick, agitated, and I guess he takes himself by surprise, because his eyes widen the second the words leave his mouth.

Not *I want* you *to be princess.* Not *you promised you'd be princess.* Not *do it as a favor for me.* Not *what does Bre have to do with anything?*

We'd have to adjust your costumes.

I don't care that he didn't mean it that way. It's how I'm taking it.

Away, away.

"Oh, fuck. Gwen, I didn't *mean*—"

"No." I hold up a hand.

When I turn to leave, whirling so he can't see the new tears spill, he doesn't stop me. As I run back to Britomart, I think of nothing, nothing at all.

* * *

Arthur calls for the sixth time when I'm in the light bulb aisle of Target.

With very few exceptions, you can walk into any Target in the country and immediately orient yourself. Some have the groceries on the left, some on the right, but the differences in organization and layout stop there.

When I was little, Mom and Dad and I used to play this game called Light Bulb. We would all start at the bathrooms in the front of the store, and whoever could find the light bulb aisle first would win. It was stupid. It was fun. It made Target feel less like a store and more like home.

I thought about this last night, when my head was running circles around the dozens of ways Arthur might react to my proclamation of fondness. Just thinking about the ways I considered telling him—of blurting it out, of finding a stupid song on my phone along the lines of "You've Got a Friend in Me"—makes my face feel hot and my body suddenly full of energy I can't use.

I have the most ridiculous impulse to shove all the light bulbs onto the floor, but that, as Dr. Jenkins would say, is not a thought we should pay attention to.

I'm an idiot. A full-fledged idiot. And so is Dr. Jenkins and Fatima, for that matter, for encouraging the idiocy.

I have too much energy to be contained in the narrow aisles, but I don't want to be home in Britomart, either. I don't want to be anywhere where Arthur might think to look for me. So I guess that means I'm going to stay here and wander the rows of sameness until I die of starvation or dehydration or, the most likely scenario, boredom.

Because I have nothing better to do, I meander to the clothes section, and the thought I had this morning—of wishing for an outfit I well and truly like—makes me pause in front of the skinny mannequins with the long limbs and disproportionate heads.

One is wearing a shirt that makes me think of fall, the kind of orangey tan that could be called "pumpkin" or "autumn leaves." The sleeves are fluttery, the neckline dips but not too far, and if it wasn't a—I check the tag—size medium on a mannequin that looks less than half my size, I'd maybe be tempted to try it on.

"You finding everything all right over there?" A woman

chewing gum and wearing a red shirt appears out of nowhere, her headset slightly askew. From the hips up, she looks like she could be one of the mannequins, long torso, long thin arms, but her khakis look like they might fit me if I had anything in my closet that made me look as good as she does.

She's only in her uniform, but she looks confident and put together in a way that I've never been able to pull off.

"I'm fine," I tell her. "Thanks."

"You sure? That shirt is also across the way," she says, pointing across the aisle to the plus size section I didn't notice. "It's *real* cute. Bought mine yesterday."

She doesn't wait for an answer and turns around in that purposeful retail-employee "follow me" kind of way. It's not like I have anything better to do, or at least that's what I tell myself instead of acknowledging the low hum of anxiety about going to the plus size section at all. Because what if people see me and look at me and draw circles in the air? My heart is too bruised to take it today, especially.

"Here we go." The lady hands me three different sizes of the pumpkin shirt. "And if you like that, you might like this, too," she says, slinging another set of sizes of a blue dress over my arm. "That will make your eyes pop. Oh, and if you need jeans, we just got a new batch. Holler if you need my help or a different size, okay?"

She's off again, rolling a red cart full of clothes and hangers from all different departments away from the fitting rooms.

I stand blinking after her until I feel my feet take me into a fitting room.

As a rule, I hate fitting rooms, and if I had been keeping the noticings for my entire life, I would need less than a page to document all the times I've tried clothes on in store. Goodwill stuff was so cheap, we brought it back to Britomart without trying on, the things that didn't fit cut up and repurposed by Mom as RV cleaning rags or leather polishing cloths. Only occasionally, like when I needed new bras or we had a special event that warranted a new outfit, did I get dragged into fitting rooms.

The light in here is aggressively halogen and bright, and my face and hair look washed out because of it, like I'm standing in somebody else's spotlight. Only my restless energy propels me to take my shirt off, then my pants, and for a second, I look at myself in the full-length mirror in only my underwear and bra.

I don't remember the last time I stood in front of a mirror this size without clothes on. There is a half mirror above the sink at home, and of course for the princess-costume fitting I was surrounded by them, but it's not the same as seeing myself in trifold dimensions, seeing myself from every angle.

But I want to look. I want to see if the picture I carry in my head is the same as what is actually there.

Spoiler alert: it's not.

My nose, for one. I *thought* I knew what it looked like, but here I can see it in profile. It's a little sharp at the top, rounded at the bottom, both of which I knew, but I didn't realize how it balances my soft chin.

I make myself look lower. In my head, my chins melt into

my neck, which—to be fair—they kind of do, but not in the hideous, shapeless way I imagined they did. No, from this angle, I can see that unless I'm, like, yawning super wide, I do not in fact look like a snapping turtle without its shell. I just look a bit like a thick-trunked tree. You can still see all my individual branches.

My stomach I dread seeing, but when my eyes fall and fully take it in, it looks like . . . a stomach? It's not supermodel thin. It's not flat and rigid with abs. But it's just . . . a stomach? It doesn't have vampire teeth. It doesn't leap out and try to maul me for looking at it. It's just skin. Like the rest of my body. I don't know why I thought it might be different.

Have I always had that freckle above my belly button? Huh. I kind of like it.

There is a surprising amount of negative space that, again, I did not account for in my head. I'm not a square-shaped blob; I have a *waist*. It's not the narrowest thing on me, but it's *there* and distinct and I kind of like how it looks like a bend in the middle of me, like my body is a fancy wine glass and my legs are the stem.

And *my legs*. Have they always been so . . . curvy? I tilt a foot onto my toes to give the illusions of heels, and I'm not sure if it's my newfound princess career and all the walking it entails or the adventures with Arthur, but calf muscles I didn't know I had bulge out and it's . . . not unattractive? Do I have good legs?

A knock on the door startles me into dropping my foot.

"Okay in there, hon?" It's the overly friendly employee

lady. She must be bored out of her mind to be checking on me.

"Just getting started," I say. "Thanks."

"Just call if you need me for anything, okay?"

"Okay," I say. And, before I can change my mind, "You said something about jeans?"

"I'll bring you a bunch of sizes to try, 'kay? Just try 'em on without looking at the tags. That's what I do."

For a millisecond, to the sound of her retreating footsteps, I panic about the three different sizes of the burnt-orange shirt in front of me, which I know are already arranged from smallest to largest. Do I get the smallest one and risk having to go up a size? Or do I start at the biggest size and risk it being so baggy I give up trying on anything at all?

I go with the middle, which fits surprisingly well, but is the *slightest* bit too tight in the arm holes.

"It's just a tag," I whisper aloud to myself as I take the larger size off its hanger. "It doesn't actually matter."

It doesn't. Not at all. My arms are more comfortable in the larger size, and for the first time in my life, I start a "maybe" stack on the door hanger of the Target dressing room.

When the woman returns with the jeans, I take her advice and don't look at the tags at all, which turns out to be the best tactic. The sizing is all over the place, for *everything*. For the first dress, I need the largest size. For the second, Suzan—the overly helpful employee's name tag says—has to fetch me a straight-size one because the smallest of the plus size options makes my boobs look weird. She brings back a variety of shirts and dresses (and a skirt that is so absurdly colored, I think she means it as a joke) for me to try on, and soon the fitting room feels not totally dissimilar from trying on princess clothes at the castle.

I leave with *two whole bags* of clothes because I literally couldn't decide which ones to leave behind. The cute linen overalls made my legs more leggy. The pleated A-line skirt made my boobs and waist look amazing. The peasant-style maxi dress made me feel like an influencer, or at least someone who knows their way around a fancy brunch. Even the brightly colored rainbow skirt with aggressive neon fabric made the cut, because it looks so stupidly fun with the white eyelet tank that is both comfy and functional in the heat.

From the car, I text pics of a couple of the chosen outfits to Fatima, putting off her last text to me of How'd it go with the boyyyyy with a Not great. I'll tell you later, but what do you think of these?

Three dots appear and then quickly disappear: WORK IT, MADS! My baby's all grown up. You can have your teenagedom card back.

She sends a separate text of the dancing lady in the red dress emoji repeated over and over and over, and I smile all the way home. It's a little forced, because it's not like I've forgotten why I ran away to Target to begin with, but I keep it in place.

That is, until I see who is in front of Britomart. I don't know why I'm surprised. He's leaning against the picnic table when I pull up, his face as serious as I've ever seen it.

"I'll go if you want me to," Arthur says when I get out of the car. "But I came to explain."

"It's okay," I say, opening the back door to pull out my bags. "I mean, you don't have anything to explain. I understand about the theater kids. And that's great your dads are going to let them work at the faire. It's cool."

My voice thankfully sounds even, devoid of light bulb–breaking tendencies. Is this what people mean when they talk about retail therapy? But really I'm just interested in getting him to *leave*.

"They were supposed to have a big fundraiser at the new aquatics center," Arthur says, his voice rushed. "But they had to cancel because the renovations are taking longer than they thought, so it won't reopen until the school year, which will be too late for them to buy stuff to get ready for the fall showcase. That's why Bre called yesterday, to tell me. So Dad and I thought—"

"Really," I say. "It's okay. I get it. But with them, you don't need me as princess anymore."

"But—"

"I don't *want* to be princess anymore," I say, and I wish my voice could sound gentle and calm like his does, but it comes out all wrong. "I didn't want to be in the first place, remember?"

"But you are now. You can't just *quit*."

When I dig out my key and open Britomart's door, he stands behind me, waiting for an invitation to cross the doorframe that I don't give him.

"I'm not quitting," I say, setting my bags on the lower bunk. "I'm stepping aside. Bre and Noah are in theater, right? So they'll be here and Bre can be princess again."

I watch his face closely, trying to gauge his reaction. He annoyingly gives nothing away.

"Why do you keep bringing up Bre?"

I set the bags on the bottom bunk. "She was originally supposed to be princess, right? So really, *that's* what is fated. Not me."

"That's not—"

"*I'm not going to be somebody's Juliet,*" I say, and it comes out louder and more forcefully than I intended.

Arthur looks a little stunned. *I'm* a little stunned.

"What are you *talking* about?" he asks.

I wish he had brought his lute. I want to smash it over his head.

"Don't be obtuse. *Romeo and Juliet*? Not gonna do it. You know the most ridiculous part of that entire story?"

Arthur raises an eyebrow, and it makes me want to pummel him more. "That two teenagers fell in love in two seconds and then died two seconds after that?"

"No," I say. "No, it's that Romeo was supposedly *so in love* with Rosaline, but the second he saw Juliet he changed his mind. He just didn't want to be alone and Juliet was available while Rosaline wasn't, and maybe everyone would have lived if Rosaline had come back on the scene."

For the first time, Arthur looks mad. Properly mad.

"So that's it, then? You think all of this"—he gestures at

the postcards from our adventures taped to my wall—"was just because I was lonely? It had nothing whatsoever to do with me actually *liking* you?"

I fold my arms. "I can't be Juliet," I say. "We don't have time to make the dress fit."

Arthur blinks once. Twice. Opens his mouth and closes it.

I step around him, cramming my arm beside him to turn the knob.

"Where are you going?" he sputters when I open Britomart's door.

"*I'm* staying here," I say. "*You're* going home."

He steps forward, just one tiny step to stand right in front of me, close, too close. I can feel his breath on my cheeks.

"Am I going home because you need space right now?" he asks, and his voice sounds angry but not. Frustrated but not quite. "Or am I going home because you're afraid to finish this conversation and hope that if you make me leave, we'll never have to?"

I'm not going to dignify that with an answer, but even if I wanted to, I can't. His eyes are falling to my lips and then bouncing back to my eyes. After a minute of silence, Arthur nods.

"You can flip your coin," he says, and his voice is the most serious I've ever heard it. "You can talk to every *wise wizard* in existence. You can make your lists and you can build all the walls you want, Madeline Hathaway, but at some point you're going to have to decide what it is *you* want and go for it and damn the rest."

With that, he leaves, and I mindlessly remove tags from my new clothes.

I don't read *The Falconer's Gauntlet* or make tea or anything.

I just go to bed.

CHAPTER TWELVE

"ARTHUR ISN'T HERE." TIM SAYS WHEN he answers the door.

I try to look like I didn't spend the entire morning sitting beside Britomart waiting to hear the sound of Arthur's terrible engine in hopes that he would leave and I could return the princess things without seeing him.

"Oh," I say. "Did he tell you about . . ."

I hope Tim will nod sympathetically so I don't have to finish, but he only cocks his head in confusion. I sigh, and kind of wish it was Martin who had answered the door with his people-pleasing smile and easy demeanor. Tim feels . . .

like the prickly parts of Arthur. I don't see those parts enough to know how to deal with them.

"Well, it's just . . . I told Arthur I don't think I need to be princess anymore," I say. "Now that you'll have the theater group here and everything, I mean."

"Ah," Tim says. "No, he didn't mention that." He steps back, holding the huge door open. "Why don't you come in, Madeline? I've *just* brewed an excellent pot of herbal tea. I can never get away with it when Martin is here. He prefers black with too much sugar."

"Oh, it's okay. I was just going to drop these off," I say, holding up the last princess dress I wore, the makeup palettes, my shoes.

"Afraid I can't carry them on my own, so you'll have to come in. That is, if you don't mind giving me a hand?" Tim smiles. He holds his hands up between us. "Spent all morning sewing for the new recruits. My fingers are sore to the bone."

It's a transparent ruse to get me inside, but I don't see how it can be avoided, so I follow.

I've never been inside the kitchen before. It looks like it belongs in *Downton Abbey* or *Bridgerton*, if they had been able to acquire stainless steel appliances hidden behind cupboard doors. There are little clumps of plants scattered around the room, and it takes Tim picking up a green glass squirt bottle to idly spray them for me to realize they are real and not like the plastic succulent Mom used to pretend to water near Britomart's steering wheel.

"Herbs," he explains. "They like the sunlight in here. Care for a cookie?"

"No thanks." I sling the dress over the back of a chair and set the rest of it on the table. "I really should be going."

"Nonsense," Tim says, plunking a gold-rimmed teacup in front of me. "Don't make me drink alone."

I sit, less begrudgingly than I would if not for the mint chocolate chip cookies Tim places between us. I take a sip of tea, and I already know the light citrus flavor will *perfectly* complement the cookies.

"Thank you," I say, remembering that I am a human with manners.

"Of course," Tim says, pulling himself to the table. "Now, what's this about you not being princess anymore?"

If you're not paying enough attention, Tim and Martin look mismatched. Martin is tall and dark and enthusiastic about *everything*. Tim, meanwhile, is short and fair and quietly thoughtful, not at all exuberant by nature.

But there are similarities, too, like how Tim is looking at me with this intense *knowing* that Martin also has, the one that they passed onto their son. All three of them look at you like you're going to tell them *everything*, like they expect it, but also welcome it? They listen. Really listen.

Which is probably why the first words out of my mouth are not *I should be helping my dad* or *I could spend the time working on summer reading*, but instead, "I'm freaked out by the theater kids."

Before I can apologize, elaborate, Tim wipes crumbs from his mouth and nods.

"Understandable. You do online classes, correct? You probably don't have many opportunities to interact with children your own age, especially en masse like this. Have you always done school in this way?"

"Yeah," I say. "Mom homeschooled me until I was in third grade, and then we switched to the online program."

Tim takes a sip of tea. "Have you ever wanted to try traditional school?"

There must be truth serum in these cookies, because I'm not sure how my plan of "drop the stuff and run" got so derailed, but I find myself shaking my head.

"No," I say. "I mean, Dad and I talked about it after my mom passed. I think he wanted me to try it, thought it might be good for me, but I didn't want another change."

"Change can be hard," Tim says. "But it is also the only way we move forward in life."

Apparently the three of them share a love of annoying wisdoms, too.

"Yeah," I say. "Yes. I just . . . kind of don't want to deal? With the theater kids, I mean."

Tim pushes the plate toward me, indicating I should take another cookie. "We certainly don't want you to be uncomfortable, should you wish to avoid it," he says, "but consider this: At some point, whether now or in college or your future career, you *will* have to interact with large groups of colleagues in one form or another. Maybe it would be best to practice now? Bite the bullet, as it were?"

He's right, of course. "But if I wait," I say, "I won't have to do it in slippers and skirts."

Tim laughs at that, sipping his tea. "Don't you mean you won't *get* to do it in slippers and skirts? And a tiara, I might add. Can't forget that."

"I don't know if fake faire royalty means anything to teenagers," I say. "Wouldn't that be a mark against me? Something they could use to make fun of me?"

He looks so lost in thought, I wonder if he heard me. But then he says, "I wish I could tell you that all of the kids will be kind and accepting and welcoming, but I can't. Kids are just humans, and humans have a tendency to vary in their levels of compassion for one another. However, I *can* promise that every instance where someone *isn't* kind is another opportunity for you to discover what is within you."

"That sounds . . . inspirational."

Tim shrugs, but he smiles a little. "That depends entirely on what's within you, I'm afraid."

So much of my fear of the future, I realize, is wrapped up in feeling unprepared, untested against the world. The wonderful thing about growing up in the circuit is that I was in our own little bubble of a family unit. The terrible thing about growing up in the circuit is that I've never had the bubble burst.

But maybe Tim is right. It's going to have to happen at some point.

"I still don't think I should be princess," I tell him. "Arthur . . ." I trail off, not wanting to bring up Bre.

"Arthur," Tim says, "is the greatest work of my life. I love him beyond measure. He is, however, not a good enough reason to lay down your tiara, Madeline."

"Oh, no," I rush to clarify. "He *wants* me to still be princess, but . . ."

"What is it *you* want?"

"I want—" I stop, because at that exact moment, the little globe charm snags on my new tank top and pulls the chain at my neck. Tim's eyes follow my movement to dislodge it as he waits for me to finish my thought.

I'm so tired of trying to evaluate what I want, because it's almost always in response to something bad or unexpected. Nobody asks you to reevaluate your life, your choices, when things are going well.

But it's not Tim's fault that he is what feels like the hundredth person in the last year to ask me how I want to proceed.

"I want to tame the world," I say, my usual, easy answer. "I want to make it kinder."

Tim is quiet, waiting, like he knows this was a canned response. I try to think of what I can add to make it sound sincere, and I'm surprised when the words are ready on the tip of my tongue.

"But I also . . . I want to take up space in it?"

Tim's smile is small but warm. He has a chocolate chip smudged on his two front teeth that I would rather die than point out.

"Do you think being princess will help you achieve that goal?"

He's giving me an option, I realize. He's not going to force me to be princess any more than Martin or Arthur would. I could walk out right now and leave the gown, the shoes, the responsibility, and—if I'm being honest—the fear behind. I wouldn't have to interact with a bunch of theater kids I've never met, I wouldn't have to put up with Arthur and Bre, and I could go back to my original plans for the summer.

I know what the Maddie from the beginning of the summer would do. She'd take that deal in a heartbeat, gleefully go back to her noticings and her tea and her routine.

Now I'm not so sure. This Maddie has had her feet propped up on the dashboard listening to playlists for hours on end while eating Tootsie Pops. This Maddie has a trunk full of new clothes that fit and show off curves instead of hiding them.

There are similarities. Neither Madeline knows what the end of the summer holds. Neither one is sure how she'll feel the day of Mom's anniversary. But this Maddie is tired of things *happening* to her.

"I want to try," I tell Tim. "I want to be the one to decide."

He gently pushes the stack of princess things back toward my side of the table.

"And so you shall."

* * *

I really need to stop making it a habit to talk to people with the gift of inspirational speaking, because their ideas always seem *so good* until I execute them.

Naturally, I'm currently reconsidering all of my life choices, and I'm blaming both freakin' Suzan for showing me the cute shirt that gave me so much false confidence when I talked to Tim, and then *also* Tim, for obvious reasons.

This is their fault. And probably also a little bit Dr. Jenkins's and Fatima's faults, too.

Because this is a *whole thing*, the group of thirty-two teenagers standing in the nave looking upward in awe at the castle's skylights, because even though I *know* we're the same age and everything, they seem like a different species.

I don't know if my palms are sweating because of the theater group or because I'll finally see Arthur.

I haven't spoken to him since our . . . fight? Discussion? Whatever it was.

And he hasn't called.

I don't know if Tim told him about our conversation or not, and I tell myself that part of taming the world and making it kinder for myself in this moment is not caring, but I care anyway.

I *so* care. I wish the lava had burned it all away, but it didn't.

I don't see him in the crowd of kids. They're so at *ease* with each other. Words pour out of their mouths like they have nothing to lose, like they could say the wrong thing and it would be forgotten just as soon as it is said. They don't look self-conscious or hyperaware when they bump into each other, when hands accidentally graze shoulders and torsos and backs. Sometimes they touch on purpose, and somehow that's even more terrifying.

I'm having a hard time identifying the weird storm cloud of a feeling it brings up in me, watching them flirt and poke at each other, but I don't have time to delve further—or to wonder which one is Bre—because Martin, Tim, and Arthur are suddenly there, king and bard attire conspicuously absent, though they look like a royal unit all the same as they descend the staircase.

"Hello, hello, hello," Martin says, and he is met with a chorus of excited greetings, the group obviously happy to see their beloved parental volunteers.

"We hope everyone is having a good summer," Tim says, and though he doesn't raise his voice like Martin, I can hear him clear across the room. "And we are glad that we are able to help you meet your fundraising goal. Today will be mostly a chance to show you the grounds, assign roles, and of course do some costume fittings. First, some introductions are in order . . ."

As they rattle off the names and roles of the couple of faire managers at the front of the room, I watch Arthur's face, more specifically his eyes.

I don't think he's spotted where I'm hiding beside a suit of armor, but his eyes are looking for me, roaming the room—and passing me twice.

He's not trying to find me after all.

This was *such* a mistake.

"And then there's our fearless princess," Tim says, smiling in my direction. "Raise your hand, Madeline. Ah, there she is. Madeline kindly offered to step into our royal party at the start of the summer, for which we are eternally grateful. I'm sure you'll become better acquainted over the next couple of weekends."

Everyone, literally *everyone*, is staring at me, and I want to shrivel up and die from embarrassment. I would if not for Arthur, standing beside his dads and looking square at me for the first time today. I can't read his expression, but something in it straightens my spine and makes me do a stupid little wave at the group.

"Hi," I say.

And before I have time to overanalyze if this was the appropriate one-word greeting, Martin is going on about faire etiquette and a crash course in faire speak when a boy, tall and olive-skinned and the kind of attractive that is almost hard to look at, comes to lean against the wall beside me.

"Hiya, Princess," he says. He folds his arms, which makes his already-bulging muscles even more prominent.

I may not know much about how other teenagers work, but I know what *this* is. He's here to suck up because he thinks I have some sort of power—which I don't—or worse, he's going to do that thing overly attractive people do to people like me, wherein he pretends I am worth his time.

There are only two reasons for this: One, he wants to feel better about himself, a god of pleasantly-disproportionate-in-all-the-right-ways body parts smiling down upon a pleb. Or two, it's one of those indirect ways of making fun of me. A joke.

"You should be listening," I say, hoping he'll leave me alone. "What if you miss something?"

His smile is bleach white and charming. "Ah, come on, Princess. Don't make me do school stuff in the summer. I'm just here to look pretty with a sword."

It sounds so much like something Arthur would say that it takes me aback and startles a laugh out of me before I can stop it. From my periphery, I can see Arthur jerk his head in our direction, and something petty and a little bit mean spreads in my stomach. Good. Let him watch.

"Besides," the boy says, still smiling, "you're the princess. You must know everything there is to know."

Again, I don't know *much*, but I'm not stupid enough to believe his flattery is anything other than self-serving.

"I know enough," I say. And then, because Arthur is watching, a girl—one different than me—who always wears cute clothes and knows how to act around humans her own age yanks me out of myself and slightly touches his arm. She laughs in what I'm pretty sure could pass as a solid attempt at flirtation. "You won't need to know much of this if you're going to be a knight character actor. Knights can get away with a lot at faire."

"I'm hoping they'll teach me to joust," he says. "Do you think they will? I wanna sit on a horse and hold the pole."

"Lance," I correct. "And I doubt it. Those guys are trained professionals."

He snorts. "Yeah, but I bet I can out-bench them."

I shoot a glance at his arms. "Probably."

He leans next to me until Martin and Tim finish their spiel, and when it's over, he pushes off from the wall and rubs the back of his neck.

"See ya around, Princess."

"See ya," I echo.

"Promise you'll cheer for me when I get to joust, all right?"

"Sure," I say.

Almost as soon as the boy is lost in the throng of kids rushing to get out the main doors of the castle and onto the moat, Arthur is at my side. It appears, for lack of a better description, like he is actively trying to swallow his tongue and choke on it.

I refuse to speak first, so he has to rearrange his mouth to finally say, "Hello."

"Hey."

"What were you doing talking to Noah?"

I file away this information for later. Arthur wasn't kidding about him being a Greek god.

"I'm surprised you noticed," I say, and the pettiness inside me grows at Arthur's obvious irritation. "Looked like you were too busy looking for someone to pay attention to what I was doing."

"Yeah, I *was* looking for someone," he says. "*You.*"

"Were not," I say, and for maybe the first time in my life I'm worried I sound like the cliché spoiled only child. I just need a good foot stamp and I'll fit the part. "You were looking for Bre."

We're alone in the castle now, Martin and Tim having

followed the gaggle out to begin showing them the grounds. Arthur and I should be with them, but here we are, beneath skylights and tapestries and a clusterfuck of feelings.

"I didn't have to look for Bre," he says. "I saw her right when I came in."

That stings a little. I flinch, but he must not notice, because he presses on, "I couldn't see you hiding over by the armor until you laughed and I heard it."

"Yeah, well, your friend Noah is a funny guy."

Arthur mumbles something, but it's too low for me to hear. "Look, we need to talk."

It's not his usual *do you want to talk* full of caveats and fail-safes to make sure that I am comfortable, that this is something *I* want to do. This is Arthur's serious face, and it is seriously freaking me out.

What I want to say is that I flipped the damn coin and it told me to stay away from him. I kind of even want to say that I had decided to go against it, that I didn't care and I was going to let myself like him anyway.

But I don't, because it wouldn't do any good. He would argue for the kind of fate that brings people together when I've only seen fate that, inevitably, tears people apart.

"I can't right now," I say. "I need to go home, work on jewelry and stuff."

Arthur blinks. "But tomorrow is . . ."

He remembers Mom's anniversary. Of course he does.

"I know," I say. "It's fine."

"You can be mad at me and still call me," he says. And it's

almost enough to make me fold right there. *Almost.* But not quite.

"Thanks," I say. And then, awkwardly, "Gotta go."

I can feel him watching me as I leave. I *should* go with him, join the group and try to help Tim and Martin, but instead I actually do head home to the smallness and the safety of Britomart.

My intention is to work on jewelry, to work my fingers numb first and then eventually my head, but after only an hour or so, I pick up my phone and call Fatima. It goes straight to voicemail. A second later, she sends me a photo of her with a group of girls in front of what looks to be an incredibly run-down theme park. **Talk later!** her text says.

What could I decide to do in this moment? Fatima not answering is something that happened to me, but what can I decide to do on my own?

My usual suspects—make jewelry, work on summer reading, go to Target—feel too normal. I want to do something with the pent-up energy left over from my stilted conversation with Arthur, with my worry of how I will feel when tomorrow comes and I wake to find myself a year removed from my last Mom hug, the last time I saw her.

I want to *move*. Days without an adventure and endless walking have made me physically restless, something I've rarely experienced in all my years living in an RV with much less than four hundred square feet to call my own.

Impulsively, I text Dad: **Okay if I take the car?**

The three dots appear quickly, though the text takes at

least a minute to appear. He's probably hunting for his reading glasses.

Sure. You going with Arthur?

I don't want to say that I'm going alone because he'll worry, so instead I say, **Another adventure.**

This reply is faster: **Have fun. Be safe.**

"Fun" seems a stretch, but I'll take *away*.

* * *

Arthur deemed Tulsa's Center of the Universe too boring to be worthy of our adventuring, even though it was one of the first things to pop up when I searched for "things to do in Oklahoma."

"It sounds cool," I had said.

"It's a bunch of concrete, a glorified walkway," he said. "How is that any better than mysterious floating lights?"

When I pull into the parking lot of a huge office building—the closest spot I can get to the "Center of the Universe"—I'm already cursing him for being right.

There's no plaque, nothing to mark this as a tourist spot or acoustical anomaly other than the couple of people milling around at the center of the concrete circle.

It's *literally* just a walkway, and I'm honestly kind of pissed about it. Here it is, my first solo adventure, something that I thought would prove to Arthur, to myself, that I am perfectly capable of doing something meaningful on my own with all the confidence of a princess, and I choose a stupid bunch of concrete in the middle of a circle of buildings.

The couple of people milling about the circle don't seem to notice or care when I sit on one of the raised concrete flower beds that's just full of those plants that mostly look like grass. It is the most underwhelming place in the world, but I've driven an hour to get here, so I figure I might as well wait a second before heading back home.

It's a group of preteens standing in the middle of the brick circle. One of them is in the dead center, the others scattered a few feet away.

"Dude, I seriously can't hear you. Seriously."

The girl in the middle cups her hands over her mouth and appears to yell something, but I can't hear her from where I sit.

"Nothing," a girl on the outside of the circle says. "Like, maybe a mumble?"

I wonder if they're exaggerating. When we were looking for stuff to do and I found the Center of the Universe, I read a short paragraph about it. Legend has it that a foghorn could go off in the middle of the circle, but if you're not inside the circle with the foghorn, you couldn't hear it go off, even if you're mere steps away.

"Let me try," a boy says, stepping into the circle.

He does, his friends shake their heads that no, they can't hear him, and then he gleefully steps outside long enough to say, "I'm going to tell a secret, then. Hold on."

This starts a new string of excitement, with each person

taking turns yelling their secrets into an acoustical void where their friends can't hear them.

"Hey," one of the boys says. "Hey, lady, do you want to try?"

When I realize he's talking to me, I startle.

"I'm okay," I say.

"You should try it," he insists, taking a step toward me. "It's awesome."

When I stand, the girl with long straight hair smiles at me. "Do you want us to stand outside and see if we can hear you?"

She's so eager, clearly enthralled to have found something to break up the monotony of summer in Oklahoma, that I can't say no.

When I stand in the middle of the circle and they stand around me, I can't help but smile.

"What should I say?" I ask. I jump a little when my voice comes back to me tenfold, echoing and loud.

"*Oh*," I say. I guess I missed reading about this part of it.

The boy directly in front of me cocks his head and smiles back at me. "Can't hear you," he says. "You sound like a teacher from Snoopy."

I'm thinking of what I want to say, if I trust the acoustics enough to dare say one of my own secrets aloud, when the kids lose interest. They wave a goodbye, the half hand raise you give to people you'll never see again, and head toward the cluster of bikes lying in the grass.

It's just me, the circle, and the horns of distant traffic.

I *do* remember reading that nobody is one hundred percent sure what causes the echo effect and what exactly distorts your voice to outsiders. The echoes probably come from the ring of concrete surrounding the brick circle, but that doesn't explain why it's a *private* echo chamber. The pathway used to be a bridge for cars, but it burned down in the eighties. When it was rebuilt, the unintentional phenomenon was created.

Nobody knows, either, who first coined the name "Center of the Universe," or even how long it has been around.

I'm beginning to feel less stupid for coming here, because though it isn't much to look at, it's so much to *hear* and *say*.

Distantly, I can see a couple with small kids making their way up the slope toward me. I probably have all of two minutes before I'll no longer be alone, and now, standing here, it feels like I really should tell a secret, something I want to stay at the Center of the Universe.

Because tomorrow is Mom's anniversary.

Because even with all of these hard, inescapable truths clouding my brain, the one secret I want to confess has everything to do with a coin flip, a bard, and my heart.

So I say it aloud, I let it echo back to me tenfold, and then, when the last echo dies, I step from the circle and leave the secret behind me.

* * *

On my way out of town, I stop at a gas station where a bored-looking attendant idly flips a quarter over and over. Each time, he makes tallies on a sticky note beneath an *H* and a *T*.

"Can I help you?" he asks, and I shake my head to wake myself from staring.

"Postcards?" I ask.

He doesn't stop flipping the coin. He draws another tally while jerking his head to the side.

"Over there," he says. "Only have a couple left."

He's right, down to the exact number. There are two lonely postcards left on the nearly empty turnstile, both for the Center of the Universe.

I intended to only buy one, but it seems wrong to leave the other behind.

"It's a dollar even," the guy says, not looking at me.

I give him a bill and turn to leave, but I can't resist asking before I do, "Why are you doing that?"

He shrugs, still not looking at me. "Dunno."

"Is it really fifty-fifty?" I ask. "Heads and tails?"

Another shrug, another toss, another tally. "Heads is winning by three flips," he says.

I nod, like this means anything, and tell him, "Thanks."

A bell jingles above me as I leave behind the guy flipping a coin and making tallies at the gas station at the Center of the Universe.

CHAPTER THIRTEEN

THE NEXT MORNING. MOM'S ANNIVERSARY. I expect Dad to be weepy and maudlin when I come sit across from him on the little picnic table next to Britomart, but he is surprisingly not.

He looks his usual self, actually. His hands are stained from the leather and a pile of dirty rags have already begun collecting at his elbow as he polishes the latest stock.

"Neil is starting to make journals, too," he says in greeting when I grab a rag. "Smart guy. Did you know he was almost an accountant?"

"How'd he end up as security at a faire?" I ask.

"Quit with only one semester of school left. Decided he preferred being outside to an office and took a job for a big outdoor venue in the city."

"Huh," I say.

"Yeah. He's a good kid."

He hands me a box of journals that he pulls up from the bench beside him.

"How are you?" he asks after a while.

Even though I *know* he knows what today is, I wasn't sure how we were going to approach it. If we were going to spend the day together without acknowledging it, or if we were going to have this big sappy, awkward conversation that neither of us knows how to handle without the person we're mourning here to fix it.

I guess we're going with the second one.

"I'm . . . okay," I say. "I mean, does it feel like it has been a year to you?"

He's goes quiet, polishing an entire journal before answering.

"When you get older, time slips away. Every year seems shorter than the last. This year seemed longer. Much longer."

"Yeah," I say. "But also, I can't believe it's already been that long."

"Depends on the day," Dad says.

"Yeah," I say. "Today feels like both."

He mumbles something that might be an agreement, and then we're back to our individual journals. The one in my hands, a standard size with a rich blue cover, catches the morning sunlight.

"Do you have any plans today?" Dad asks.

I don't stop polishing, and neither does he. Neither of us wants to look at the other when we talk about this stuff, for which I am grateful. Eye contact right now would be too much.

"I thought I'd walk around the faire a bit," I say, which is a half-truth. "Just . . . remembering."

"Your uncle Jack has invited us to his place," Dad says. "If you wanted. He's going to make the meatballs your mom loved."

Dr. Jenkins asked me once if I resent Dad when he goes to be with his friends, and truthfully, I don't. Not at all. He needs them, his chosen family. But even though I'm not a little kid anymore, it's hard for their friends to see me as anything other than the baby they met all those years ago. It's hard for Dad, too, but it's less hard when it's just the two of us working like this, side by side.

Being with him and his friends on the anniversary of Mom's passing would make me feel like a spectator.

So I say, "It's okay, Dad. You go. I'm going to go for that walk."

Dad nods, and I think maybe that's going to be the end of the conversation, but then he says, "I miss her, Maddie."

"I know," I say. And even though it feels like we're reading lines from an invisible script to the world's most predictable TV show, I add, "Me too."

Sometimes there is nothing else to say but what has already been said.

Maybe other families would spend the whole day remembering her together, laughing and crying all mingled together until they went to bed exhausted but rejuvenated. They'd probably visit a graveside—which Mom doesn't have because she requested her ashes be scattered in the Pacific Ocean—or maybe go eat at a restaurant their loved one used to enjoy.

But Dad and I . . . we're okay. We don't need each other in this specific way.

It's a relief to admit. I'm *not* mad. I'm not disappointed. This is just how we are . . . Slowly finding our footing in this new Mom-less world, together but apart.

It's a weekday, but the faire is still strangely quiet. Usually there are one or two groundskeepers walking around even on off days, polishing lampposts, power washing walkways, or trimming hedges.

But today it's like Stormsworth knows I want solitude. Its princess—reluctant as she is—requires peace.

In my head, I've already chosen the trees at the edge of the jousting ring for what I have to do. They're thick enough that nobody will wander over to them, and out of the way besides.

They're *so* far away. It takes me a good twenty minutes to walk from the gated entrance, past the shops, to the jousting ring. Another two to make it to the redbuds.

Mom would like it here. It would probably remind her

of the original entrance to Stormsworth, but she would love, *love* the view of the new castle.

As for me, I try not to think about who lives inside the castle.

The tree I choose looks the most asymmetrical, the kind Mom would be drawn to because it looks slightly less put together than the others. *More original*, she would say. For a second, I let myself stand and remember.

I miss Mom. I miss the way her hair smelled when she stepped past me in Britomart. I miss her laugh and the way it always made me and Dad laugh along. When I squeeze my eyes shut, I swear I *can* hear it, her laugh. If I cover my ears, still holding the journal, maybe I can keep it in my head forever.

Maybe from now on I'll try to remember that *one thing* the hardest: the laughter of Dad and Fatima and maybe even Arthur and Tim and Martin. Maybe if I can remember what someone's laugh sounds like, it will be enough.

This feels like a revelation to me, as I slowly unbutton the purse at my hip and draw out the book of noticings, but I must have known I was going to leave the noticings here, because it's the only part of my travel journal I brought with me. The rest I left in Britomart.

Because it's not the doodled facts, the school notes, or even the poetry that I *know* Mom would love just as much as I do that is keeping me from moving forward. It's the noticings.

I know. I've *known*. I'm not stupid. It was always going to be this crutch, this way of remembering without *actually* remembering anything at all, that was going to have to be laid to rest.

But it hasn't felt right until now. If I'm being honest, it still doesn't feel good, the thought of leaving it here, but I know it's the right thing to do. I didn't even have to flip and ask the coin.

I'm still unsure of what Mom would want for me if she knew I would have to be without her, but I know she wouldn't want me to obsess over tallies.

Suddenly, I have the prickling feeling of being watched, that weird leftover awareness that must come from a time when humans were afraid of being hunted by saber-toothed tigers.

Arthur stands at the far end of the jousting ring, hands in pockets, lute strung on his back, and for once, I can tell he's not going to say his usual spiel: that he doesn't have to be here, that he will do whatever I want, whatever makes me happy.

He's just going to stand there and wait.

He's going to wait for *me* to say something.

We stand there just staring at each other for a full minute, maybe longer. It's one of those charged standoffs which must just look stupid, two kids on opposite sides of a dusty, sandy jousting ring holding a long-distance staring contest. But to me, at least, it feels important, like there is nothing to do but stand here and let this moment happen.

Why is it that eye contact makes time slow? Another Lark poem feels startlingly relevant:

*To say that eyes are windows is to believe that they are still.
No, eyes are grappling hooks that will sink their barbs into
you and pull without letting go.*

"You don't have to stand over there," I say.

"What?"

I raise my voice. "You can come over here, if you want."

He gives a slight nod, and I look back to the tree to avoid
watching him as he approaches with his long, lanky strides.

We're quiet for a minute, awkward, and I can practically see him sifting around in his head for something to
say, something *appropriate*, and I'm too nice to let him
suffer for long.

"There's nothing you can say," I tell him. "'*I'm sorry*' is
stupid because it's not your fault and also it doesn't help. '*How
are you feeling*' is worse because then I have to try to explain
the unexplainable to you."

Arthur says nothing, so I continue.

"You could always go with the '*She's in a better place*,'
which is also dumb, because unless I can buy a plane ticket to
get there, it doesn't really help *me*, and I'm the one suffering,
now, not her. Oh! You know what? You should *definitely* play
a song. Something relevant to the big emotions but flavored
with just a *smidge* of humor that will make me laugh and
make me forget my mom is gone."

The noticings are shaking in my hands. I don't notice until Arthur leans forward, and—without his usual gentleness—
pulls me into a hug against his chest, hard. The journal is

wedged between us, still shaking, but the weird thing is, tears don't come. I just let him hold me in his vise of a grip as I shake.

When we part, he gently brings his lute around to the front.

"I was kidding about the song," I say. "Please don't sing."

"It's not . . . I wasn't going to sing. But, if you wanted, could I play you something? For your mom?"

I don't have the emotional energy to do anything but nod.

"Okay. You can tell me to stop and I will," he says.

And then he's playing. I don't recognize the song, but I can feel the words of it deep in my bones all the same. It's about heartbreak. It's about grief. The low chords thump repeatedly like a heartbeat and pulse through my ears, teasing tears from my eyes as the key changes to something a little less sad, a little more like . . . remembering.

When I was a kid, I had this toy that you held up to your eyes, and each time you clicked a button, the picture you could see inside would change, the wheel on the outside turning frame by frame so that you could focus on nothing but the photo in front of you.

My childhood toy was full of animals, scenic landscapes, and movie stills, but listening to Arthur play is like watching a slideshow of Mom, each moment, each flash the only thing before my eyes.

Here, she sits at the work bench with her tongue sticking out from the side of her lips as she threads a needle. Here, she squints at the instructions on the side of the macaroni and cheese she makes at least once a week. There, she puts her hands on Dad's shoulders and pulls herself up to kiss him. And here, she folds herself up small to sit next to me on my top bunk when I cry over a bad grade.

All of these I have seen before, but as Arthur plays, it's like the music drags a memory from deep within my brain, somewhere I couldn't go if I tried, but one that his playing opens like a gate.

When he finishes, I'm crying, the noticings journal clutched between my fingers so tightly that my fingernails leave an imprint.

Arthur puts his lute behind his back and then digs around in the pocket of his jeans.

"I brought this for you," he says. "I . . . I just wondered if you would want something to honor your mom. Physically, I mean. So I thought . . . Well, here."

He thrusts a slim wooden box that slides open to reveal a shallow bed of silk into my hands, almost dropping it.

"The box is from John's Woodshop," he says, and it's the most nervous I've ever heard him. "Remember? You said you liked that padauk jewelry box he made? Well, I asked him to make this in case you wanted to, I don't know, bury it or something?"

I stare at him wide-eyed. He tries to read my expression, but plows on, sliding the box the rest of the way.

"Silk," he says. "Pops says it's the kind that they used for

royalty. And this"—he unwraps a tiny corner of the fabric—
"one of the glassblowers made this for me. It's a camel, see? I
know you said she loved little animals, and I thought maybe
you would want to put one in the box with a note or something so you could always have something to remind you of
her at Stormsworth."

My tears have stopped, and I'm too busy trying to piece
together the *how* of this. How could he have known I was
going to bury the book of noticings? How could he have paid
so much attention to know exactly what to do?

Arthur's eyes search mine, and he must misread my silence because he says, "Oh shit. You hate it. Look, it was just
an idea. I'll give it to Dad. He can hide the camel around the
castle to irritate Pops and—"

He makes a slight strangled noise as I throw my arms
around his neck.

"Thank you," I whisper. "Thank you, Arthur."

It takes him a second, but he hugs me back. I feel his head
tilt into mine. "You're welcome. You don't hate it?"

I wipe my nose, shake my head. "I was going to bury the
noticings here," I say. "Do you think the journal will fit in
the box?"

Arthur's eyes widen, but he only says, "I'm not sure. We
could try."

"It probably won't," I say.

But of course it fits. It's tight, and the little camel bends
one of the edges of the journal, and once we slide it closed it

will probably never open again, but it *fits*. Just barely, but it's enough.

We both look down at it in my hands.

"Gwen?"

"Yeah?"

"I know you have complicated feelings about fate or whatever," he says. "But I swear to god I had no idea you were going to want to put the journal inside."

"Just this once," I say, "we'll call it fate."

The burying of the box proves to be a challenge. In movies, don't people just scoop up dirt with their hands until they have an appropriately sized hole? But the Oklahoma dirt is dry and packed, and even with Arthur's help, it takes us a good five minutes of digging and chipping fingernails to make a dent deep enough to bury the box.

When we're finished, both of us kneeling in the dirt, Arthur is the first to get up, wiping his hands on his shorts and grabbing his lute.

"I'll leave you alone," he says.

And part of me wants him to stay, or better yet, take me somewhere in his hideous car and listen to his eclectic playlists and eat too many suckers. But besides not being sure where we stand, if we're still mad at each other—for the Noah thing, the Bre thing, the whole *thing*—I know that today is for me, for Mom.

There will be more days to figure out the Arthur thing, but today I just need to remember.

So instead, I say, "Thank you. For the box, I mean."

Arthur nods. "Anytime. Whenever you need me."

He hesitates, like he wants to say more, but he doesn't. He gives me a salute before turning to walk back to the castle, his feet making a rhythm that matches the song he plays as he leaves. It's the same song he played for me minutes ago, and as he and the song fade away from me, I let the memories wash over me. I let myself notice the way the wind moves in the trees, how it picks up the dirt in little eddies that are almost magical in how they swirl around me, and I don't write it down.

I'll remember.

Part of me feels like I should stay, keep a short vigil over the buried box and really soak in the moment or whatever.

But it's hot and I'm thirsty, so I don't stay long after Arthur leaves, beginning the long walk back to Britomart.

I kept thinking that this year's anniversary would be an arrival of sorts, that I would get here and know more about how to handle Mom's absence and maybe how to move forward. But even though the missing of her doesn't seem particularly heavy today, of all days, it still feels like a companion, a silent stoic presence that's not going anywhere soon.

As I walk through the trees at the entrance of Stormsworth, the trees my mother loved so well, I try to notice every leaf, every branch. Knowing I can't—*won't*—write down any of the noticings makes me hungrier to look, but also a bit lighter. Somewhere along the way, what I meant to be a coping mechanism became shackles.

Maybe it is enough to honor Mom today by letting myself be a little more free.

Maybe it's fate.

* * *

I almost welcome the chaos that is the first Friday of faire with the theater kids. Even though I'm okay—more than okay—with my decision to bury the journal of noticings, it's a good distraction from my thought spirals of Mom and anniversaries. The cacophony of people pouring out of the castle as the day's work orders are shouted drowns out any chance of overthinking, or thinking at all.

It's in the midst of this swirl—in all my princess finery— when a girl in a costume a step above peasantry comes straight toward me, smiling.

"I am your lady-in-waiting, Your Highness." Her curtsy is absurdly deep and graceful, which makes me feel awkward beyond measure.

"Oh," I say. I don't know why, but I take a small step back, my skirts brushing against the mouth of the moat. "You don't have to do that. Especially when we're not in front of customers or whatever."

Her smile is bright white against her dark brown skin, her teeth perfect and straight in a way that reminds me of Noah's toothpaste-commercial teeth. Does Arthur go to school with disproportionately gorgeous human beings? No wonder he's insecure. It must be a school of supermodels.

"I like the manners and stuff." She giggles. "This *so* beats a fundraiser at the aquatic center."

"I'm sure," I say. "What was your name again?"

Her smile doesn't change when she mushroom-clouds my tenuous grasp on stability. "Breanna, but most people call me Bre."

"Who assigned you to be a lady-in-waiting?" I ask, and I can barely make my voice even, because inside the lava is mixing with dread and making me sick. My globe is already sticky with sweat between my fingers.

If Bre notices my agitation, she doesn't say anything.

"Oh, I volunteered! Honestly, it was either this or be a tavern wench and serve French fries, which, no thanks. Proximity to royalty is a huge plus."

And here, she smiles a perfect smile that I find both dazzling and completely irritating.

"Arthur mentioned you," I say. "That's why I asked."

"Oh, I *looooove* Arthur," she enthuses. "He's such a good guy."

I decide to play dumb, completely, wholly dumb. I realize this could backfire—I don't know when they last spoke or if they spoke about me at all—but I have to ask, just to see her reaction: "Are you guys together or something?"

"Me and Arthur? God, no. I'm totally with my boyfriend, Noah, and his . . . well, assets."

On cue, Noah rounds the corner from the direction of the jousting ring, his armor abnormally shiny in the high afternoon sun. Nearby, a group of three girls in Halloween-grade princess costumes collectively swoon. He catches their eyes and finger-guns them, walking toward us.

"Hey, babe," he says, leaning down to kiss Bre.

"You're sweaty," she protests. She mimes pushing him away.

"You like me sweaty," he says, shaking his hair at her.

I'm grossed out, but Bre laughs. "Ugh," she says to me, like we're conspiratorial friends. "The things I put up with."

"A knight and his princess!" A small girl wearing a huge, pointed princess hat with a long braid dangling out of the top comes careening into our small triangle. I assume she means Bre and Noah until she—with all the bossiness of a child with zero social awareness—drags me closer to Noah by my skirts.

"Picture!" she announces, holding up a cell phone that's a newer model than my own.

I shoot a worried glance to Bre, but she's only laughing at the precociousness of the little girl and Noah's obvious preening.

"Can you see me flexing in this armor, babe?"

Behind me, I hear him clanking as he changes poses with each artificial shutter click of the little girl's camera. I try to spot her parents, but if I had to guess, they're the ones sitting on a bench across from us. They're both red-faced, taking turns drinking from a too-small water bottle.

"Okay," the tiny photographer says, "now it's time for the princess and the knight to kiss."

"Oh," I say. "No, that's okay. It's—"

But suddenly Noah's lips are on my cheek. In the periphery, I can see that he's flexing the arm farthest from me.

This time I am certain Bre will be very displeased, but she is still laughing. "I need you to text me that one," she tells the girl.

I'm smiling, like *actually* smiling, at the camera when Noah announces, "I'm gonna pick you up, 'kay?"

I don't even have time for a *wait, what?* or a *I'm too heavy* before my feet leave the ground and I find myself squished—uncomfortably, I might add—against Noah's armored torso.

It's ridiculous. The whole thing. So of course I'm laughing and of course Noah looks down at me and smiles his megawatt grin and leans in for another kiss on the cheek . . .

And *of course* Arthur chooses *now* to come strumming around the corner directly toward us.

As if she can sense the discomfort when Arthur's eyes meet mine and quickly dart away, the little girl with the camera disappears in a flash of ribbon, leaving me, a proud knight, a laughing lady-in-waiting, and a very, very irritated-looking bard.

We haven't talked since the box and the song and what I now realize was an unofficial Stormsworth memorial service for Mom. I half thought he would text or call me last night, that we would clear the air.

He could tell me that he was sorry if his excitement hurt me, but Bre coming to work at faire was too good a chance to pass up. I could tell *him* that of course I want him to be happy. I want him to smile his too-large smile always, but he would just have to accept that I couldn't stand by and . . .

Watch him smile *not* at me.

"Hey, dude," Noah says. He puts me down in a smooth motion and walks over to Arthur, shadowboxing at his lute. "Can you play Metallica on that thing?"

In an impressive show of disinterest, Arthur ignores him entirely, instead staring straight at me.

I almost think he's *jealous*, and then his eyes jump to Bre and he smiles. Just a little, but it's enough.

"Your dress looks nice, Bre."

"Thanks," she grins. "Your dads are geniuses. Are you hanging out with us for the day?"

The quickest of glances back to me, but since I don't have time to adjust my features beneath his gaze, I'm frowning.

When Arthur's focus returns to Bre, it's like the sun comes out from behind a storm cloud. He's practically beaming.

"Nah, I've got to help Pops with something at home. But I'll catch you later."

He strums once and sketches a bow to Bre. He doesn't look at me before turning on his heel and plucking at the strings in what sounds like a poor rendition of Olivia Rodrigo's "Happier."

I don't have time to process, to even think about calling him back to talk, because Bre is suddenly on my left and Noah on my right.

"We should go," Bre chirps. "Schedule to keep!"

And this is how the weekend goes, with the Bre-is-charming-and-more-than-perfectly-nice-to-me show with frequent guest appearances from Noah. All the while, my brain bounces to Arthur and just as quickly away.

Bre walks me from appearance to appearance with all the grace of a true lady-in-waiting, making sure I have a water bottle, that I feel comfortable taking pictures with the passersby who hold their cell phones up in question, and generally just being a kind human.

The easiest thing would be if I hated Bre. If movies and books have taught me anything, it's that the mean girls deserve whatever they get: they deserve to lose the love interest, to be excommunicated from their social groups, to have their insides rotted by their beautiful outsides, to be hit by a bus. If I'm being honest, the existence of mean girls is a big part of the reason I've always been happy—*more than happy*—to avoid the whole actual high school thing.

But Bre is so, *so* kind. She's a lot like Arthur, really. She's careful and watchful and looks for ways to help before you even know to ask for it. And she's drop-dead gorgeous. I'm a little in love with her, I think. Dark skin, long graceful fingers, and spirals of dark hair that point down her back to a tiny waist that is accentuated by her voluminous faire skirts. She looks like Brandy's Cinderella. She looks like she belongs in these princess skirts, not me.

She's everything I want to be, everything Arthur deserves,

everything the faire-goers expect when they see a princess on the throne. Next to her, I feel frumpy in my dress in a way I haven't felt since the beginning of the summer.

But even between fighting my brain's persistent chatter about how I look, I can't help but start to really like Bre. She talks constantly, oohing and ahhing over every little thing we pass at the faire. I should find it irritating—because I've seen all of this stuff for years—but instead I can't help but scope out the path ahead to guess what will snag her attention next.

Best of all, she's the perfect distraction from where I currently find myself on the other side of the one anniversary I both dreaded and anticipated. *And* she is apparently an effective Arthur repellant.

Since the theater kids got here, I've only seen Arthur in passing, sometimes playing Adele on his lute, sometimes showing around the theater newbies, but though we've locked eyes a couple times, his eyes will fall on me, and then Bre, and then quickly flick away. Which makes the last time we spoke the anniversary, with his overly thoughtful box for my journal and the tiny glass camel.

I wonder if he buried any feelings he had for me in the box, too.

When I rode with Tim and Martin in the parade, Arthur's absence bothered me more than it should. Bre was more than happy to take his place, grinning as she blew kisses at anyone who looked our way, and for once I wasn't worried about who was looking at me. Because against my better judgment and the ruling of the coin, I found I wanted *Arthur* to be looking at me. I didn't care about anyone else.

I know why he's making himself scarce: he very obviously still has feelings for Bre, and as much as I tell myself I should be happy that he does, that I'm not going to be somebody's Juliet rebound or else die for love, it makes my stomach turn to think of it. It might not be dying, but it definitely feels like being suspended from a tree by a net.

Despite knowing this, I find it difficult to be mad at Bre. By the end of our first weekend together, I find myself enjoying having her at my side, not least of all because Noah often abandons his duties of being a knight who's supposed to be stationed near the front entrance for photo ops in order to follow us around.

If I ever thought of Arthur as a hopeless flirt, it was only because I hadn't yet met Noah and his will-flirt-with-anyone-with-lungs self. It's shameless, really, how he finds a way to lean against *anything* and make it look attractive.

He demonstrates this Sunday evening, which has always been one of my favorite times of any faire. Sunday evening tends to be the lightest because so many people have to return to work or—when it's not summer—school on Mondays. The crew that remains are often college students and older folks who have come to faires for years and know that Sunday night is their best chance to visit a less busy faire.

Noah seems eager to try his various charms out on an eager college crowd.

"Good morrow, gentlemen," he enthuses to a passing group of three guys, just as Bre and I are taking a break on a bench from walking the grounds.

"I used to keep track of stuff," I tell Bre as we both watch Noah lean an elbow on his bent knee, smoldering at the boys.

"What do you mean?"

I don't know why I said anything about the noticings, but it's too late to take it back. "Lists and stuff mostly," I say. "But if I had to make a list of all the times Noah has flirted with someone in the last three days . . ."

"You wouldn't have enough paper." Bre laughs. "Yeah, I know."

I don't ask if it bothers her, because it very evidently doesn't. Even now as he shamelessly waggles his full, black eyebrows at one of the guys, Bre looks on fondly.

"He's a good guy," she says, answering the question I won't ask. "I know he seems kind of like an airhead, but he has this way of making everyone feel at ease. I like being around people that make me feel happy. It's not going to last forever or anything. I know we'll break up when we go our separate ways for college. But right now, it's just . . . fun. Is that selfish?"

One of the guys is now attempting to pick Noah—armor and all—up at the waist. They are all laughing, trying to take a video of it on a phone.

"I don't think so," I say. "He's got his own way of making the world feel like a kinder place, so I say go for it."

Bre's smile is lopsided, and it's the dopiest I've ever seen her. It's also the prettiest I've ever seen her, as her face glows while watching Noah.

I want to ask her about Arthur, but the words get stuck in my throat when the three guys ramble off and Noah rejoins us, kissing me on the cheek and then Bre on the lips.

"My ladies," he says, and he sketches an impressive curtsy, especially considering his armor.

"Our fearless Sir Noah of Leos." I laugh.

"No, *of* Oklahoma," he says. "Remember? Leos is my last name?"

"That's not . . . ," I start, but I quickly decide it's not worth it. "Yes, exactly. Thanks, Noah."

Bre rolls her eyes at me before taking Noah's arm, and just as Noah pivots to link his other through mine—an image of Dorothy and her brainless scarecrow walking arm in arm down the yellow brick road flashes through my head—we nearly collide with Arthur.

His expression is the stormiest I've seen it since the night we first met, when he was determined to be morose and moody about being stood up. It makes sense, considering Bre—the original source of his complicated feelings—and me—probably at least a *slight* ongoing concern—are each on a side of Noah.

"Arthur, my guy," Noah says with far too much enthusiasm, unlinking arms with Bre to draw Arthur into one of those back-thumping bro hugs. "Good to see you, my man."

I've never seen Arthur's face so murderous, but all he says is, "Hey."

He won't even look at me, instead looking down at his lute. He strums one hard stroke, forceful enough that I worry a string will break.

I want him to look at me. I want to tell him how I have a new postcard from the Center of the Universe above my bed next to the ones we collected together. I want to tell him I bought him one, too, that there was only the pair left and it felt like fate.

But then I see the way he directs his murder-laser-beams at Noah, and I know deep in my gut—in the same place where I always knew that the noticings were never going to be enough to save me from grief—that he is still jealous of him and pining for Bre.

So instead, I say, "Hey," and try to put all the regrets I have into my voice.

What I wouldn't give to be *just* friends with him right now, but he won't even glance my way.

"Princess." He nods formally. "The kings have begged an audience with you tomorrow for a dress fitting."

"A fitting?" I ask.

He still doesn't meet my eyes. "Yes, I believe it is for your dress for the ball."

Even with the awkwardness, a thrill that isn't entirely excitement goes through me at the reminder. *The ball.* I keep forgetting it's a proper thing, even though there are little posters *covering* the faire advertising tickets.

Beside me, Bre makes a sound that is somewhere between a squeal and a wail.

"*Ooooh*, that reminds me, I need to stop by and see if they can whip something up for me."

Arthur meets *her* eyes, and a smile I haven't seen in I don't know how long flashes across his face.

"They've partnered with a couple of the other costumers on vendor's row to make stuff for the theater kids, since you'll be the ones serving the dinner for the fundraiser portion."

"Yes," Bre says, "but we all get to *dance* at an actual, IRL *ball*."

It kills me a little, to see Arthur laugh for her when he won't even look at me, but my insides light up all the same to hear it.

"It'll be fun," he says. His fingers drum on the bottom of his lute and he gives me the quickest of glances before half waving at us. "Gotta go."

As he walks away, Noah loudly says, "You girls are gonna be my dates. A princess and a hottie!" He pauses almost immediately. "You're a hottie, too, Maddie. A princess hottie." Another pause, and I can smell smoke as the gears in his head try—adorably—to make sense of his ridiculous statements. "But you're my princess, too, babe. So, double princess. Double hottie. Deal?"

"It's a date." I laugh.

Bre pats his arm, her ice-blue, very-time-period-inaccurate nails tapping against his armor.

"Whatever you say, Noah."

And I'm surprised at how comfortable it feels, the three of us, walking side by side as we head toward a castle in the middle of Oklahoma. I remember Tim's words, about how some humans are kinder than others, and I decide that Bre with her generosity and Noah the lovable airhead are making the world tamer just by being here.

Even though Arthur is mad at me or embarrassed by my presence or proximity to Bre, and even though my heart is still not quite sure what to do on the other side of a year without Mom, I believe she would be proud of me. I *know* she would pull on Dad to have him *come and see, come and see Madeline with her friends.*

It's almost like feeling her presence, but not quite.

CHAPTER FOURTEEN

"I JUST *CAN'T BELIEVE* I'VE NEVER BEEN to a Renaissance faire before this," Bre tells me *again* the next Saturday, the penultimate day of faire. "This is like the best thing ever. You're so lucky."

Her enthusiasm makes it doubly impossible to ignore that she *chose* not to be princess of faire and is now a lady-in-waiting. I finally get the courage to bring it up, when we're both sitting inside the castle in our little dressing room on the second floor, trying our best to cool off before the final camel joust of the season.

I want to keep Arthur out of it—make this about the faire,

not him—so of course the first words out of my mouth are "So . . . Arthur?"

Bre's entire face lights up.

"Oh my *god*! I thought you'd *never* bring it up." She flounces—actually *flounces* in her skirts like we're in a Jane Austen movie—from her seat across the room to sit beside me. "I've been *dying* to ask you when you two got together since last weekend when he was all moody and pensive and *sexy* around you when he came to tell you about your fitting."

"Oh, we're not—"

Bre cuts me off with a pretty gasp. "*No?* The imbecile. He's so obviously in love with you."

"Funny," I say, "I was going to say the same thing about him and you."

Her smile melts from an excited grin to a Mona Lisa smirk. "Okay, we absolutely should have discussed this sooner. What did he tell you? And when?"

"He mentioned at the beginning of the summer that he thought you liked him and agreed to be princess and then backed out at the last minute." Bre opens her mouth, but I can't resist adding the part I'm most curious about. "He also said that you stood him up for a date."

Bre rolls her eyes. "I'm not sure if you've noticed, but Arthur has a slight flair for the dramatic."

Her voice is so dry, I can't help but laugh. "Oh, I'm aware."

"I liked Noah all summer. Before that, even. And I know Arthur was aware of it because I *told* Arthur I liked Noah. I thought we were friends. *Just* friends. And I knew he liked me a little, but I was always careful to redirect."

"What made you change your mind about being princess, then?"

Bre leans forward, like if she's closer to me she can make me see her side more clearly.

"Noah invited me on his family's camping trip last minute. I would miss the first three weeks of Stormsworth, and it didn't seem fair to anyone for me to ask them to keep the spot empty for that long. I told Arthur all of this, but he still wanted to meet for dinner to try to convince me to not go on the trip."

"So you stood him up?" I ask, and it's the very last thing I have to possibly be cross about with Bre. If she stood up Arthur, I can happily keep a corner of my brain labeled *mean girl* and put her in it. I can pretend she isn't a person at all but a caricature of a princess I can never be and one that broke Arthur's heart.

"Of *course* not," Bre says. "He texted me and asked if I was coming and I reminded him that I couldn't because Noah and I were going to the sporting goods store to pick up last-minute things for the trip. Did he tell you I stood him up?"

It seems like an eternity ago, meeting Arthur in the dead of night in an empty Stormsworth. The particulars have mostly been sifted out of my head.

"I just know he said he waited at the restaurant for you," I say. "And that you didn't show."

"That's because I *told* him I couldn't come. But you know Arthur . . . He said, 'I'll be there if you change your mind,' or something. I can't believe he told you I stood him up." Bre laughs, and it's a kind, fond sound. "That kid: he thinks everything good that happens to him is because of fate and anything else must be a mistake."

I want to ask her more—and just *talk* to her because now that I don't unfairly hate her, I really do like her—but Tim raps on the open door.

"Ladies, may I escort you to the joust?"

"The camel joust, you mean," I say, grinning at his grimace.

"As if I will *ever* need reminding," he mutters icily.

I feel lighter than the bubbles that soar overhead from Ms. Cynthia's Bubbles New and Olde stall, though I'm not sure why. Nothing much has changed other than Bre is lovely, she isn't secretly keeping an undying love for Arthur, and for once, despite my usual hang-ups, the skirts, the makeup . . . They don't feel quite so restrictive. They feel almost natural, like maybe I *was* meant to be the Princess of Stormsworth.

When we arrive at the camel joust, I jolt a little to see Noah already at the side of the sand, puffing his full lips at a camel that could not be any more apathetic toward his coddling.

He's filling in for one of the HACKs who was too sick to ride today. Noah—of course—leapt at the chance, and when he ran to tell Bre and I about it while we were overseeing the fairy garden kids this morning, he made a loud shout of victory that all of our dainty, flower-crowned fairies immediately copied.

"*I'm finally going to be a knight!*" he shouted.

It turns out the fairy garden is not unlike the Center of the Universe in that it will echo triumphant war cries back tenfold. I saw more than one parent smile but flinch at the noise.

Maybe his pure joy is why—when it's time to pick a knight—I pick Noah instead of my usual HACK Tyler to tie my token of favor (an old bandana) to his lance. Maybe that's why, when Noah steps forward to accept it and winks at me, I wink back. Somewhere behind me, Bre laughs.

And maybe it's the elation of knowing I'm capable of making friends, of playing or flirting or being an active participant in teenagedom, but whatever the reason, I don't notice when Arthur opens the door to the royal box and makes a face, which later Bre will recount as "a truly awful scowl" that made her "fear for Noah's life."

I *do* notice when Arthur is mysteriously absent the rest of the afternoon. It worries me enough that I risk Tim's wrath and take my phone out from the hidden skirt pocket Martin made for me and shoot a text of **Hey, you okay?** It's the first text I've sent him in two weeks, and there's no answer. He doesn't even read it.

When I ask Bre if she's seen him as we walk to the evening joust, she raises an eyebrow.

"I expect he's off hitting a tree repeatedly with his lute or whatever it is bards do to de-stress."

I set down my water bottle with its sun-faded Stormsworth crest. "What? Why is he stressed?"

"You didn't notice?"

"Notice *what*?"

"To be honest, if I didn't know him, I would be concerned that he was plotting to throw both you *and* Noah in the moat after you gave him your handkerchief at the joust. Arthur looked . . . livid."

"Arthur doesn't know how to *be* livid," I say. "Look, there is no way he was pissed about that. It's just Noah. *You* are very obviously with him. What does Arthur have to be mad about?"

Bre raises an eyebrow. "I want to make it very clear that I don't feel any sort of way about any of this, but you *do* have a great laugh. If I had to guess, it was probably the laugh when you gave Noah the bandana that did it. That's when Arthur left like he was being chased by a swarm of bees."

"Noah slung *mud* on me with his lance," I say. "I was surprised! It was a surprised laugh."

Bre shrugs. "Arthur did not seem to care what kind of laugh it was."

I roll my eyes. "No offense, but that doesn't add up. *He* made me laugh like a million times this summer."

"Who understands the ways of men?" She sighs. "Not me, certainly. I'm just here for a good time."

I can't resist teasing, "With *Noah*?"

If Bre thinks I have a great laugh, it's only because she can't hear her own, hearty and full. "He's a bit of an idiot," she admits. "But he's built like a linebacker and pays when we go on dates. Like I said, I'm keeping him for now."

It's all the conversation we have time for before we arrive at the final joust of the day, the *real* joust. When we get to the box, Tim and Martin are already seated on their thrones, arguing in that whisper-hush way parents do when they think their kids can't hear.

"What is going on?" I ask.

When they see me and Bre, they break apart. Martin quickly pastes a smile on his face. Tim keeps scowling.

"It seems we are down two *real* knights," Martin says. "Not to worry: Everyone has agreed *not* to consume week-old barbecue leftovers for the remainder of the faire. It seems a good bout of food poisoning is indiscriminate of what the knight rides: camels or horses, it will take them all and lay them low."

"What are we going to do?" I ask. "Just work with the two professional guys plus Noah and be down a knight? Noah is filling in like he did for the HACKs, right?"

"Well—" Martin begins.

"We're not down a knight," Tim says. "Because—"

The trumpeters enter the jousting ring, their instruments held high. It's Martin's cue to stand at the front of our box and announce the knights as they ride in.

I think that will be the end of whatever they're arguing about as two of the regular knights ride in on their huge horses followed by Noah, but then the second substitute knight rides in and . . .

"No," I say. I turn back to look at Tim. "He is going to get hurt. Like *actually* hurt."

Tim opens his mouth, and his expression tells me he agrees, but Martin answers first. "The other knights know he is untrained. They will be careful. There was no talking him out of it. He was very insistent that if Noah could be a knight, so could he."

I don't think my mouth has closed since I saw Arthur, the armor and yellow heraldry practically swallowing his slim body whole atop a horse that somehow looks ten times larger than the others, ride into the arena.

"This is . . . This is *absurd*," I say, turning to Bre. "Can't you go down there and talk reason to him?"

I half expect Bre to look as outraged, as fearful as I do, but she's making doe eyes at Noah and her mouth is twisted up in a smile. "God, but don't they look hot on horses?"

"*Bre*."

"What?" she asks, shrugging. "There's nothing I can do about it. I'm just a lady-in-waiting."

The four knights are leading their horses to face each other in the middle of the arena, all the lances held straight to the sky—except for Arthur's, which leans at a sharp angle.

"Can he even ride?" I ask Tim.

Tim grimaces. "He had lessons."

"When? When he was six?"

Tim and Martin's silence is answer enough.

"Madeline, let him have his fun. It's not as if they are *actually* going to hurt him. The other knights know to look out for him," Bre says. "What's the worst that could happen? Look, even his parents aren't worried."

Arthur's dads shoot each other a speaking glance but don't correct her.

"It's not the others I'm worried about," I say. "He looks like he's about to topple off his horse. Nobody can save him from getting trampled."

The crowd's cheers jerk my eyes to the movement in the arena. Arthur leads his horse to the other end of the jousting ring, opposite one of the professional knights. As I watch, Arthur straightens the helmet that looks too big for his head *twice*.

"He can't even see," I tell Martin. "*Do* something."

Martin reaches up from where he now sits and pats my arm. "He'll be just fine. Let him have a go at it."

I want to spike a volleyball at his head, because my mind is conjuring up images of Arthur beneath hooves, Arthur with an arm in a sling and no way to play his precious lute or his video games or drive his terrible avocado car. And I know it's not likely that he would be *more* than injured in this farce of a joust, but my fear is enough to hurl me to the front of the box, just as the knights lower their lances and ready to charge.

"*Stop!*" I yell. "By order of the princess, I command you to stop!"

They do, both removing their helmets to look up at me. The trained knights look bored—and maybe a bit sickly green like they, too, consumed the perishable barbecue and are powering through—but Arthur's face is unreadable, stone.

If it were just us, I would tell Arthur *exactly* what I'm thinking: that he's being stupid and foolish and careless, that this is no way to impress Bre or—if Bre is right about him being jealous of my laughter, which is *absurd*—me.

But it's not just us. The audience is looking up at me, their faces interested in what could cause a royal to put a stop to their games.

They think it's part of the show, I realize, and I'll have to make it one.

For once, I don't feel any judgmental stares and the silent questions of *how can* she *be the princess.* I don't worry about whether this dress is the most flattering of my princess dresses. I don't worry about looking stupid in front of a crowd of people. I don't suck in my stomach. I don't see or hear anything but Arthur in his too-large armor and my own heartbeat thumping in my ears.

"Good people of Stormsworth. There is a threat upon your royal family. The exiled sorcerer"—I am forced to pause as I search my empty brain for a name—"the Unwise Old Wizard has sworn revenge for his exile." Behind me, Martin coughs out what might be a hidden laugh, but I press on, making my voice louder. "He could attack us at any time. I ask you: Will you sacrifice a champion of my choosing for our protection? You will have the thanks of your kings and the love of your princess."

My voice rings out loud and clear, echoing the slightest bit, and for a moment—as my voice comes back to me—it feels like I've created an artificial Center of the Universe in a jousting ring instead of Tulsa.

The crowd doesn't react, but then Tim—*Tim*, not Martin—stands up beside me and yells, "Huzzah!" and the crowd, eager to please the royals (and probably just to shout huzzah), answers in kind.

"You must choose your champion to protect us," Martin says from behind me.

I raise my voice once more, pointing down to Arthur. "The yellow knight shall have the honor of guarding our box during the joust. And the fair red knight will take his place and joust twice. Find you this agreeable, good sirs?"

The red knight, one of the last remaining professionals, nods and yells, "Sure," before remembering himself and correcting, "It would be an honor to fight for our majesties."

"Good," I say. "It is done. Enjoy the festivities, good people of Stormsworth. Sir Yellow, your presence is required in the box immediately."

I've been so busy trying to patch over Arthur's removal for the audience, I haven't had a chance to really look at him since he took his helmet off. But now I have nowhere to look but his eyes as they burn up at me, angry and hot, but he knows that I have effectively killed any chance he has of competing. It wouldn't make sense to the faire-goers, and it would just disrupt the whole joust even more if he put up a fight.

If he was anyone else, he might hurl the reins of his horse at one of the squire attendants and throw his helmet against the ground in anger. But even though he is very clearly mad, Arthur dismounts, pats the horse's side, loosely passes over the reins, and then trudges out of the arena toward our box.

The helmet with the yellow feather is still under his arm when he enters the box, coming to stand as far away from me and Bre as possible, near his dads, while the joust begins below us.

It feels like we're on display in the box, which in a sense we are even as the audience is completely absorbed by the jousting. I don't have the chance to call Arthur to my side, to explain and ask *him* to explain what it was he planned to accomplish by entering into the joust with zero training.

Instead, I am left to watch his profile from my periphery. It's strange, because I've seen him from this exact angle so many times in his car on road trips, but now it's like he's an entirely different person. His jaw is raised, his eyebrows lowered, and without his sunglasses and a lollipop stick jutting from the corner of his mouth, he almost looks like a knight who shouldn't be crossed instead of a bard who frequently crosses others.

When the joust is over—with a triumphant but very exhausted red knight—I assume Arthur is going to sulk back to the castle. But as soon as his dads leave the box and the final patrons leave the stands—two tired-looking parents with *five* little kids—he leaves Bre's side, dashing to the low fence of the arena, his armor clinking with every step.

"Noah!" he calls. "I challenge you to hand-to-hand combat!"

Noah looks up from where he is trying to knock muddied sand from his boot in the arena. "Huh? But the fight's over?"

"For honor!" Arthur shouts. "And glory!"

It would be a more impressive pronouncement if his foot didn't catch on the top rung of the fence and cause him to faceplant into the sand.

Noah rushes forward to help him, grabbing Arthur beneath the armpits and dragging him upward. Arthur pushes him away, snatching a wooden sword from the weapons rack and turning to face Noah.

"Dude," Noah says as Arthur begins circling in the sand. "You know I play football, right?"

Noah's arms are up, unarmed, but Arthur still leaps at him, somehow missing Noah entirely and landing in a small heap before springing back to his feet with his muddied wooden sword held at an angle that I *think* is meant to be threatening.

"Yeah, well, I play the lute."

Oh, for Christ's sake.

Part of me wants to put a stop to this, to stand up and find the royal, commanding voice I used to make Arthur leave the ring to now make them put down the swords. But a bigger part of me, the immature will-surely-be-chastised-by-Fatima-when-I-call-her-later part of me, wants to watch Arthur get lightly pummeled.

If he wants to be injured so badly, who am I to stop him?

It doesn't take much effort on Noah's part. Arthur, for all his bluster, hasn't moved his left leg since he stood back up. That doesn't stop him from waving the sword at Noah and yelling what I guess are supposed to be medieval taunts, though.

"Have at thee, you foul fiend," he says. "My mettle is stronger than yours."

Noah blinks. "Your sword is wood, though. Not metal."

Arthur doesn't pause to explain. "I'm named after an ancient king who united the kingdoms and had a magic sword. Is *your* sword magical?"

Noah laughs. "That sounds messed up. I'm not comparing swords with you, my guy."

Bre, who is still munching on popcorn she bought from a walking vendor during the joust, leans over and offers some to me. "Should we stop them?" I ask, grabbing a handful.

"God, no." Bre says. "I wish I could say it's because this is kind of hot, but it's honestly so pathetic, I just want to see how it plays out."

She's not wrong. A second later, it becomes abundantly clear that Arthur has not moved because he has done something to his ankle. There will be no fighting for him today.

"Arthur—" I begin, moving toward him. "Hey, let's get you back to your house, okay?"

His jaw is clenched, and he's sweating like crazy in his armor. "Can't," he says.

"Is it that bad?" I ask.

Arthur opens his mouth, and for the first time in what feels like forever, he locks eyes with me and half smiles. "I do believe I'm going to faint, Gwen."

"You're *not* going to—"

Noah might be a bit of a dolt, but he's fast on his feet. He catches Arthur, armor and all, and scoops him up in his arms so quickly, it takes me at least five full seconds to realize what's happened.

"Did . . . He really fainted," I say. "Like, *actually* fainted."

"Good catch, babe," Bre says.

"Thanks, babe."

"Guys, he *fainted*. Can we save the congratulations for later?"

Bre nods. "He probably just needs some water. Let's get him to the castle."

"Babe," Noah says. "Do you think if I kiss him, he'll wake up? Like in movies?"

"Only one way to find out," Bre says, just as I say, "Noah, *no*."

CHAPTER FIFTEEN

ARTHUR IS IN PAJAMAS ATOP HIS bed that evening when Martin taps on the door and says quietly, "You have a visitor, son."

"I don't want to see anyone," he says.

"It's me," I say, and from the sliver of space around Martin, I can see Arthur's eyebrows lower farther, his face focused on the console in his hand. I bet he's playing *Splatterbomb*.

"Especially not you," he says. "Come back when I'm manly and haven't swooned like a maiden with a touch of the vapors."

"I'll leave you two alone," Martin says. "And son: remember what we discussed earlier."

When the door closes softly behind me, I don't know what to do with my body. I've changed out of my princess-wear, but instead of putting on one of the cute outfits, I slipped on the ratty pair of sweatpants and an old shirt. My hair is still wet from the shower I absolutely *had* to take to get the sweat off me, and I just now am remembering that I forgot to rub off the acne cream on my chin.

Lovely.

"You can sit down," Arthur says, still not looking up from his screen. He scoots over conspicuously on the bed. "My ankle isn't broken or anything. Just sprained. And Pops says I probably fainted from dehydration more than anything else."

I come and sit on the edge, as far away from him as I can. I've never been in his bedroom. The walls are a soft shade of green beneath the layers and layers of band posters. I didn't even know band posters were actually a thing people bought, but Arthur has at least two dozen crammed onto the windowed wall beside his bed.

Above him, but beneath one of those cheesy black-and-white canvas photos of a very small (adorable) Arthur and a significantly younger Tim and Martin, our postcards are thumbtacked to the wall. Unlike mine, they're a little off-center, like maybe he planned for there to be more added later.

"I'm not mad at you," he says, and I drop my eyes from the mementos of our adventures.

"I find that hard to believe. You haven't talked to me in days. Not since the box."

Arthur blows a long stream of air from his lips. "I'm *not* mad. It's just . . ."

"You're upset that Bre is still with Noah," I finish for him. "And maybe you're a little upset that we all hang out together. I get it. But I must warn you: having spent two whole weekends with them, they're pretty devoted to each other."

Arthur's blinking is so comical, so slow, I worry that it's some sort of sign of a concussion. Maybe he hit his head against Noah's armor when he fell.

"You think that I still like *Bre?*"

"I mean, it seems pretty obvious," I say. "You were so excited to have the theater group come here—"

"—because they are my *friends* and it sucks that their original plans got canceled."

"But then you looked ready to strangle Noah every time he touched Bre—"

"Every time he touched *you*," Arthur says, and now he's tossed the video game to the side and is leaning toward me. "You *flirted* with him. All summer long I've been so *stupidly* careful to not cross any lines, to try to make sure you felt comfortable and safe and all the things I *knew* you needed to feel because Stormsworth was different and your mom's anniversary and then day *one* of him being at faire, he's *kissing you, Maddie*."

"On the cheek!" But Arthur doesn't stop.

"You let that . . . that . . . walking pile of tin *pick you up* and *kiss you*."

He breaks off, collects himself, and says more calmly, but still passionately, "I like *you*. I liked you from the second I saw you wandering around Stormsworth. I liked you before I knew you liked Tootsie Pops and before I knew that you collected facts and poems and things you noticed. I liked you before I saw your necklace. I liked you because of *you*. Not because of how I felt about Breanna or anything else. I liked you because you noticed *me*. Is that so wrong?"

"I—"

"And then you noticed Noah," he says. "Stupid Noah with his stupid rippling pectorals or whatever, and his stupid thick neck, and his stupid thighs that are bigger than my rib cage. And how am I supposed to compete with that? I couldn't with Bre, and I couldn't with you."

"Do you want to know *why* I couldn't like you?" I say, and my voice is rising to meet his, angry and broken and hurt. Because this feels like it's all my fault, but it's too late for me to back down. I don't know how. "I flipped the coin. And I know it's a stupid reason not to like someone, but that's why I was coming to tell you I *did* like you anyway. Like you, like you, probably. Probably even more than that. But then I came to the castle and you were *so* excited about Bre and the theater group and then you said that terrible thing about my clothes not fitting her and—"

"That's *not* what I meant, and you know it," Arthur says. "You know *me*. At some point you're going to have to stop assuming the worst about yourself and everyone else around you."

"Funny," I say, fuming. "I could say the same about you."

We're both breathing hard, furious, with our faces inches away from each other. When did we get so close?

Arthur's eyes drop to my lips and I wonder if he even notices, because his gaze doesn't move when he says, "I think it's probably best if you go home."

I snort. "Am I going home because you need space? Or am I going home because you're afraid to finish this conversation and hope that if you make me leave, we won't have to?"

I can feel his breath on my lips when he says, "Both."

Now *I'm* looking at *his* lips, all pillowy and soft and . . . And I'm thinking very unfeminist thoughts, like he should just kiss me to end this argument and every argument.

I'm thinking I wish he would have kissed me sooner.

Like he can hear me, Arthur leans forward, but then quickly jerks back, rolling onto his side and literally turning his back on me.

"I'm tired," he says, a clear dismissal.

As I leave, no song—sung or hummed or strummed— follows me out the door.

* * *

As far as the end of faires go—besides my sinking, convoluted feelings about a certain bard—this one is fairly anticlimactic.

I come home, Dad and I share our customary end-of-faire dinner of whatever local burger place has the highest Yelp reviews, I shower, I hair mask, I lotion. My eyes skim a couple episodes of the adventures of Adelina and Cornelius. I sleep.

I expect the next day to be usual, too, packing up the rest of our stock and preparing to go to the next stop.

I'm trying to forget about the ball. Despite my best efforts, it's not going well.

Yesterday, when I changed into my regular clothes and left my princess dress behind, I ignored the garment bag with the beautiful ball gown that Martin and Tim had pinned and tucked to perfection.

It's not a pity party. It's a ready-to-move-on party. An I'm-tired-of-trying-so-hard-to-fit-in party. To say nothing of Arthur and the way he dismissed me. I can't say that I blame him.

I thought Dad knew nothing about the ball, but when he comes in and sees me in my bunk, he stands below, eyes darting to me with my headphones and down to his feet until I pause the music and say, "Yes?"

"Maddie," he says. "The ball?"

"What about it?"

"You're the princess. Aren't you invited?"

"Not going," I say.

"Why?"

I move my thumb to turn my music back on. "Not interested. I texted Tim and Martin and told them I was sick. There's some bad barbecue going around, you know. You go if you want. Have fun."

Ha. As if Dad has any interest in a ball.

Only a few seconds of music pass before Dad reaches up to take my phone from my loose-fingered grip and pauses it.

"Hey—" I say.

"You should go," he says. "Your mother . . . She would want you to go."

"She's not here," I say, and it stings a little, but not so much that I clam up. "I don't mean that melodramatically," I say. "But she's not here, so why should I go if that's what *she* would want?"

Dad's lips move, but nothing comes out. I wait, then wait a bit more, and I'm about to ask for my phone back when he finally says, "*I* want you to go."

For some reason, this makes me mad.

"Why?" I ask. "Why do you—the master of hiding from everyone other than your oldest faire friends—want me to go to a *literal ball* with a bunch of strangers who are too obsessed with themselves to know if I'm there?"

Dad blinks, and I wonder if I've hurt him until he says, "I'll go with you."

Now it's my turn to blink. "Um, what?"

"I'll go with you," he repeats. "As your escort. If you'll have me."

"*Why?*"

Dad doesn't cry very often. He's not one of those never-cries people, but it's almost like he doesn't care enough about stuff since Mom died to let anything else bother him.

But he's crying now.

"I miss your Mom," he says. "And I worry that means I've let you miss *me* this past year."

"Dad—"

"No, let me finish." He breathes shakily, and though I know it's hard for him, he holds my eyes when he says, "I'm sorry if I haven't been there in the way you've needed me."

"You had to work," I say. "You can't blame yourself for that."

"Yes," he says, "but I still could have been here when I *was* here."

I don't argue with that. Instead, I say, "It's okay, Dad. Really. And you don't have to go to the ball to make it up to me. I just don't want to go."

Dad shakes his head, disbelieving. "You still haven't said why."

In the interest of avoiding an hour of catchup or, worse, another talk about *relationships* with my father, I tell him the truth. Well, the half-truth.

"The coin said I shouldn't."

Which isn't entirely correct. It said I shouldn't like-like Arthur, and if I go to the ball tonight, even though he is still mad at me, there's no guarantee that I will come out of it without shouting my feelings at him.

Dad's eyebrows shoot up. "You flipped it?"

I sigh. "I've flipped it twice this summer."

"Huh," he says. "I didn't know you did that."

"Yeah."

"So it said no ball, huh?"

I nod.

"And you listened?"

I gesture around me at the bunk and then at my pajamas. "Looks like it."

"You know, the coin was never supposed to be an edict. Your mother and I never used it that way."

I sit up a little straighter, agitation flooding my fingers. Suddenly I want to fidget with something, which of course reminds me of Arthur. "You did, too," I argue. "You said you flipped it when you decided to get married and to have me and to join the faire and all that stuff."

"We did," Dad says. "We just didn't listen."

I blink. "Excuse me?"

Dad motions for me to come down to the bottom bunk. I do, and he folds his huge form in half and sits next to me, his hands carefully placed on his knees. After a second of thought, he moves one to my knee. It covers the entire thing and I feel like a little kid.

"The coin *did* come up in the affirmative when we flipped to see if we should get married, but the rest of it . . . It was a no, kid."

My brain is short-circuiting, the synapses flashing bright as they wink out completely.

"But . . . But Mom said it told you what to do. *You* said that."

"In a way it did." Dad sighs. "We knew we wanted to join the circuit. We knew we wanted *you*. Flipping was more of a way of making sure. We knew before it landed what our answer was going to be, both of us. But sometimes you do something just to make sure, you know? We were surer in the second before the coin 'told us' something than we were before we flipped it."

I stand up just enough to reach above me and pull out the coin.

"But what about all that stuff about only flipping it once and how it has magic powers and stuff?"

Dad's head tilt is made all the more comical by the limited space of the bottom bunk. "Magic . . . powers?"

"Yeah," I say. "That's what you and Mom told me growing up. That's what you said."

"Sounds like your mother must have embellished a bedtime story or two," he says. "It's a family heirloom, but it's not magical."

I blink hard, trying to stop the emotions swirling inside of me from bubbling over. It could go either way, the hurricane: I could laugh like a maniac or sob, and I don't want to do either one in front of Dad and freak him out.

"Maddie, you know I love you, right?"

"I know you love me, Dad," I manage.

"So, let me show you, okay? Trust me. Forget the coin. Come to the ball with me. We'll go together, the princess and the humble book maker." His smile is watery, but it's not small. "Besides, Neil told me the catering is worth more than a king's ransom."

I count to ten. Then count again.

"We're only going for the food," I finally say. "We eat, then we go. That's it."

Because I'm still trying to wrap my brain around the coin thing.

And because I don't want to see Arthur, and maybe I can get in there and get out fast enough to avoid him. And because I *want* to see Arthur, and maybe I can go and tell him everything I meant to tell him before the theater kids came to Stormsworth.

"For the food," Dad agrees.

CHAPTER SIXTEEN

YOU WOULD THINK THAT BY NOW I would not be in the business of underestimating the lavishness of Tim and Martin when it comes to all things faire, and yet here I am, stunned.

The entire bottom floor of the castle has been rid of the usual overstuffed leather couches, the rugs, the bits that made it a home. In their place, at the entrance, are suits of armor leading to the grand ballroom that usually functions as a living area and dining room. Huge chandeliers dripping with artificial candles and pearls soar above our heads in the entrance, and from the spot where Dad and I are rooted, we can hear music and laughter pouring from the room.

We're late. The posters said the ball started at six and it's nearly eight. There are no heralds ready to announce us, no medieval dressed attendants or knights or ushers pointing the way. We're alone in the entrance, a girl in a peasant dress from Target and her father, who is wearing his single pair of dress pants.

"We could still go home," I say. "It's not too late."

Dad looks at me. "We should go and see. For Mom."

"And for our stomachs?" I ask smiling. Even in the entrance, the smells of spices, herbs, and bread reach us, and despite my nerves and doubts that we should be here at all, I find that I'm starving.

"For the food," Dad intones again.

The room looks impossibly larger. Tables line the perimeter of the room, laden with all the sources of the sweet and savory scents. It looks like there are at least one hundred people, some dressed in modern cocktail dresses and suits, some in medieval garb, all eating from plastic plates that look wooden and shuffling around the dance floor to the gentle sounds of a string quartet.

Silently, I tally the many, *many* historical inaccuracies, starting with Noah's sports coat paired with medieval leather boots and ending with the DJ I can already see setting up his gear to the side of the quartet. I wonder how much of a fit Tim threw over the latter, but when I spot him and Martin sitting on makeshift thrones presiding over the soiree, Tim only looks besotted with his smiling dark and handsome king.

It takes me a moment to find their young bard, if only because I did not expect him to be sitting beside them.

He's in a prince costume, one of the outfits I saw on a mannequin at the beginning of the summer when he was still Teenager #3 and not Arthur. His dads' costume magic must be amplified on their offspring, because his long silver tunic and red-striped vest somehow make him look more the part of the brooding hero than the playful bard.

Not for the first time—and surely not the last—I wonder how I ever thought he wasn't drop-dead gorgeous.

My heart is in my throat, and I'm agonizing over what to say when suddenly I feel myself yanked sharply sideways.

"Not so hard, babe," Bre says. "Don't dislocate her arm."

"You said go grab her," Noah says. "So, I grabbed her."

Dad, who had the presence of mind to let go of me, follows us behind the large potted tree.

"Maddie?" he asks.

"Sorry, Mr. Princess, sir," Noah says. "But we've gotta get her ready for the ball. Babe got her dress ready and everything."

Bre shrugs at my questioning glance. "I figured you were running late, but I didn't think you'd be *this* late."

Dad looks at me. "Are these your friends?"

I look at Bre with her beautiful gown and Noah in the tunic beneath his sports coat that stretches conspicuously across his chest and hides zero percent of his muscles. "I think so."

"Then you go have fun," Dad says. "I'm going to go see if that's a punch fountain I spot."

* * *

I hope Dad found some friends to talk to, because my second-rate fairy godmothers are going to take approximately sixteen hundred hours to get me ready. Not that I'm helping.

"Just put it *on*, Madeline," Bre says for the third time.

"What's wrong with what I'm wearing?"

I expect Bre to answer, but it's Noah who gently pushes me behind the changing screen with my grand finale ball gown.

"You're a princess," he tells me. "You gotta dress like it."

Maybe it's unfair to call them second-rate, because in the span of fifteen minutes, my ball gown is on, Bre twists my hair into some fancy updo that she makes look deceptively easy in the mirror, and my makeup—applied by both Noah and Bre with lots of *looks good, babe* thrown in for good measure—is the most flawless I've seen it since Martin did it the first week of faire. The only thing I insist on keeping is my necklace, forgoing the jewelry I made to match the dress myself.

This feels like taming the world, and I want the globe to be here to see it.

"Now to take you to dance with prince charming." Bre smiles. She straightens my tiara and nods, satisfied.

"Oh, you want me to dance with her, babe? I thought we were taking her to Arthur?"

I snicker at the look Bre shoots me. "I *meant* Arthur," she tells him. "You're my knight in shining armor, remember?"

"I'm not wearing my armor, though."

Even though my stomach is a pit of nerves mixed with some anxious lava that threatens to crawl up my throat, I can't help but laugh.

When they lead me down a hallway I've never been to, I assume it's because they know a different way to the ballroom. They've miscalculated, though, and the door they shove me through opens wide onto a balcony overlooking the moat with its fairies and dragons and the sleeping Stormsworth beyond.

I turn to walk back into the long hallway, but the door is already shut behind me, making Bre's voice muffled when she calls, "Make good choices!"

"*Guys*," I call, and I'm about to knock on the door when something—maybe the wind, maybe fate—makes me turn.

He's here. I don't know how they knew he was here, but here he is, sitting with his knees bent before him on the raised stone of the balcony, looking out at Stormsworth and the endless Oklahoma sky. I never thought of this part of the country as being particularly romantic. It's rather flat and sparse in the way of plants and trees, but there is something boundless about being under such an open sky, something freeing and heady and full of possibility.

Maybe if I had better eyesight, I could see straight to wherever Mom lives now. If I could squint hard enough, focus hard enough, I wonder if I could see her smile.

I *can't* see it, of course, but I swear I almost feel it when I gently tap on Arthur's shoulder.

He doesn't move.

"You could have startled me," he says, his lack of movement indicating he clearly is *not* startled. "I could have fallen to my death."

"I would have grabbed you before you fell," I say.

"Sure, Madeline," he says, still not looking at me. His voice is the dullest I've ever heard it.

"Hey," I say, and I gently turn his shoulder toward me so he has to look me in the eye. "You're not the only one who gets to be angry here."

"Sure I am," he says, dropping my gaze. "You really think everything this summer was just because I needed a replacement for Bre, don't you?"

When I don't answer—because I'm trying to find the right words and they're not coming—Arthur looks at me again, shaking his head at what he must see. "You do. I *know* you do."

"It's not that," I say. When I step away from him, my skirts whirl around my ankles. "I guess I just . . ."

Arthur comes off the wall in a shockingly fast unfolding of limbs, especially considering I can see the medical tape wrapped tightly around his ankle. "What? Let yourself have fun? Let yourself open up a little? Let yourself *live* instead of trying to write every single thing down in your journal? Tell me you didn't enjoy this summer. Tell me you didn't love the zoo and the fake Stonehenge and the sunglasses and the suckers. If you can *honestly* say that you hated it, that you felt dragged along from beginning to end, then I'll shut up. I'll leave. I won't bother you anymore, if that's what you think I'm doing."

"Arthur," I say, but he keeps going. I wonder how long he's kept his own lava bottled up, because it's erupting almost too quickly for me to keep up.

"You know what really gets me?" he presses on. "The Juliet comment. Which is really, really funny that you see yourself that way, because does anyone even *remember* Rosaline? No. Not the audience, not Romeo, because the second he *saw* Juliet, it was endgame."

"Yeah, literally," I mutter. But if Arthur hears my smartass comment, he doesn't stop to acknowledge it.

"Is it his fault they were fated? Is it his fault he had a crush that ended badly just before he met Juliet? Should they not have loved each other at all because he should have had more of a . . . a buffer between the two?"

Now seems to be a bad time to bring up their inevitable-death thing again, but Arthur must be able to read it on my face, because he says, "Yes, I *know* it's a really poor comparison, but *you picked it*, not me. If it were up to me, we would be like Princess Buttercup and Westley or somebody who was fated *and* gets to live in the end."

I can tell he's going to keep ranting—forever, if I let him, I think—so I interrupt, making my voice louder to compete with his. "You keep saying that. How do you know we were *fated*? How are you so sure? Because yeah, I should have maybe told you we were friends instead of trying to self-protect or whatever, but I still . . ."

My voice trails off as Arthur brings his hand to his neck and dips it below his tunic. I'm about to ask what he's doing, concerned that he's going to faint again, when he does the impossible.

He pulls my necklace from his tunic, a tiny globe suspended at the end of a gold chain.

My own hand leaps to my neck, where *my* necklace is still fastened in place, the globe sitting just below my collarbone.

My thoughts are running in a thousand different directions.

"How . . ."

"Once upon a time," he says, and it's the bard voice he uses for the small kids at faire, "there was a young prince who lived in a plain old house." His eyes burn into mine. "But even though the house was plain, one of his dads would disappear for days on end, always leaving with a big red trunk with wheels.

"And the boy would ask where the trunk came from, what was in it, and his dad would say, 'When you're older.' His pops would watch him, of course, while Dad was away, but one day, in junior high, the boy had a particularly hard day at school. The other kids made fun of his squeaky voice. They made fun of him having two dads instead of one. And distraught at his son's tears, Pops took him out of school for the day, put the boy in the car, and drove far away to a land where castles were real and knights still rode horses and royalty still had fabulous outfits.

"But they didn't stop at the castle or the joust. Instead, the boy's pops took him straight to a stall with a curtain over the door, and there, beneath a beard and a slouchy wizard hat and surrounded by smoke, sat his beloved dad."

I don't know how to feel, but I take a step closer, like Arthur is physically drawing me closer with his words.

He continues, adopting a deep voice that is a dead ringer for Martin's. "'It's just pretend,' the boy's dad said. 'But sometimes pretend can help us with the truth.'

"The boy didn't understand," Arthur says. "Not really, but he was so excited to see the faire and his dad dressed as a wizard—and to have missed a day of school to do it—he wanted something to remember it by. When his dad finally let him look in the trunk, he saw a tiny globe of the earth like the ones at school hanging on a chain."

I let out a shuddering breath.

"When he asked if he could keep it, his dad smiled and said, 'I only had two of those necklaces, and it looks like both have found their homes in the same day. I'll tell you what I told the young lady who has the other: Tame the world, son. No one else is going to do it for you.'"

Arthur's eyes refocus on mine. "I did lie to you," he says. "I said the first thing I noticed about you was your Gwen hair, but it wasn't. I saw the globe and I knew what it was. I knew it was the other half of the matching set. And I just . . ." He breaks off and laughs, finally losing the smoothness of his story-telling voice. "I knew, Maddie. And then I got to know you and from the second you sat beside me in the car and put on those sunglasses, I. *Knew.*"

"Because of fate?" I ask.

His eyes are bright in the torchlight.

"Because of you. And fate. And the Tootsie Pops. And the hair. And the way you fought so hard to not be my friend."

"What did that have to do with anything?" I ask.

We're close again, almost like we were on his bed last night. If I were a little taller—and if my ball gown weren't so wide and my bust so large—our matching necklaces could probably touch.

"The lady protested too much, I think," Arthur smiles. "If you didn't care, you would have agreed and just . . . not cared. But you *did* care. So you fought it."

His smile eases the tightness in my chest, the hum in my brain. There is too much to process, and it's made all the harder because I'm in a ridiculously poufy dress.

I don't know what else to say, so I say the first thing that pops into my head. "I have a story, too," I say. "And it's about a girl with a globe necklace and a coin. She . . ." I stop, fumbling for words, because I'm not Arthur and smooth and quick on my feet. But he waits patiently, of course, and his hand drifts to mine and takes hold.

"She flipped the coin early in the summer. I think—I think she must have known even then what the boy could mean to her. But she was scared: because she missed her mom and didn't want to miss anyone ever again, and because she let the world tame her instead of the other way around.

"I—she—said she didn't believe in fate because fate had been cruel to her, and she didn't want to give it a chance to be cruel again."

I'm picking through my thoughts, trying to sort them out, when Arthur whispers, "And now?"

I breathe in deeply and then let the air out on a sigh. I drop the storytelling voice. "Dad told me that he and Mom used the coin to confirm what they already knew, not to tell them *what* to do. So . . . maybe it's fate, but also not? Maybe fate is what happens after you choose something for yourself?"

Arthur takes another step impossibly closer, his voice deep as he takes my other hand. "And what do you choose now?" he asks. "Are we friends, then, Gwen?"

I pretend to think about it, and his eyes narrow.

"We already have matching necklaces," I say. "I guess there's no going back."

"Nope." He pops the *P.* "Only forward."

And then his hands are on my waist, and I'm not thinking about anything but how I *swear* I can feel their warmth through the layers of fabric.

"Maddie," he breathes, his head tilting downward. "*How* good of friends are we, do you think?"

I think about saying *very.* I think about being snarky and telling him to go ask his already-good-friend fate. But in the end, I know deep in my bones what taming the world looks like.

For a moment, I'm standing outside of myself, letting the everything-ness of the evening, of the past year, of my life wash over me: of Arthur, yes, but also of my mom and how she and Dad met at faire, the coin they ignored, the love of poetry she passed on to me, meeting Arthur, our tiny globes, and the way everything has boiled down to this.

He's looking at my lips again, like he has done so many times before, but this time I'm looking back. Maybe taming the world means liking this boy, and maybe letting him like me back.

He shifts toward me, his already parted lips opening farther. "You don't have to—"

I stand up on tiptoe and pull on our joined hands to bring his lips to mine, cutting off whatever he was going to say.

It's urgent, less of a peck and more of an accidental collision, two meteors orbiting a planet that just so happen to be in the same exact space at the same exact time. Beneath my wandering fingers, I can feel the way his neck warms and— when he grabs my hand and pulls it down to his chest—his necklace nudges my thumb.

When we pull away, his eyes are bright and his breathing fast.

"So," Arthur says. "Like, good enough friends to go to Marfa and look at the mysterious floating lights?"

"Absolutely not."

"*Gwen*, it's cultural."

"*Arthur*, it's really not."

I know when he opens his mouth it's to argue, so I try my new Arthur-quieting technique of kissing him instead. This time it's a little less clumsy, a little more of something I can't name, but it works.

* * *

Of the two of us, Arthur looks the most happy-but-dazed for the remainder of the ball. We don't get to dance together for more than one slow dance, and his sprained ankle makes it the least romantic dance that has ever happened, because he keeps dragging his foot and it keeps getting caught in my skirts.

And maybe it's the culmination of like thirty different confessions at once—Arthur and his secret of the matching necklace, me and the realization that the coin is not, in fact, magical, and that we have probably been more than friends for a while—but I feel lighter. I feel beautiful in my gown. I don't feel the least bit self-conscious or awkward or out of place.

Even when Fatima video-calls my phone and demands to be introduced to Arthur, Bre, and Noah.

Even when Dad asks to dance with me and it's possibly even more stumbling a dance than the one Arthur and I shared.

Even when Martin comes forward and—seeing Arthur's necklace resting on his shirt—kisses my cheek and steals the uneaten non-medieval chocolate chip cookie from my hand.

When I protest, he leans down and whispers knowingly into my ear, "Magic is not free." I take the cookie back and say, "I'll un-tame the world if you touch my dessert again."

And even when the night is over and I worry—just a little—that Arthur is going to want to have some heavy Romantic-with-a-capital-R moment to cap off the night and we instead go to the basement with Bre and Noah and play *Splatterbomb* until our fingers are numb and Noah falls asleep slumped against my side, I feel nothing but right.

If this is my fate, with Noah's snoring in one ear, with Dad and Arthur's parents laughing somewhere upstairs echoing in the other, with Arthur and Bre cursing each other out on op-posing *Splatterbomb* teams, and with Arthur's crown and my tiara balanced precariously next to each other on the arm of a sofa . . . I'll take it.

EPILOGUE

I DON'T WANT TO FLIP THE COIN in Britomart, but I *do* want to flip it.

Arthur must have anticipated this turn of events without my mentioning it, because the morning after the ball, he is at my door with his key ring spinning around his finger.

"Fancy a drive, Gwen?"

"Please," I say. "Have you been to this park?" I ask Arthur.

"A couple times," he says. "It's just a regular park."

"Perfect," I say. "Let's go."

This morning, before Arthur came to pick me up, Dad

cooked us both breakfast and insisted we eat together at the table. Britomart will smell like bacon for a week because he forgot to prop open the door, but it was worth it to sit in an awkward-but-not-too-awkward silence with him for most of our meal.

"Have I mentioned I like him?"

I took a sip of orange juice. "Who?"

"Arthur."

"Yeah, he's nice," I said.

Dad made a gruff noise that sounded like an affirmative. "He reminds me of your mother."

"Yeah," I said. "He's a good guy."

Another mumbling sound from Dad, and I thought that would be the end of it, but he said, "You're a lot like me, kid."

I put down my fork, abandoning my last bite of eggs. "What are you saying?"

Dad shrugged. "Nothing, I guess. Just that a bit like me and a bit like your mom seems to have worked before."

"We're not getting married or anything, Dad."

"You're too young," he said, like that's the only reason.

It's not, of course. There's the fact that we've only known each other for a couple of months and we spent at least a quarter of that wary of each other, or at least I was wary of Arthur. And then another quarter was spent with mixed feelings and hurt feelings and in-between feelings that had a lot to do with each other, but also nothing at all.

But that quarter where we laughed and road tripped and shared postcards and quiet moments with memento boxes by trees . . .

"What happens to us?" Arthur asks—like he can read my mind—and I'm surprised it has taken him this long to ask.

"I don't know," I say. We are standing on a small, weathered dock that juts out into a pond that might have once been a lake. Ducks swim through the heavy green algae beneath us. I take the coin out of my pocket and dump it from its pouch into my hand. "Should we flip for it?"

Arthur's grin is slow. "Heads, we stay in touch. I road trip to see you at any and all faires that are less than five hours away."

"And tails?"

"Tails, we follow each other on Instagram, like each other's posts for a while, and then you ghost me and pretend I don't exist when you become a major fashion influencer with millions of followers."

"That seems—"

"Wait," Arthur interrupts. "I'm not done. So you have this major following, right? And then one day you decide you're going to start making your own line of jewelry and it starts selling like crazy because it's amazing and also you're an *Influencer* with a capital *I*. And then, when you need to start your own stores to sell your stuff and keep up with demand, you think, 'Hm. What should I call this?' And then you think fondly of our one golden summer together. And you call it"—he pauses and stretches his hands out in front him slowly, like he's unfurling a banner—"Marfa Lights Jewelry."

I groan. "I don't care if we flip it and the coin is literally abducted by aliens that spell out 'go to Marfa' with their UFOs. I'm not going."

Arthur clutches at his chest dramatically. "But, Gwen, my love, it's fate."

"You're absurd," I say, "and I'm flipping this."

I'm about to when he stills my hand. When I look up at him questioningly, he leans forward and kisses me.

"You can flip all the coins in the world," he says, "but it's going to take more than fate to get rid of me."

I smile. "Coincidentally, I don't really believe in fate."

Arthur's smile is blinding. "So you say."

In the end, I do flip the coin. For one glorious second, it hangs as if suspended between us, Arthur and me.

In that second, I imagine all sorts of possibilities and let all of the variations of what could be roll out before me like an impossible atlas. There are so many options, so many ways this could go, and no routine or single choice will guarantee a particular destination.

Another Lark poem flashes me by; this time I swear I can hear Mom's voice reading it to me as it does:

All flowers are beautiful in their time,
But none bloom so brightly—so obstinately—as those planted
in the soil of grief and watered by stupid, irrational, inexorable
hope.

When the coin lands back in my palm, Arthur smiles at me before slowly uncurling my fingers so we can both look down at what fate has decreed.

ACKNOWLEDGMENTS

If you're lucky, your acknowledgments often include a similar mix of people from book to book. I'm one of the *very* lucky ones; this is my third time thanking most of these lovely humans, so please forgive both the English language and me for our lack of creativity when it comes to saying "thank you."

Firstly, to Thao Le the Great. It's an honor to work with you. I swear I never think it's possible to appreciate you more, but I'm more grateful to have you in my corner with each passing year. THANK YOU FOR EVERYTHING!!!

Secondly, to Vicki Lame and Vanessa Aguirre, for being my editorial fairy godmothers with this book. Your enthusiasm for this world and these characters buoyed me during another year of being an author in unprecedented times, and I know I'm already out of ways to properly express my gratitude, BUT THANK YOU!!!

To Team Wednesday, with their ever-changing festive logos, their tolerance and encouragement of my Bridgerton obsession, their ability to turn a graphic around in record time that would have taken me roughly twelve hours to make on my own, and their extreme kindness and professionalism in the face of my stickers and eagerness; y'all are the absolute best. Special thanks to Eric Meyer, Carla Benton, Jeremy Haiting, Alexis Neuville, Brant Janeway, Sarah Bonamino, Kerri Resnick, and Devan Norman. And extra special thanks to Hannah Good for so lovingly lending her magical artistic talent to Arthur and Maddie!

And because I grow old . . . I grow old . . . I'm going to save myself—and you—some time, here, and just say thank you to the family, friends, and in-betweens who make this life worth living and worth writing about. If you're wondering if this includes you, it absolutely does.